P9-DGS-279

CLUBBED TO DEATH

Ruth Dudley Edwards was born in Dublin but now lives in London. After a period of teaching and academic research, she worked in telecommunications and then the Civil Service. Since 1979 she has been a freelance writer. Her other Robert Amiss mysteries are *The Saint Valentine's Day Murders*, *Corridors of Death* and *The School of English Murder*. She has written a number of biographies, including the official biography of Victor Gollancz, and is the author of the official history of the *Economist*.

CLUBBED TO DEATH

by

Ruth Dudley Edwards

GOLLANCZ CRIME

First published in Great Britain 1992
by Victor Gollancz Ltd

First VG Crime edition published 1993
by Victor Gollancz
A Cassell imprint
Villiers House, 41/47 Strand, London WC2N 5JE

A catalogue record for this book
is available from the British Library

ISBN 0 575 05583 9

Printed and bound in Great Britain
by Cox & Wyman Ltd, Reading

To James and John – the most direct inspirations for this book

Disclaimer

The gentlemen's club to which I belong resembles
ffeatherstonehaugh's in its architecture – emphatically
not in its membership or staff.

Since Death on All

Since death on all lays his impartial hand
And all resign at his command,
The stoic too, as well as I,
With all his gravity must die;
Let's wisely manage this last span,
The momentary life of man;
And still in pleasure's circle move,
Giving our days to friends, and all our nights to love.

   Then while we are here let's thus perfectly live
   And taste all the pleasures that nature can give;
   Fresh heat when life's fading our wine will inspire,
   And fill all our veins with a nobler fire.

When we're sapless, old and impotent,
Then we shall grieve for youth misspent;
Wine and women only can
Cherish the heavy heart of man.
Let's drink on till our blood o'erflows
Its channels, and luxuriant grows,
Then when our whores have drained each vein
And the thin mass fresh spirits crave, let's drink again.

   Then while we are here let's thus perfectly live
   And taste all the pleasures that nature can give;
   Fresh heat when life's fading our wine will inspire,
   And fill all our veins with a nobler fire.

JOHN WILMOT, EARL OF ROCHESTER

Prologue

'Are you still out of work, Robert?'

'Yes I am,' said Amiss blackly. 'Things aren't looking up.'

'Oh good,' said Ellis Pooley. And then, hastily recollecting himself, 'Sorry, Robert. Of course I didn't mean that. I just meant, oh good, that means you're likely to be free for lunch today.'

'Are you sure that's all you mean? You wouldn't by any chance be coming up with job suggestions for me again, would you?'

'Don't be so suspicious, Robert,' said Pooley firmly. 'A friend should be able to ask you to lunch without his motives being impugned.'

Amiss snorted. 'Not when that friend is Sergeant Pooley of the CID. However, if you're paying, yes, I am free for lunch today. When and where?'

'One o'clock at the Repeal Club.'

'The Repeal Club? Blimey! What's a nice young policeperson doing in a place like that?'

'There's nothing wrong with the Repeal Club.' Pooley sounded slightly offended. 'My father put me up for it when I came down from Cambridge. It's really terribly economical and convenient. Of course if you'd prefer me to invite you to the snack bar in the police canteen . . . ?'

'No, no,' said Amiss hastily. 'Incidentally, what's it trying to repeal?'

'The Corn Laws.'

'Weren't they repealed in the mid-nineteenth century?'

'Indeed they were.' Pooley's patience seemed to be wearing thin. 'However, we're still celebrating. Now, Robert, I'll see you at lunch-time. Oh, and please wear a jacket and tie.'

'Where is this place anyway?'

'At the Regent Street end of Pall Mall opposite the Travellers' and the Reform. See you.' Pooley put the phone down firmly.

Thankfully abandoning the application forms he had been filling in half-heartedly, Amiss wandered into his bedroom to begin the process of changing himself into something resembling a gentleman. He felt cheered by this break in his demoralising daily routine. A momentary fear struck him that Pooley might be in the austere mood that characterised so many people at lunch-times in these puritanical days. Would it be the cheerless litre of mineral water and grudging offer of a single glass of wine? He shook the notion off as unworthy. Gentlemen didn't behave like that – especially when entertaining the indigent.

1

'Once a toff always a toff,' observed Amiss as he settled back in his high-backed leather armchair and accepted graciously the glass of champagne Pooley had satisfyingly pressed on him.

'Meaning what?'

'Meaning only a toff would assume that I'd know the where-abouts of the Travellers' and the Reform.'

'Well you mixed with toffs when you were in the Civil Service,' said Pooley.

'You sound defensive, Ellis. Yes, I did indeed. But they didn't take striplings to their clubs. They were places for the sere – the men of *gravitas*, those bowed from selflessly bearing the heat and burden of mismanaging the country. Nor can I remember any civil servants whose fathers were in a position to put them down for clubs when they were twenty-one. But then, the Department of Conservation was perhaps a touch plebeian.'

'Stop talking nonsense,' said Pooley good-humouredly. 'Anyway you got here, and on time.'

'Well yes, but I had to investigate swanky buildings randomly because none of them had their names on the door.'

'I think,' said Pooley, 'that the principle is that if a chap doesn't know where a club is, he shouldn't be allowed into it.'

'There's no arguing with that logic. Anyway, since I was early I threw myself into the spirit of things and peered into several clubs along here. I'm sorry to have to tell you that this club is the least imposing of them. I think I'd go for that Grecian pile at the corner myself.'

'Ah, the Athenaeum,' said Pooley. 'You'd hate it. It's crammed full of bishops.'

'Well, what about that Italian palace across the road?'

'The Reform? Too many economists, civil servants and PR men.'

'Well, the slightly smaller Italian palace to its left?'

'The Travellers'? Wall-to-wall Foreign Office.'

'Very well then. You've made your point.' Amiss sipped his champagne appreciatively. 'So what's this joint full of?'

'I suppose mostly people who can't stick consorting with civil servants, diplomats, bishops or economists. It's an amiable outfit full of people from no particular walk of life with no particular principles.'

'But surely if you're founded in order to repeal the Corn Laws you must be anti-protectionist, internationalist and all that kind of thing?'

'No, no, no. Certainly not. We were invented by a few people who couldn't get on with the worthy people who had set up the Reform and wanted a reasonably respectable excuse to set up a club of their own. By adopting a faintly serious cause just when it was won, they were free not to have to care about anything ever afterwards. That's why my father became a member. You don't think he'd have anything to do with a high-minded, outward-looking or forward-looking organisation?'

Amiss reflected on what he'd heard from his friend about the politics of Lord Pooley, and nodded comprehendingly.

'Does he come here much, your old man?'

'Good Lord, no. I wouldn't be here if he did. He's an enthusiastic member of the Carlton, Boodle's and the Cavalry Club, all of them jam-packed with people just like himself. He keeps up his membership here as a nostalgic gesture to his raffish, radical youth.'

Amiss grinned as he looked around at the busts and portraits of the early Victorians classified by Lord Pooley as dangerous radicals – the deadly serious Manchester traders who had fought for free-trade principles and the profits they believed would go along with them.

'If this place ran on any kind of rational principles,' he observed, 'it would be sprinkled with new heroes all the time – fearless negotiators for free trade within the EC, leading lights of the GATT talks . . . smugglers.'

'Fortunately, this place is not run on rational principles.' Pooley suddenly leaned forward. 'I've just realised what's odd about you. You aren't smoking. What's happened? Have you given up again?'

'I am not smoking at the moment. Note the cautious turn of phrase. I invested some of my overdraft in a course to help me stop and have learned all sorts of wheezes to assist the process. I could bore on about it for hours, but only a smoker or ex-smoker could find the subject interesting.'

'Well done, Robert. I'm delighted. It wasn't doing you any good.'

'Ellis, I am extremely fond of you, but sometimes you try me sorely. There are two things that make me desperately want to reach for a cigarette. One is someone saying the kind of thing you've just said. The other is the persecution of smokers by sanctimonious fascist twats – among whom, I hasten to add, I don't number you: you've always been tolerant – anxious, health-conscious, but tolerant. Whereas those buggers who ban smoking from their houses, bellyache about passive smoking at work and demand that smokers be excluded from the National Health Service drive me crazy.' Amiss was sitting bolt upright, quivering with indignation.

'I think it's time for lunch,' said Pooley.

Amiss was both grateful and suspicious when Pooley ordered a fine bottle of claret.

'Have you taken a half day, Ellis?'

'Yes, I have, Robert. You know I don't drink when I'm on duty. Now try this. Our wine cellar really is one of the best things about us.'

'Yum, yum,' said Amiss. 'The same, however, cannot be said for your chef, if you'll forgive my saying so. Clearly a man of simple traditional values, unsullied by nasty foreign notions.'

'If you think our chef is bad, you should experience some of the others. In some clubs our menu would be considered positively *outré*. Anyway, come on, that's a perfectly decent pâté. The vegetables – although they will be frozen – will not be tinned, and if you look at the puddings you will see that in addition to apple tart and bread and butter pudding there are such delicacies as crème caramel and fresh fruit salad. You don't know when you're well off.'

'Sorry, Ellis. All those visits to Paris to see Rachel have spoilt me. In fact, latterly I've been eating far too well for an unemployed chap with no capital and few prospects.'

'What's going on?' Pooley looked concerned. 'Isn't the plan still as it was when we last met, i.e., Rachel comes back any day now, you set up home together and you maybe go back into the Civil Service?'

Amiss emitted a loud snort, snatched up his wine-glass, took an unmannerly large mouthful, swallowed it with a little difficulty and said, 'Hah. What's gone wrong? The fucking Foreign Office, that's what's gone wrong. In fact, now that you've tipped me off that the Travellers' Club is awash with the buggers, I might go and set fire to it after lunch.'

'Well, go on. What's happened?'

'Well, as you rightly remember, Rachel, after quite a long time in Paris, was due to come back to London for a home posting of two to three years. We would live together, I would go into a relatively serious job, and we would be ready at the end of her term here to make decisions about whether she stayed in the Foreign Office and I travelled with her, or she took a job here – that sort of thing. But three weeks before she's due back she's informed that the second secretary at the High Commission in India has cracked up and it's her duty as a loyal and single person to step into his shoes immediately. If she resists she'll get labelled "insufficiently dedicated to the Service and to the nation as a whole" or some such crap. So she's going. She doesn't really think she's got much choice, it will help the promotion prospects and it's a fascinating job. Therefore, on many scores, it's an offer she can't refuse.'

'How long will she have to stay there?'

'Probably only about six months if she's there as a stopgap. Maybe a whole two years. Nobody's clear at the moment. Depends on whether this chap recovers.'

'What's wrong with him anyway?'

'A lot. Delhi belly, malaria, dysentery, the whole shagging lot – everything short of the bubonic plague as far as I can gather. He's going to be spending quite some time in the Hospital for Tropical Diseases.'

'I thought no one got those sort of things any more, what with vaccinations and all the other wonders of modern medicine.'

'Well, so did I, but whether he forgot to take his pills or drank the water or what happened to him I don't know and I care less. What I do know is that it's screwed up everything good and proper as far as our short-term future is concerned.'

He shoved his plate away as the waiter arrived bearing the Steaks Repeal – the club speciality that Pooley had urged him to try. Amiss looked incredulously at his, which was smothered in a sauce in which sweetcorn featured prominently.

'Repeal – Corn Laws – geddit?' Pooley was pleased with his joke.

'I don't think a sense of humour is any advantage whatsoever in a chef,' said Amiss sourly, after he had tasted the dish and scraped all the sauce off the meat. 'Nor, on this occasion, in a host. However, the claret is so good that I can forgive practical jokes.'

'So why don't you go with her?' asked Pooley.

'Well, I might in a few weeks – maybe,' said Amiss. 'But I don't know, and I don't know whether it's wise to give up the chance of getting a sensible job, and I don't know what it will be like out there, and I don't know what the accommodation is like, and I don't know if local sensibilities would require us to get married, and I don't know anything. So it's impossible for us to make up our minds until she's been there for a few weeks and finds out how the land lies. At the moment I don't even have the bloody air fare, and I've no idea whether I could get any kind of work out there.'

'So a temporary job would fit the bill really, wouldn't it?' said Pooley thoughtfully.

'Oh yes. In fact I've been back doing some bartending. It's better than being on the dole, even if not much better paid.'

'I have something in mind that might suit you, Robert.' Pooley saw Amiss looking at him with an expression of the deepest distrust. 'Let's not talk about it now. Let's just finish our lunch and catch up on other news and afterwards, over coffee, I'll try my idea out on you.'

'Before I listen to another one of your ideas, Ellis, I'm going to require you to buy me the best brandy this club can offer.'

'Gladly.'

'You're only saying that because you expect to make me so drunk that I'll agree to go down the salt-mines, infiltrate the Pentagon, become a Beefeater, or go wherever you are minded to install me as a copper's nark. That's what you're up to, isn't it?'

'Broadly,' said Pooley. 'Now how about some cheese? And do let me refill your glass. There's still some claret left.'

2

'The great thing about those huge, lumpy English meals is that they soak up the booze effectively,' said Amiss. 'My mind is as clear as a bell, as sharp as a razor and – it goes without saying – as cool as a cucumber. I will have no difficulty in turning down this latest daftness of yours as soon as its full horrors have been explained to me.'

He leaned back contentedly, swallowing as he did so the last of the claret he had carried from the dining-room. Pooley, who had drunk about a third as much as his friend, tried to conceal his grin and rang for a waiter. A few minutes later the brandy was in front of them and they were left in peace in the small salon. It had a plaster ceiling with an intricate pattern of gilded fleurs-de-lis, a polished floor strewn with Chinese silk rugs, comfortable Victorian furniture and book-lined walls. It boasted one other inhabitant, who lay prostrate in a vast armchair at the far end of the room, snoring diligently.

'Now be careful,' said Amiss. 'That old buffer down there might be in the pay of . . . well, of whom, now that I come to think of it? Dammit, ten years ago one was safe in saying he'd be an agent of the KGB, then attention switched to the CIA and now there aren't any predictable baddies at all. It's very tiresome.' He yawned.

'Surely the new enemy is a representative of international business of the environmentally unsound variety?'

'And you've come here today to ask me to help you save the Amazonian rain forests.' Amiss sounded a little sleepy.

'I haven't,' said Pooley. 'And I wouldn't worry about old Watson down there. He's about ninety-three and has been sleeping away the afternoons in that corner for, I believe, the last twenty years. I can't think he's doing it just on the off-chance that one day he'll pick up something useful to the enemy. Now come on, concentrate.'

'Oh, all right. What do you want me to do?'

'I want you to become a waiter.'

'Silver service, I hope,' said Amiss, with a hint of hauteur. 'My mother would be most upset if I sank any lower than that.'

'Certainly silver service – club waiters always are.'

'You want me to become a club waiter?'

'Yes.'

'This club.'

'No. Fanshaw's.'

'Fanshaw's. Where's that?'

'Just off St James's Street. Very close to the centre of clubland there.'

'I can't remember ever reading anything about Fanshaw's.'

'No. But that's probably because it isn't spelt Fanshaw's. That's how it's pronounced. It's actually spelt Featherstonehaugh's. You understand that, don't you? It's the same as Cholmondley being pronounced Chumley and Marjoribanks Marchbanks. Oh, yes. And it begins with two small "ff"s.'

'Nothing begins with small "ff"s outside fiction.'

'Oh, yes they do. Just hang on a minute.' Pooley jumped up, walked over to a free-standing bookcase and returned within moments flourishing a large volume. 'Can't find *Who's Who*. One of the old buffers out there probably has it: some of them like reading their own entries over and over again. We'll have to make do with *Debrett's Distinguished People of Today*. They won't have so many aristocrats, unfortunately. Some tomfool notion of merit applies. Let's see . . . Ah, yes. Here we are, the double "ff"s. Ffolkes, Ffooks, Fforde and Ffolkes don't use a double small "f", I grant you. But let's look at the ffrenches.' He frowned. 'Good Lord!'

'You look shocked.'

'I am shocked. The country's going to the dogs. What would my father say? The ffrenches have ratted. Look.' He thrust the book at Amiss and pointed.

Amiss perused the offending entries. 'Dear, dear. Not only are a clutch of ffrench-born now styling themselves Ffrench, but even ffytche has turned Ffytche.'

'Still, at least they're keeping on the two "ff"s.' Pooley removed *Debrett* and went off to put it back. When he returned, Amiss's eyes had closed. 'Wake up, Robert.'

'Sometimes I don't believe England,' said Amiss dreamily. 'I think the whole country has been invented by a deranged Hollywood impresario with intellectual pretensions and we're all living in a theme park.'

'Well, he certainly deserves full marks for inventing ffeatherstonehaugh's. D'you know anything about the history of clubs?'

'Oh, just the usual stuff.' Amiss sat upright, stretched, and picked up his glass. 'Some of them were gaming-houses; weren't they, and some of them are descendants of coffee-houses? Yes? Others, like this one, were founded quite late on to bring like-minded people together. Roughly it?'

'Yes, that's roughly it.'

'Well, I hope that ffeatherstonehaugh's is going to be one of the more interesting ones. If you've got to tell me a story, let it be a story about a club which descended from mad Regency bucks – a place that embodies the spirit of the chap I remember reading about who threw a waiter out of the window and told the club steward to put him on his bill.'

'Ffeatherstonehaugh's is much closer to that *beau ideal* than here, I can promise you. Unusually enough, it was founded largely on the proceeds of a legacy from Lord ffeatherstonehaugh, who even by the standards of his time was pretty *louche*. He fell out with the proprietors of the clubs he belonged to because of what he regarded as their unreasonable restrictions on the importation of wenches, their timidness about the anti-duelling laws, their killjoy objections to three-day parties and so on and so on. Fearless ffeatherstonehaugh, he was called about town.'

'Fearless with two small "ff"s, no doubt. Jesus, the aristocratic sense of humour is almost enough to make one send for the tumbrils.'

'Anyway, after a particularly ferocious row he swore that he would have a club set up in his honour to perpetuate the principles of a full-blooded aristocrat. And sure enough, much to the rage of his family, the unentailed part of his very considerable estate was found to have been left for the foundation of a club.'

'Well, if it was set up in the spirit in which he apparently wanted it set up, I'm surprised it's still in existence.'

'Ah, yes. But those to whom he had left this delicate task were slightly less reckless than he had been. Indeed a couple of them seem, from all one hears about ffeatherstonehaugh's, to have been uncommonly keen on rules and regulations, even by the standards of gentlemen's clubs, all of which, you probably know, are absolutely hide-bound by daft conventions, rules and nomenclatures. You know the sort of thing: it's true of most of them. The dining-room is called the Coffee Room, but it's the place where you can't have coffee. The place you sit in after lunch is likely to be called the Morning Room. The cold food restaurant is called the Strangers' Room because a hundred years ago you couldn't

20

take strangers into the Coffee Room. The room with all the books in it isn't called the library, it's called the Smoking Room. And so on and so on.'

'Yes, what's the point of all that? Hangover from boarding-school presumably.'

'Quite a lot of it is. I mean, it's not just that it's a matter of keeping up traditions. This is a way of confusing the new boys as well as the outsiders and making members feel superior and part of a private conspiracy. Anyway, ffeatherstonehaugh's has more than its share of that sort of carry-on. Whatever ffeatherstonehaugh's decided to do they did with more enthusiasm than any of the other clubs.'

'How long am I going to have to wait to find out why you're telling me all about this place?' asked Amiss.

'There's been what I think is murder, but it can't be proved. Shall I go on?'

'Situation normal. Go on.'

'So of course I said yes,' reported Amiss to Rachel on the telephone that night.

'What do you mean, "of course"?'

'Because the place is preposterous and what he wants me to do is equally preposterous. I need stimulation. I'm bored, I'm fed up and you're going to India tomorrow.'

'So it's my fault that you're going into a haunt of thieves and vagabonds?'

'Of course it isn't, you silly bitch,' said Amiss affectionately. 'I'm not placing on your shoulders or even on those of Her Majesty's Secretary of State for Foreign Affairs the responsibility for my electing to become, or rather, to try to become, a snooping waiter in a lunatic asylum. However, you have made it possible for me to do this and I can't resist it. Don't be cross.'

'I won't be cross. What's the point? Clearly there's some old *Boy's Own* adventure urge rampant in you at the moment. I suppose you might as well get rid of this inclination while you're an unemployed bachelor rather than finding yourself in ten years' time – a senior civil servant or a captain of industry – stripping off to your red underpants in telephone kiosks.'

'More likely to be a down-and-out than a captain of anything, the way things are going,' said Amiss gloomily.

'Well, maybe you won't get the job and you'll have to apply for something sensible.'

'I'm afraid there isn't much chance of my not getting the job. I understand from Ellis that the turnover in staff in ffeatherstone-haugh's is spectacularly high even by club standards. They treat them badly and the inmates are madder than the norm, I gather. So at the moment they are short of about five underlings. It would be very strange indeed if they were to reject a WASP like me.'

'I don't know what to wish you on this one, other than a short and safe tour of duty.'

'Look on the bright side. I'll be gaining some useful experience for being an embassy husband. I'll know from which side to present the canapés.'

3

At 9 a.m. Amiss began ringing employment agencies specialising in the catering trade. By ten o'clock he was standing in a short queue on the premises of the one that had sounded most hopeful. To his delight no one seemed to want to fraternise, so he was able to read his *Independent*. From the snippets he picked up from overhearing interviews, there appeared to be few fluent speakers of English among the job hunters.

The surroundings were plain; the interviewers crisp. By ten twenty-five he was sitting in front of a large woman wearing an enormous grey Aran cardigan that bore all the unhappy signs of having been knitted by an over-ambitious amateur.

'Experience?' she demanded.

'Not as a waiter,' said Amiss hesitantly. 'But I have been a barman.'

'Hum,' she said. 'Testimonials?'

He passed over rather sheepishly the five-line encomium from his landlord friend, awash with lavish praise of his probity, upright-ness, sobriety and general reliability.

'So why don't you stick with bartending? Why d'you want to be a waiter?'

'I need a live-in job and I heard there were more as a waiter. And anyway, I want to increase my experience.'

She glowered at him through her heavy spectacles and tapped impatiently on the desk with her pen. 'I don't know what the world's coming to,' she informed him crossly, 'when a young fellow like you is wasting himself on this kind of job. Why aren't you a schoolteacher or something? You're obviously educated.'

Amiss gazed at her defiantly. 'Because I'm a poet,' he said firmly, 'so I can't afford to expend any of my creativity in my work.'

'I suppose I should be grateful you're not doing it on my taxes. Now why did you say you wanted clubs and not hotels? You can live in in either of them.'

'I prefer the kind of person you get in clubs.'

She looked unimpressed. 'They're more cultured,' he offered, rather desperately. 'You can get to know them.'

She eyed him dubiously. 'Well, it's your funeral. All right. Here are details of the jobs available at the moment.'

Amiss leafed through the cards, which listed vacancies in half a dozen or so clubs.

'Hurry up. Choose two.'

He took out the cards for the Repeal and ffeatherstonehaugh's.

'Don't take ffeatherstonehaugh's,' she said. 'You won't like it. The staff get rotten food and rotten conditions and everyone there is mad. It's got the highest turnover of any of our clients. Being English, you'd easily get into one of the others.'

Amiss was touched by her concern and impressed by her brutal honesty. 'Nevertheless, I like the sound of it. It has a romantic aura.'

'Romantic aura my granny. But maybe you're daft enough for it,' she declared sourly. 'Don't complain to me when you walk out in a week's time.' Scribbling his name on a couple of introductory cards, she handed them over, nodded curtly and called for the next applicant.

He was outside ffeatherstonehaugh's by eleven o'clock. It had proved particularly difficult to find, being in a kind of mews off an alley off a side-street. However, there was nothing discreet about the building: it was a brash, daring and vulgar parody of the Athenaeum. Where the Athenaeum entrance was dominated by a huge figure of Minerva, ffeatherstonehaugh's had Venus. In place of the Athenaeum's faithful reproduction of the Parthenon frieze, featuring the pride of Athenian youth on beautifully sculpted horses, ffeatherstonehaugh's had reproductions of erotic Hindu sculptures. On either side of the five steps leading into the building there loafed a marble Grecian youth, unclad, and well-endowed, wearing a provocative leer.

Amiss found it impossible not to enjoy the joke: call it art and you can get away with anything, even if you are Victorian. Still smiling, he went up the stairs into the rather dark and grimy lobby, where he was stopped by a stooped and gnarled ancient in a dingy frock-coat.

'How can I help you, sir?'

'I should like to see the club steward, please.'

The ancient, who was wearing what was presumably his normal expression of obsequiousness, altered it instantly to one denoting shock and contempt. 'And what might your business be?' he enquired, the unsaid 'sir' hanging between them.

'I've come about a job.' From the glare cast at him, it was clear that he would have to work hard to be forgiven for allowing himself to be mistaken, even momentarily, for a gentleman.

'Well, you can't see him,' announced the porter with satisfaction. ''E's gorn.'

Amiss noted that the posh accent had disappeared along with the courtesy. 'When you say gone . . . ?'

'I mean gorn . . . fired.' The old blighter looked pleased.

'Well then, may I see the secretary?' asked Amiss, aware that this was an even more futile request, since it was the secretary's demise he was hoping to investigate.

''E's dead,' said the porter with even more pleasure.

'Dead? Was it sudden?'

'As sudden as it can be. One minute he's upstairs having a drink and a chat with some of the members. Next minute he's jumped off the gallery and splat, he's all over the floor of the Saloon.'

Amiss affected shock. 'How horrible. Killed instantly, was he?'

'Well, what d'you expect to happen when you jump sixty feet on to a tiled floor?' asked the sage.

'Splat,' said Amiss.

'Splat's right. And you should of seen the skidmarks. 'E travelled a fair bit, I can tell you. It was a real mess.' By now the porter was clearly softening towards his appreciative audience.

'I suppose you'd better see Commander Blenkinsop. He's doing the secretary's job till we find a new one. He used to be secretary until the new git took over.'

'You didn't like him?'

'Interfering bollocks.' The porter was throwing all dignity and discretion to the wind. 'Trying to go changing things. I don't see the point. Now the Commander, he understands what the club is about. He's one of the old school.' And with an approving nod at his own sagacity, he beckoned to Amiss and led him into the interior of the building.

Amiss was pleased that Pooley had been able the previous day to take him into the body of the Reform Club to prepare him for the lampoon of that noble interior perpetrated by ffeatherstonehaugh's. Without a reasonable knowledge of the original, the subtlety of the caricature would have been lost on him. As it was, he recognised immediately that the great square central hall with colonnades, a fine staircase and an upper gallery closely resembled the original. It was in the incidental adornments that the differences were strikingly obvious. Where the Reform's mosaic floor featured a geometrical design, ffeatherstonehaugh's favoured frolicking nymphs and shepherds, draped lightly, or in some cases, not at all.

'He fell on to this?' Amiss asked.

'He sure did.' The porter grinned evilly, revealing several gaps among his greeny-grey front teeth. 'Made a right mess of that crowd over there, I can tell you.' He directed Amiss's attention to what appeared to represent a bacchanalian orgy. 'Put a bit of a stop to their gallop, if you ask me,' he said with a malevolent chuckle.

Amiss was fascinated by this display of prurient fancy. Its creator gestured at him to wait and disappeared through a door in the corner of the hall. Amiss gazed around looking for evidence of fresh travesties. Like the Reform, ffeatherstonehaugh's had enormous portraits inset into the walls. Amiss speculated wildly as to who would feature in place of the Reform's great liberal statesmen. Satyrs? Strippers? From where he stood the outlook seemed disappointing. Although he could see one woman, she was fully clothed, and the chaps looked like most chaps in varying kinds of historical

25

kit. Unable to contain his curiosity he dashed over to the portrait that dominated the hall, the one that a cunning arrangement of huge mirrors ensured could be seen from every angle. The picture was enormous, probably one and a half times life size, and it featured a chap with voluptuous lips whom Amiss didn't recognise. He read the plaque underneath: 'John Wilmot, Earl of Rochester, 1647–1680'.

Good God! thought Amiss. Ellis didn't tell me this. Rochester, the great dirty poet. What an extraordinary un-English patron saint for a club. He felt a sudden rush of certainty that he was going to enjoy his time at ffeatherstonehaugh's – whatever horrors it might bring.

'Young fellow, come here,' thundered a voice behind him. 'Come on, come on, come on. Don't keep me waiting. That's the trouble with you young fellows these days. No respect. No get-up-and-go. No idea of right and wrong. Deafened by pop music. Heads crammed full of ideas above their station. Now stop gaping, gaping, as I said. Stop gaping and come over here double-quick and tell me what you're good for.'

Christ, thought Amiss. Another parody. And with as much speed as dignity would permit he walked over to the Commander.

4

The Commander had the florid complexion one expected of an old sailor, though Amiss guessed it more likely to be attributable to an excess of alcohol rather than sun, wind and sea. His extreme portliness tended to confirm the diagnosis, though he had the height to carry it well. He wore a blazer of some antiquity and his loud pink-and-black-striped tie sported several stains.

It was not an exacting interview. As the Commander explained from the start, it was a nice change to have somebody white and English-speaking looking for a job.

'That's one good thing about all this unemployment,' he remarked cheerily. 'Every cloud has a silver lining, what?'

Being unable to think of a response which would please his conscience and the Commander, Amiss resorted to a weak smile.

'Mind you,' said the Commander, proving himself to be a more even-handed man than Amiss had expected, 'at least some of these blacks have some get-up-and-go. Whereas a fellow like you looking for a dead-end job like this must be a bloody layabout.'

'I need the free time for my poetry,' said Amiss bravely.

'A poet!' The broken veins on the Commander's face seemed to stand out in an even deeper purple. 'A bloody poet?'

'Yes,' said Amiss. 'Like the Earl of Rochester.'

A few seconds passed before that sally connected with the befuddled brain of the Commander and then light broke through. 'Well, you young dog,' he said. 'Rochester, of course, our great patron. He was a good poet, right enough. Let me remember. I used to be able to recite this when I was a younger man.' He fell back on to the nearest bench, his eyes glazed over with the strain of concentration. Moments passed and then he erupted into a noisy gabble. 'So bring me a seat and buy me a drink and a tale to you I'll tell.' There was another long pause followed by a further burst: 'Of dead-eyed Dick and Mexico Pete and a whore named Eskimo Nell.' He beamed proudly.

Amiss was usually prepared to put up with the unspeakable opinions of those he needed to woo, but such an assault on his intellectual integrity proved more than he could bear. 'I beg your pardon, sir,' he said, adopting as craven a tone as he could muster, 'but "Eskimo Nell" was not written by the Earl of Rochester.' Seeing the Commander begin to swell like a bullfrog, he added tactfully: 'It is of course, sir, a splendid poem, and close to the kind of thing that the Earl went in for, but he did not write it.'

After a couple of seconds the Commander clearly decided that this was no time for a dispute about literary attribution. 'Oh well,' he said, 'you're one of those long-haired chaps. Dare say you're right. It was just something I learned at one of the Rochester evenings that we used to have in the good old days of the club. Dear, dear. We never have any fun any more.'

A question rose and died on Amiss's lips. What he needed was a job. 'Is there anything else you'd like to know, sir?'

'Well, what can you do? Can you do anything? I mean dammit, what are you? Are you a waiter? Are you a valet? Can you cook? What're you good for? Except poetry, that is. Not much call for it in the club these days.'

'Well, I have experience working behind a bar, sir, and I expect I could quickly learn to be a valet or a waiter.'

The Commander was clearly losing interest. Judging by the occasional fumes that had reached Amiss's nostrils, he suspected his putative employer had been interrupted in mid-drink.

'All right, all right. That's fair enough. We'll try you out now. Do you want to live in or out?'

'How does it work out financially?' asked Amiss with some trepidation. It was a pretty poor show, being a snoop who got no money from the people who asked him to do the job, while being expected to live on whatever grotty earnings he got from ghastly jobs that made him ineligible for the dole.

'Makes no difference. Either way you get one hundred and twenty quid a week for a full shift with your meals. If you live in you get full board, except for weekends, when you get nothing unless you're looking after the residents.'

'You mean I get paid the same regardless of whether I live in the club or out of it?'

The Commander gurgled with merriment. 'When you've seen where you'll be living you won't be surprised. Now come on in here and let's try you out in the bar.'

He led Amiss into what was, on the face of it, a pretty straightforward club sitting-room. In fact, it closely resembled those Amiss had seen in the Repeal and the Reform. Standard-issue green leather armchairs, long velvet curtains, oriental rugs, splendid mirrors and lots of bookshelves. He realised that the occasional busts of elderly gentlemen were likely to be those of old roués rather than pillars of the establishment, but then, he reflected, if you don't know who these old codgers are, an aged libertine looks much like an Archbishop of Canterbury any day. Standing obediently by the door as the Commander lurched over to the far end of the room, Amiss ran his eye over the nearest bookshelves. While the Reform had sported hundreds of volumes of Parliamentary reports, the Repeal had favoured Victorian novels. Ffeatherstonehaugh's bindings resembled those in its sister clubs, but the contents were more raffish – *The Golden Bough*, *The Decameron*, *The Story of O*. His studies were interrupted by a hiss. 'Come on, come on. Over here, what'syourname!' The Commander obviously felt that he was issuing his instructions *sotto voce*, but their effect was to awaken a patriarch slumbering near the door. Imposingly built, mighty-domed, multi-chinned and about a hundred and forty-five years old, he shouted, 'Yes, Father. Yes, Father. I'm coming, I'm coming.'

'It's all right, Glastonbury,' shouted the Commander.

'What?'

'It's only me. Go back to sleep.' Obediently Glastonbury collapsed back into oblivion.

Amiss sped silently over to the Commander's corner.

'Come on, come on. No time to lose. Got to introduce you to the bar wallah and see how you make out in his place. All right then, sort him out.' And with a brief nod at the young and handsome Asian behind the table, the Commander set off at a smart pace to rejoin his glass of whisky.

'Welcome aboard,' said the youth.

'Thank you,' said Amiss. 'D'you think I'll like it?'

'Anything's possible. Now we'd better get a move on if I'm to show you the ropes. I'm Sunil by the way and you're . . . ?'

'Robert.'

'OK, Robert. Well now, what you'd better do is get downstairs, introduce yourself, get a uniform, get your lunch and get back here as quickly as you can.'

Amiss looked at him apologetically. 'I thought the Commander wanted me to learn about the bar.'

'The Commander doesn't know anything,' said Sunil, 'and he cares less. Come on. Follow me.' He led Amiss out of the room and across the hall. 'Go in to the dining-room over there and ask for Mr Gooseneck.'

'Mr What!?'

'Of course it takes some getting used to. Ask for Gooseneck, the head waiter. He's standing in for the catering manager. He seems a bit dotty, but he isn't really. He'll show you where the uniforms are kept. And don't forget to mention lunch.'

'It's a bit early, isn't it?'

'If you don't have it before you start your shift you won't have it at all. You must remember that the only way to get anything in this place is to demand. They're so short of staff and the place is so frightful, they have to be a bit obliging. See you back here in about half an hour.'

*

The opulent but rather seedy dining-room was dominated by portraits of voluptuous ladies. Most of the tables were small, but three were large and circular: each had an immense silver centre-piece of entwined bodies. Amiss spotted in the far distance an old person who had to be his quarry. No one could be that old and be a junior waiter.

'Mr Gooseneck?' he enquired as he arrived at the octogenarian's side. 'I'm not Gooseneck.' The old man seemed deeply insulted by the suggestion. Through his ill-fitting false teeth, he whistled, 'What d'you take me for? An old faggot?'

'I'm terribly sorry. I don't know my way around here. I'm new.'

'Well, don't worry. You won't last long. If you want Gooseneck, try the kitchen.' He jerked a dirty thumb towards the swing doors.

Being little more than sixty, Gooseneck was a stripling by ffeatherstonehaugh standards. He had a certain saturnine charm, and all his hair, and he seemed to lack the malevolence of his colleague in the front hall or the irascibility of his subordinate in the dining-room. Amiss judged him a man resigned rather than soured by his fate.

'I assume you have no experience,' Gooseneck observed.

'Only as a barman.'

'I cannot pretend surprise. If you're young and clean and speak English there has to be some obvious drawback. Why are you here?'

'I need time for my poetry.'

'You need time for your poetry. How delightful. Unfortunately I am but a simple head waiter. How should I employ a poet?'

'The Commander said I should relieve Sunil.'

'Splendid. I can always rely on the Commander to make the key decisions. Very good, young man. Come along with me. It's getting late.' He led Amiss into an adjoining room where several dozen uniforms hung alongside three or four frock-coats, at which Amiss looked appraisingly.

'Aha. I discern that you would like the more sober garb. I'm sorry, but I fear you are required to wear the more vulgar uniform. Frock-coats are for the old guard.'

Amiss felt depressed. He'd already taken a rooted objection to Sunil's uniform, a red and cream affair dotted with brass buttons which was reminiscent of a bellhop in Chicago during the era of Al Capone. The only thing missing was the cap and the elastic band.

Gooseneck was assessing Amiss's size with a practised eye. He took two uniforms off the rail. 'Very good, dear boy. Choose and don the better fit and then ask someone to send you to the staff dining-room. You may have lunch before you start work.'

Amiss was deeply touched by this evidence of compassion.

'Thank you. And my own clothes?'

'Consign them to the corner. There is no time to waste. You will be able to retrieve them when you come off duty at five. Are you going to live in?'

'Please.'

'There is no accounting for taste,' said Gooseneck cheerfully. 'May I leave you now?'

'Just one thing.' Amiss began to remove his jacket and trousers. 'I need to make an urgent telephone call.'

'Very good. Return to the main hall and Ramsbum will show you a public box.'

'Ramsbum,' said Amiss faintly.

'Mr Ramsbum to you, young man. He is, after all, the head porter.'

'Thank you, Mr Gooseneck,' said Amiss.

'Do you have a moment, sir?'

Detective Chief Superintendent James Milton looked up from his depressed perusal of the latest guidelines for senior officers and smiled at his young sergeant.

'Yes, Ellis. Come in.'

Pooley bounded across the room, his face wearing that expression of pent-up excitement that always filled Milton with a mixture of amusement, curiosity and apprehension.

'Sit down. What's going on?'

'I've had a phone call from Robert. He's been given a job at ffeatherstonehaugh's.'

'Oh God!' Milton ran his hands wildly through his hair. 'You mean you went through with that mad idea.'

'Well, you did say I could, sir.'

'I said I wouldn't forbid it, Ellis, but I suppose I was banking on Robert not being so malleable this time.'

'It's not so much malleable. I think he's actually developing a taste for this kind of undercover operation.'

'Does it ever occur to you, Ellis,' said Milton rather crossly, 'that I might feel bad about my friend being exploited and indeed possibly put in danger in this way?'

'Well, he's my friend too,' said Pooley stiffly.

'You obviously expect your friends to be made of very stern stuff.' Then, seeing the disappointment on Pooley's face, Milton pulled himself up. 'It's OK, Ellis,' he said. 'You're doing your job, if in a decidedly unorthodox way, and Robert is a consenting adult. How did he sound anyway?'

'Incredulous,' said Pooley. He had already forgotten their dispute: his features were transformed with a broad grin. 'I told him it was a bizarre set-up, but judging by the gargling noises he was making, belowstairs is as daft as above. Anyway he wants to meet us, this evening if possible. He reckons he'll be free early evening and he needs some moral support and advice.'

'I could do eight o'clock,' said Milton.

'For dinner?'

'Where?'

'Ah,' said Pooley, 'Robert was most explicit on that subject. He said that if anybody thought that after a day toiling in Dickensian surroundings he was to be fobbed off with a twentieth-rate meal in a tenth-rate restaurant they could . . . ' He looked embarrassed.

'Take a flying fuck, I imagine. You really are very proper, Ellis.'

'Anyway, sir, I think he was getting a bit worked up.'

'So what's he looking for? The Savoy?'

'Too public,' said Pooley. 'I mean, I know I took him to my club the other day, but now that he's actually been seen in ffeatherstonehaugh's, it would be bad news to have him spotted anywhere salubrious outside. Awfully suspicious. I suggested we meet in my place. I'll have something sent in.'

'By a bevy of Hooray Henriettas, no doubt,' said Milton absently.

'Well . . . I do have a cousin.' Pooley seemed rather abashed. 'She wasn't awfully academic but she did terribly well on the cordon bleu. Quite a nice little business she's got going now with directors' dining-rooms and that kind of thing.'

'You cheer me up, Ellis,' said Milton. 'I'll see you at eight. But make sure that you've got celery salt to go with the quails' eggs and that the *boeuf en croûte* is rare. Now clear off and get on with some of the work you're actually supposed to be doing.'

5

Milton had just rung Pooley's doorbell when a taxi drew up and disgorged Amiss, a large suitcase and a noisy wicker basket. 'Hallo,' came Pooley's voice over the intercom.

'It's Jim Milton and friends.'

Milton pushed the door as the buzzer sounded and held it open for Amiss. Wails and crashes sounded from the basket.

'Good evening, Robert,' said Milton, holding out his hand for the suitcase.

'Good evening, Jim.'

They made no attempt at conversation on their way upstairs, since the screams of the tormented animal had reached an ear-splitting crescendo. Pooley's smile of welcome died as he opened the door and identified the noise.

'Come in,' he said. 'All of you.'

Without invitation, once the door was shut, Amiss undid the straps of the basket and a great ginger creature erupted from it; it spent several minutes racing wildly round the living-room. The three men stood awestruck as the cat soared on to table tops, swung from the mantelpiece, cleared the top of the sofa, dangled from the top of Pooley's favourite armchair and clambered up the long velvet curtains, to come finally to rest on top of the pelmet.

'You remember Plutarch?' enquired Amiss affably.

'Indeed I do,' said Pooley. 'I hadn't realised she was coming to dinner.'

'Well, she's not so much coming to dinner,' said Amiss, 'as coming to stay. They don't let servants keep pets in the club.'

'You're expecting me to give house-room to that?' expostulated Pooley.

'Let's have a drink and discuss this like gentlemen,' said Milton hastily.

'Sorry to have given you such an unpleasant shock,' said Amiss, when the three of them had settled down with their gin and tonics. 'Unfortunately, when I got back to my flat to pack my effects I found the obliging neighbour was away and there was no time to corral someone else into taking over; you were the obvious choice.'

'But for Pete's sake, Robert, how can I keep a monster like that? Damn it all, this flat isn't like yours. It's full of breakable objects.'

'Search me,' said Amiss genially. 'You must work it out between you. My conscience is clear. Not only do I need a cat-sitter wholly and absolutely because of you, but I wouldn't even have the bloody cat if you hadn't involved me in that last hideous intrigue.* I don't mind whether you put her up yourself, send her to an hotel, or stick her in a zoo for the duration, just as long as she's properly fed and watered. I feel an obscure sense of duty towards Plutarch, though I can't pretend a deep affection yet: her appetites are gross and her manners coarse.'

'You seem a little sharp, Robert,' said Milton. 'Have you had a hard day at the club?'

'More demeaning than hard,' said Amiss. 'I know you chaps are used to dressing up in silly clothes, but nobody ever attracts your attention with a "hey you". Or not without getting a swift blow with a truncheon.'

'Character-forming,' said Milton.

'I don't know why I'm letting you two dictate the pace at which my character is being formed,' said Amiss sourly. 'You always seem to be putting me in circumstances which do no good for either my bank balance or my career.'

'But for heaven's sake, Robert,' said Pooley, 'you don't have a career. If you were still in the Civil Service I wouldn't be trying to yank you out of it to do undercover work. I'm just providing you with challenges while you've nothing worthwhile to do.'

'Well, you can provide me with some more gin,' said Amiss. 'And I hope the food's good. They feed club servants on pig-swill.'

The food was very good: the wine was even better. Amiss was mellow. 'Well, I'll give you this,' he remarked, 'the coppers' charity for the care and feeding of informers has been most generous on this occasion. Long may it continue.' He waved his glass and drank a toast.

Pooley was getting restless, his humour not improved by his searing experiences of Plutarch's behaviour. Not only had she hurled herself against the door of the dining-room until admitted, but she had set up such howling demands that, failing any other

*See The School of English Murder

34

suitable food, she had had to be placated with substantial amounts of smoked salmon and *blanquette de veau*. That was bad enough in Pooley's view, for he had firm aristocratic views on the foolishness of cosseting domestic animals, but Plutarch had then taken a fancy to him and was now stretched across his knees, purring vigorously. He stroked her reluctantly and grimaced.

'She's shedding, Robert,' he said.

'Indeed she is, Ellis,' said Amiss. 'You'd better give her a wash-and-brush-up in the morning. I'm sure she'll enjoy that.'

'Now look here, Robert. We've really got to get down to brass tacks. It's nine-thirty and your narrative has only got as far as your arrival at the servants' lunch. We've got some strategic decisions to take.'

Milton intervened hastily before Amiss could explode. 'Now, Ellis,' he said soothingly, 'we are dealing with a volunteer here you know, not a conscript, so we should let him play it at his pace and in his way.'

'Very good, Jim,' said Amiss. 'I hope you're taking notes, Ellis, on how modern managers keep their troops happy. You can't throw your weight around as with the peasantry. But then of course you haven't had Jim's advantages. Lower-class upbringing, a management consultant for a wife and all those courses for senior rozzers on caring and compassionate leadership.' He caught Milton's eye and grinned. 'All right,' he said. 'I'll get on – even speed up a bit. But it is important that you understand the context and that's not explained quickly. Let me give you a visual aid. I've brought a menu from the dining-room. And please grasp that what we have here is not a series of choices: luncheon includes the lot.'

Set Luncheon
Mulligatawny soup
Lobster salad
Boiled cod
Veal cutlets
Cold roast beef
Mashed potatoes
Stewed celery
Bread & butter pudding
Cheese

'And what did you get for your lunch?' enquired Milton.

'Macaroni cheese and rice pudding.'

There was a silence, which Amiss interrupted. 'Now, as you'll imagine, that obviously left them a bit peckish. Here is today's set dinner,' and he read: 'Oysters, turtle soup, turbot, orange sauce, boiled leg of mutton, broccoli, turnips, mashed potatoes, carrots, caper sauce, queen of puddings, anchovy toast, cheese and coffee.' Milton and Pooley seemed dazed.

'Oh! I forgot to tell you that the set meals include wine. At dinner they had madeira with the soup, champagne with the fish and claret with the entrée, followed by a dessert wine and a rather decent port. All included in the price.'

'Which is? It doesn't say on these menus,' said Milton, who was perusing them in complete bewilderment.

'Lunch costs four pounds and dinner six. Pretty impressive, isn't it? More heavily subsidised even than the House of Commons. And incidentally, servants have supper, not dinner, and I'm told it's worse than lunch.'

'I think you've made your point, Robert,' said Milton. 'You're going to need supplementary provisions. Ellis, perhaps you could arrange a tuck-box?'

Pooley was spluttering. 'Yes, yes. But this is absolutely ridiculous. They're not paying ten per cent of the cost. They must pay ferociously high subscriptions.'

'Anyone eating there regularly would need to pay a subscription of about ten thousand a year to avoid being a financial liability,' said Milton. 'This makes no sense. These menus are completely anachronistic.'

'Straight out of Mrs Beeton's *Household Management*,' observed Pooley. 'The first edition, I mean. My mother has one and I was looking at it only recently. These menus are typical, although Mrs Beeton was in favour of giving servants meat along with the macaroni cheese and rice pudding.'

'Well, what else do you have to tell us from today, Robert?' asked Milton. 'Before we get down to making plans.'

'Oh, nothing very important,' said Amiss. 'Sunil showed me the ropes, taught me the prices of drinks and how to make the club cocktail, the ffeatherstonehaugh special – a nourishing drink, made mainly with rum, brandy, champagne, green chartreuse and angostura bitters.'

'And what do the drinks cost?' asked Milton.

'Well, they're cheap but not incredibly cheap,' said Amiss. 'As far as I can see, members are cosseted, but not guests. So what I've shown you are the menus from the dining-room – aka the Coffee Room – where guests are not allowed. Members wishing to feed guests have to take them to the Strangers' Room, which has a much less lavish menu and higher prices.'

'Odder and odder,' said Milton.

'Anyway,' asked Pooley, 'does this mean that you're now assigned to the bar?'

'Before lunch, yes. Although I'll be expected to help out in the dining-room at breakfast and on the gallery in the afternoons.'

'What's your room like?' asked Milton.

'I haven't seen it yet, but according to Sunil, it's appalling. We're sharing, but thank God, it's just the two of us. Apparently some of the others are four to a room, and I have to admit that I'm a trifle turned off by many of my colleagues. Personal daintiness is not among their priorities. But then one's standards are inclined to slip in an institution that has dungeons for kitchens and, I am told, infestations of cockroaches, not to speak of the occasional rat.'

'You'd think the public health authorities would be down on the management,' said Pooley.

'Who's going to complain?' asked Amiss. 'Most of the staff are thankful to have been given a job. Even me. And since nearly everyone is foreign, they presumably think ffeatherstonehaugh's is typical.'

'Well, I certainly don't think you'll be wasting your time there,' said Milton. 'Ellis's murder will probably turn out, despite him, to have been a suicide, but you're going to have plenty to tell your grandchildren in the long winter evenings.'

Amiss got up and filled their glasses with Pooley's Armagnac. 'Thanks,' he said, waving his glass in the direction of his host, still unhappily pinioned to his chair by the cat. 'Now, Ellis, since I've got a grasp of the geography and the ambience of ffeatherstonehaugh's, will you run me through the story of the secretary's death again?'

Pooley leaped to his feet, much to the rage of Plutarch, to whom he apologised absentmindedly as he began to stride up and down the room. The cat headed straight for Milton, jumped on his knee and commenced lacerating his thighs. With only a muttered oath, he extracted her claws, stroked her gently and had her lying placidly within half a minute. Amiss looked at him in some surprise.

'Actually, I like cats, Robert,' Milton said. 'Even this one.'

'Excellent. You can take her to keep you company when Ann's away.'

'You're wasting your time, Robert. Regard me as an occasional friendly uncle. I will not adopt this encumbrance.'

Pooley was champing at the bit. 'The secretary, Trueman, was having an after-lunch drink on the gallery, this day two weeks ago, with two of the members, Blenkinsop and Fagg.'

'Is Blenkinsop actually a member?' asked Amiss.

'On and off. When he gave up being secretary he reverted to being a member. Where was I? Yes – Trueman was talking to Blenkinsop and Fagg.'

'With two "f"s no doubt,' said Amiss.

'No.' Pooley sounded rather long-suffering. 'Two "g"s. According to their story he didn't seem in very good form; he was pretty inattentive and uncommunicative. But naturally, being English, they didn't ask him if anything was wrong. They just carried on regardless, talking about general club gossip. Then apparently, he leaped to his feet without a word and strode right down the gallery out of their sight. Next thing they heard a scream and a thud and to their horror saw his body lying on the floor of the Saloon. They rushed downstairs, felt for his pulse and concluded he was dead. Both being military types, they were not too distressed by the mess.'

'Did anyone actually see him jump?' asked Amiss.

'No.'

'Was anyone else on the gallery?'

'Only Glastonbury, who was asleep very close to the spot from which Trueman descended. In due course he also descended to view the corpse and lament.'

'And your only reason for thinking that it's murder rather than suicide is your intuition and the lack of a suicide note.'

'Or a motive. Here's a comfortably-off, apparently quite happy bachelor, with no known entanglements and an affectionate family. Why should he jump?'

'It happens, Ellis,' said Milton, 'as you well know. Lots of people never understand why their loved ones kill themselves.'

'But you know there's much more to it than that, Jim. As I've said to each of you, Trueman was unpopular in the club owing to his reforming zeal. Robert has already had confirmation of that. There just could have been one or even two people lying in wait for him. It wouldn't take much to do it. You'd only have to invite him to look over the balustrade and with a bit of a heave, if you were reasonably fit, you could shove him over in a trice.'

'I didn't think there was anybody fit in ffeatherstonehaugh's,' said Milton. 'Certainly we didn't see anyone.'

'Maybe there was a coven of geriatrics formed to do the deed,' said Amiss. 'Maybe he was actually clubbed to death with crutches, and chucked over afterwards. It still seems very thin to me, Ellis. However I'll grant you, first, that your intuition is normally good and second, that even if he did commit suicide, I'd like to know why. And there certainly are some very odd things about ffeatherstonehaugh's.'

'I'm not really *au fait* with the details,' said Milton, 'but didn't Ramsbum claim to have seen him fall over, and to have seen no one near him?'

'Did you check out his eyesight?' asked Amiss.

'I did,' said Pooley. 'It's poor enough to make his evidence worthless. My guess is he was just looking for attention.'

'That wouldn't surprise me,' said Amiss.

Milton was frowning. 'But wouldn't Glastonbury have heard a struggle?'

'From what I know of Glastonbury already,' said Amiss, 'you could throw a troop of boy scouts over that balcony in the time it takes him to emerge from sleep to reality. Still, it's intriguing. What do you most want me to find out?'

'If there is anything crooked going on,' said Pooley.

'How the club is financed,' said Milton.

'Who Trueman's enemies were,' said Pooley.

'How threatening his reforms were to the members,' said Milton.

'What beats me is how he could possibly carry through any reforms,' said Amiss. 'I'd have assumed the committee was packed with die-hards and no-surrender types. In fact, I can't even imagine how he came to be appointed.'

'I'm hoping,' said Pooley, 'that the chairman of the club might help to explain that. We haven't been able to talk to him yet because he's been abroad on a golfing holiday, but he should be back within the week.'

Amiss looked at his watch and sighed. 'Give me one for the road please, Ellis, and then I'll be off. I don't want to get back too late and disturb Sunil and I've got to unpack and be up at some appalling hour. The servants breakfast at seven-thirty in order to clear the decks for the serving of members' breakfasts.'

Pooley poured him a generous drink and excused himself. He came back a moment later with a little package wrapped in foil and a cake tin.

'Take these with you, Robert,' he said. 'It's the remains of the smoked salmon and a cake my mother sent me the other day. She refuses to believe that my tastes have changed over the years so she still provides me with the plum cake I used to be sent at school. I hope you like it.'

'I'm not big on cakes,' said Amiss, 'but the way things are looking in Dotheboys Hall, I'll probably be organising midnight feasts for my colleagues. Thank you, I'm touched.' He took another swig of brandy. 'Here goes,' he said. 'Order me a cab. I'm ready to go over the top. It's one way of fitting in at ffeatherstonehaugh's.'

6

Ramsbum was still on duty when Amiss got back to the club.

'Goodness, Mr Ramsbum,' said Amiss obsequiously, 'what long hours you work.'

'It's what I'm used to. Anyway, how else am I supposed to earn a living if I don't do the overtime?'

'D'you have a family to support?' asked Amiss sympathetically.

'I bloody well do not,' said Ramsbum, clearly offended. 'Don't 'old with that sort of thing at all. Women and kids, never saw the point. I'm 'appy 'ere with my gentlemen.'

Amiss wondered wildly if the old fool had been provided by Hollywood Central Casting. If so, they hadn't expended much on a decent script. At this moment Ramsbum's relaxed posture changed dramatically. He became completely rigid, arms by his sides, legs together and eyes shut tight: he appeared to be awaiting inspiration. At a loss, Amiss stood there irresolute. After a minute or so, Ramsbum opened his eyes, gazed fixedly at Amiss and recited:

> 'To all young men that love to woo,
> To kiss and dance, and tumble too;
> Draw near and counsel take of me,
> Your faithful pilot I will be;
> Kiss who you please, Joan, Kate, or Mary,
> But still this counsel with you carry,
> Never marry.

There's a poem says it all. One of my gentlemen taught it to me. It's by that Rochester bloke.'

Amiss had a fruitless stab at trying to imagine Joan, Kate or Mary tumbling with Ramsbum and then wisely concluded that it was time to go to bed. With the amount of alcohol he had on board he could not be sure of playing any further conversation with Ramsbum as tactfully as he would wish.

'That's excellent, Mr Ramsbum. Thank you. I enjoyed it and I understand how you feel. I've often wondered why all these chaps want to get tied down. Now could you be very kind and direct me to my room.'

Ramsbum smiled the smile of pure malevolence that Amiss had come to expect of him. 'Oh yes, your quarters, m'lord,' he said. 'Yes indeed. I 'ope your lordship'll find everything to your satisfaction. 'Old on.' Donning a pair of small round plastic spectacles which he had extracted from a hidden pocket in the skirts of his frock-coat, he shambled over to the porter's desk and ferreted around.

''Ere we are,' he said. 'You're in with young Sunil. Room seventeen on the fifth floor.'

'So what do I do, Mr Ramsbum?' asked Amiss respectfully. 'Take the lift to the fifth and then . . .'

'Lift!' said Ramsbum. 'Lift! You're a servant. The committee don't 'old with servants using the lift.'

'But I've got a very heavy suitcase, Mr Ramsbum.'

'Well, you'll just have to hump it up the stairs as best you can, won't you. The back stairs, that is. The gentlemen wouldn't like to have the likes of you going up the front stairs out of uniform.'

A red haze swam in front of Amiss's eyes, but he remembered the dead Trueman and waited until it had passed. 'Very well, then, Mr Ramsbum. So it's straight up the back stairs. Five flights?'

'More like eight,' said Ramsbum. 'Anyway, you can't miss it. But mind you go quietly and don't wake any of the gentlemen. Colonel Fagg, he goes mad if anyone wakes him up. Comes out of his room like a rocket and you're out on your ear.'

'I'll be careful, Mr Ramsbum. Thank you for the advice,' said Amiss levelly. Picking up his suitcase he headed towards the back staircase.

He had reached the top of the fourth carpeted flight of stairs when he realised he was now in the members' bedroom corridor. A wooden board entitled 'Bedroom Orders', with slots for names, was on the wall to his left. He recognised the names of Blenkinsop, Fagg and Glastonbury and was interested to learn that the three witnesses to Trueman's last moments all appeared to live in the club. As he tiptoed to the next flight he was distracted by a dreadful howling sound, worse than Plutarch at her most aggrieved. It was immediately succeeded by snorting and choking, a silence, then a repetition of the howl. Amiss stood aghast. Suddenly the sequence was interrupted by a crash, an oath and an answering oath, under cover of which Amiss began to climb silently and wearily up the next staircase. He made a mental note to find out who was the snorer and who the complainant; certainly the latter would have a very sound motive for murder.

There was no longer any carpet underfoot – merely drugget, a material he recalled from nineteenth-century novels dealing with servants' quarters. However, it ran out in its turn as he reached the next storey, occupied, Sunil had told him, by upper servants. The next lot of stairs were very narrow and sported bare boards. He climbed them sadly until finally he reached a low corridor, which many years ago had been decorated in dark brown: the paint had been flaking off for years. A dim light enabled him to find room seventeen. It was locked. Amiss tapped softly but there was no answer. He felt tempted to cry but that wasn't going to solve his immediate problem. Instead, he sat down on his suitcase and fell asleep.

An hour later he was awakened by Sunil, who unlocked the door and ushered him in apologetically. 'Sorry, I was in the library. Didn't Ramsbum give you a key?'

'No. Should he have?'

'He really is such a miserable old bastard. Oh, well, you'll just have to get it off him tomorrow. Meanwhile, welcome to our happy home.'

Amiss had by now become so accustomed to the horrors of ffeatherstonehaugh's that the appearance of their bedroom came as no surprise. It contained two narrow iron bedsteads furnished with dingy bed-linen and grey army blankets. The tiny window had dusty, sagging black curtains which he guessed must be black-out curtains from the Second World War. There was one small woodworm-infested wardrobe, which could be reached only by squeezing with great difficulty past a huge, dirty-pink chest of drawers and a marble washstand with a big enamel jug and basin. The floor had mottled dark brown lino but sported an unexpectedly cheerful Afghan rug. Equally cheerful was the large, garish picture on the wall of a jovial elephant wearing orange pantaloons, an elaborately jewelled head-dress and several necklaces: his four arms were festooned with bangles and bracelets. Attractive young women fanned him as he simultaneously read, wrote, waved an axe and held a flower aloft.

Sunil saw the direction of Amiss's gaze. 'This is Ganesh,' he said. 'He's my only friend here. He is a Hindu god of great *joie de vivre*.'

'I presume that neither he nor the rug were provided by the management,' said Amiss.

'You presume rightly. Now to the division of space. That's your bed on the left and you can have the two bottom drawers of the chest.'

Amiss heaved his suitcase on to his bed, unlocked it and began to unpack.

'Why is Ganesh an elephant? Or do I mean, why is an elephant a god?'

'Because Shiva, his father, who'd been away for a long time, found him in the wife's bedroom on his return and assumed that he was her toyboy. Shiva is a bad-tempered chap—not for nothing is he known as "the Destroyer". He chopped his son's head off on the spot. Mother was furious and demanded the situation be put to rights. The only way that Father could do this was by giving his son the head of the first living creature he met, which happened to be an elephant. However, that handicap never held Ganesh back. He made the most of things.'

'Are you religious, Sunil?'

'Anything but. Don't worry. You'll be spared the flowers and the incense-burning and general carry-on. But some aspects of my family religion and culture appeal to me. Here, let me help. It's very hard to get clothes into this wardrobe until you get the knack.' Deftly he inserted Amiss's suit and sports jacket into the minuscule space.

Amiss finished flinging the rest of his belongings into the allocated drawers and lay down on his bed. 'So why are you in a dump like this?'

'I was about to ask you the same question.'

'I want to be a poet.'

'I want to be a novelist, but first I want to get a degree and ffeatherstonehaugh's makes that possible.'

'Do you drink?' Amiss took out of his pocket the hip-flask that Pooley had thrust upon him as he left. 'Whisky, that is.'

'Rarely and very little,' said Sunil, 'for pragmatic reasons. However, I'll make an exception in this case,' and he accepted the hip-flask, took a swig and returned it.

'So are you actually at university?'

'Yes, indeed.' Sunil began to undress. 'I'm taking a full-time degree at London University. I do nothing except work here, go to lectures and study.'

'Couldn't you get a grant?'

'I didn't qualify. My father earns too much money and he was not prepared to subsidise me to do what he thought was a ridiculous waste of time.'

'But I thought Indians were always terribly keen on education for their children?'

'My father would have paid for years and years to have me become a doctor, a lawyer or an engineer. He was appalled that I wanted to study English and history, both of which he thought not only pointless but a danger to my identity. He thinks I'm Indian because he is. I think I'm English because I was born here.'

'Have you fallen out over it?'

'Yes, for the moment I've been cut off. And that's a relief to me really. It saves me getting involved in all that endless round of relatives. And when I get a first-class degree, which I hope to do, I'll be forgiven because I'll bring status to the family. There will then be an outbreak of peace until I refuse to get involved in an arranged marriage.' He shrugged. 'I don't let it get me down. I regard the situation as part of the normal growing-pains of an immigrant Asian family.'

'You're very philosophical.' Amiss took off his jacket.

'Comes of being a Hindu. Even a lapsed one. What about you?'

'Well, I have a degree, but I have no idea what career I want, if any, and for the moment I'm taking undemanding jobs and writing poetry.'

Amiss hated lying to this nice youth: he changed the subject rapidly.

'Sunil, do I gather from that jug and bowl that we wash in our bedrooms with cold water?'

'Not necessarily. We have a choice. On this floor there is one bathroom, but there are twenty of us. The good news is that there are two lavatories. So I wash in the morning here and bathe when the others have all gone out. You can have the cold water here in the bedroom tomorrow morning if you like. I'll be getting up early anyway. I've got an essay to finish.'

'But how can you get to your lectures? Surely they clash with work.'

'Because Gooseneck is actually very decent to me.'

'Well, if he's so decent,' said Amiss, as he donned the pyjamas he had specially bought for the purposes of room-sharing, 'why does he allow us to be fed so badly?'

'That's nothing to do with Gooseneck. That's the provender committee. They decide on all the menus for members, guests and staff alike.' He got into bed.

'Well how can a whole committee be composed of shits?'

'That's not difficult in ffeatherstonehaugh's. But this is a special case. The chairman is that old brute Fagg.'

'What does he look like?'

'He's the one who's always covered in snuff. You can tell where he's been by the trail. And his pockets clank with snuffboxes. He carries about fourteen of them. Occupies most of his day really, pulling them all out, sniffing at what's inside, choosing the one for the moment. That's when he's not stuffing himself with breakfast, lunch and dinner and occasionally calling a meeting of his cronies to think of more ways of misusing the club funds and treating the servants as he believes they should be treated.'

'But doesn't the chairman of the club object?'

'Very tricky business politically. Would you mind turning the light out, Robert? I'm knackered. A new chairman came in a few months ago. By accident they chose someone who was half-way human. And he brought in a secretary who was at least three-quarters human. They were trying to introduce changes and then the secretary goes and kills himself and we're back with the Commander, God help us.'

Amiss switched off the light and climbed into bed.

'Do you have a copy of the constitution and rules of the club?' he asked. 'I'd like to see them – just out of curiosity.'

'Sorry,' said Sunil. 'They wouldn't be available to servants. Anyway, I use this place as a convenience. I haven't got time to get curious about it. If you want to dig the dirt your best hope is old Gooseneck, especially if he finds you attractive. Goodnight.'

'Goodnight,' said Amiss. 'And, of course, goodnight to Ganesh. He seems to be the sanest bloke in this place, next to us.'

'You ain't seen nothing yet,' said Sunil.

7

'How did you sleep, Robert?'

Amiss opened his eyes to see Sunil standing over him looking solicitous.

'Fitfully,' said Amiss gloomily. 'I think this is the hardest bed I ever slept on in my whole life.'

'Ah! Then you obviously didn't go to public school like I did. The great advantage of such institutions is that they fit you for prison conditions. I can sleep anywhere for just as long as I've got. Did I snore?'

'Well, a bit.'

'Oh, dear. I was afraid of that. Sorry. The remedy is quite straightforward.' Sunil walked over to the far side of his bed, searched among the books that stood in piles in the corner and selected half a dozen paperbacks. 'Here you are, Robert. Just toss one of those at me any time I snore and I'll turn on my side and shut up. Something else I learned at school.'

'You're very kind, Sunil.'

'We need to be kind to each other. Nobody else in this place will be. But now, come on. It's time you got up. Breakfast in twenty minutes.'

'Oh, shit! And I'm on duty immediately afterwards.'

'Aha! You're doing breakfast, are you? Well, I think you're going to find that an interesting experience. I've got the morning off. I'm going to lectures.'

Amiss jumped out of bed. He queued miserably outside the nearer of the two occupied lavatories for five minutes until it was vacated by a depressed-looking oriental, washed and shaved unhappily in cold water, put on his ridiculous uniform and ran down to breakfast.

Gooseneck presided over a table of thirty, one-third of whom were female. All except Gooseneck, Amiss and one of the girls were in ordinary clothes, and having looked at what was available for breakfast Amiss wondered why they had bothered turning up at all. Then he realised that they were presumably so poor that even a choice of cornflakes or lumpy porridge, along with underdone toast and margarine, had the overwhelming attraction of being free. He sat down beside the uniformed girl who introduced herself as Elsa from Hamburg. Unlike most of their colleagues she had fluent English, and they chatted politely as they ate. At five to eight Gooseneck took Elsa and Amiss aside for a briefing.

'I normally try to avoid having two new people on duty simultaneously,' he said. 'However, on this occasion I thought it not unreasonable to take a risk. You both need training and you both speak English. It is, I can assure you, a rare event in this establishment to have not one but two newcomers with such a qualification. As you will have noticed, most of your colleagues possess an English vocabulary of no more than a dozen words.'

Amiss wondered vaguely why ffeatherstonehaugh's head waiter should speak like a prep-school master of the 1950s. Gooseneck noticed his look of preoccupation. 'Pay attention, dear boy. Now here are the key instructions. You serve from the left, and you lose no opportunity to call the old bastards "sir".' He paused, bowed towards Elsa and said, 'I do beg your pardon. You try to keep them happy, use your common sense and come to me if you have any problems. Elsa, you will deal with tables one to seven; Robert, you take the remainder. I will help each of you according to the pressure you are under. I will also relieve you, Robert, at eight-thirty, when you take Mr Glastonbury's tray upstairs to his bedroom. Come to me then for instructions.'

As they moved towards the green baize door he added as an afterthought, 'Oh, and Elsa, if anyone asks you what nationality you are, say you're Swiss.'

'Why? I don't want to say I'm Swiss. I'm proud of being German.'

'Be guided by me, my dear girl. If you wish to keep your job, Swiss is what you need to be. Oh, and one thing more, Elsa. I have given you the section of the room in which Mr Fishbane does not sit. Always try to avoid him.'

'Which is he?' she asked.

'His appearance is a trifle anachronistic. Rather dandyish. He sports Edwardian sideburns and wears embroidered waistcoats during the day and in the evening always a black tie.' Elsa looked completely confused. 'Sorry, Elsa. I mean by that a tuxedo, as I think you will probably know it. Should he call you over to him, Elsa, I advise you to stay as far away from him as possible, and at all costs, never turn your back. Unless, that is, you enjoy being pinched. Mr Fishbane is obsessed with sex and while I imagine he can't do a great deal about it any more, poor old boy, until he's finished his breakfast he's almost out of control if he spies an attractive girl.'

Elsa directed at Amiss a look of desperation. He shrugged and together they went into the dining-room. One by one, the aged tottered in, each one seemingly more decrepit than the one before. Amiss made a mental note to find out what the average age of members was. To judge by his observation so far, it was somewhere in the region of eighty-seven.

Their charges proved pretty uniform in their habits. They each came in and looked expectantly at Gooseneck, who showed them to a table with great ceremony and handed them a newspaper. Amiss was not surprised to see that all the members – even the residents –

had separate tables. The members of this club might be odd, but they were English: the notion of socialising at breakfast would be anathema. They sat behind their newspapers. To his surprise, very few of them took the quality papers: middle-of-the-range tabloids were the norm. Fishbane was one interesting exception. He took both the *Telegraph* and the *Sun*. Indeed, as Amiss saw with fascination, his first act on sitting down to breakfast was to open the tabloid at page three, fold it and prop it against the sugar bowl in such a way that the topless pin-up of the day was there to be looked at every time he got bored with the *Telegraph*.

Having taken the orders and observed the quality of the breakfast on offer to members, Amiss was relieved that Colonel Fagg had been allocated to Elsa rather than to him. A man who could decree that the waiters should be given a disgusting breakfast prior to serving their masters with cold ham, kedgeree, scrambled eggs with smoked salmon, grilled wild mushrooms, devilled kidneys and much, much more, was a man who deserved to have his teapot emptied over his scrofulous head. It was while he was bringing a second helping of kedgeree to Fishbane that the row broke out a few tables away.

'I asked is the haddock finnan?' said a querulous voice.

'I am sorry,' said Elsa. 'I do not understand. Could you please repeat it again?'

'Finnan. Surely you know about finnan haddock. What's this club coming to when a fellow can't get a straightforward answer to a straightforward question.'

'Girl sounds like a bloody Kraut,' said Fagg, joining in. 'Are you a Kraut, girl, eh? Come on, come on. Tell the truth. Are you a Kraut?'

'A what, sir?'

'Kraut,' roared Fagg. 'Boche, Hun, bloody German. Are you a bloody German?'

'I am Swiss,' said Elsa, backing away nervously and turning and fleeing to Gooseneck. Amiss hurriedly joined them.

'It's all right, Elsa,' Gooseneck was saying. 'Old Mauleverer is obsessed with food. I should have warned you that regularly as clockwork, whenever he stays in this club, he checks if the haddock is finnan, if the skin around the black pudding is made of hog's intestines and so on. For your information, finnan is merely a superior variety of smoked haddock.'

'Yes,' said Elsa, sobbing. 'But why does that horrible old man shout at me?'

'I warned you,' said Gooseneck. 'Colonel Fagg has never quite come to terms with the end of the Second World War, I'm afraid, Elsa. He has ruled that the club should not employ anyone from a nation which fought against us. We ignore the rule and deceive him. Now dry your eyes and get back to work.'

'And try to look Swiss,' said Amiss encouragingly. 'It's eight-thirty, Mr Gooseneck.'

'Ah, yes. Now listen carefully, Robert. Have you come across Mr Glastonbury yet?'

'Yes,' said Amiss cautiously. 'I've seen him asleep and I've seen him waking up. That's about it.'

'Ah, then you probably have the general picture,' said Gooseneck. 'Now go into the kitchen and take the tray which you'll find waiting on the table on the left and take it up to room five on the third floor.'

'Can I go in the lift?'

'May you,' corrected Gooseneck absentmindedly. 'No. I fear you may not go in the lift.'

'Oh, shit!' said Amiss under his breath, beginning to turn towards the kitchen.

'Not so fast, my fine fellow,' said Gooseneck. 'There's more. When you get to room five you knock loudly and shout "Good morning, Master Boy. Here comes Nanny with your breakfast."' Their eyes met: there was a brief silence. '"Master Boy",' said Amiss.

'"Master Boy",' said Gooseneck.

'"Nanny".'

'"Nanny". Now perhaps you understand why it helps to have the occasional English person working here. Try explaining that to a Greek.'

'What happens then?' asked Amiss apprehensively.

'All plain sailing after that,' said Gooseneck. 'He will call, "I'm awake, Nanny". If he doesn't, you go through the drill again until he does. Then you go in and by the time you've arrived at his bedside, he will have acquired a dim grasp of where he is. You then revert to the norm and say, "Good morning, sir". It's perfectly simple, really.'

*

As Amiss placed the tray on the table beside Glastonbury's bed, he quickly sized up the room. Window wide open, no curtains and a narrow iron bedstead that looked no more comfortable than the one he had himself. Otherwise, the room was quite pleasant. An armchair, desk, a couple of straight chairs and other bedroom furniture were all Victorian. On the wall there were a few decent water-colours of the English countryside and in the far corner, several framed group photographs. Glastonbury was clearly not a scholar. Out of the corner of his eye Amiss could see that the single bookshelf seemed to contain mainly school stories and adventure yarns. Poor old devil, thought Amiss, as he fussed around the old man, removing dish-covers, undoing the napkin, helping him settle himself upright. His compassion intensified when he saw the other inhabitant of the bed – a small, shabby teddy-bear.

'Thank you,' said Glastonbury. 'Thank you. Now you're new, aren't you? Aren't you? I haven't seen you before, I don't think. Who are you?'

'Robert, sir.'

'Ah! English chap then. Jolly good, jolly good. Don't get many of them any more. Can't think why.'

'Would there be anything else, sir?'

'No, no. Thank you.' Glastonbury gave him a vague smile of great sweetness and then fell upon the vast mound of ham and eggs. 'Thank you, thank you.'

Amiss was stunned by the courtesy and curiously uplifted to find that not everyone in this establishment was like Colonel Fagg. He returned to his dining-room duties in a state bordering on good humour.

8

'Sometimes I think I'm becoming institutionalised,' wrote Amiss to Rachel a week later. 'I'm forming habits and staking claims to little pieces of territory. Sunil has shown me places in the club where the members rarely go and where, therefore, it's safe to read or write or sleep as long as you wear your uniform and can pretend to be doing something vaguely official if someone comes in.

'I wait at breakfast every morning, including weekends, when only the long-term residents get fed. I've graduated to serving at lunch-time also: some even newer employee has been put in charge of the bar. In the afternoon I attend to the needs of the inhabitants of the Smoking Room and the gallery. Three or four nights a week I also wait at dinner. I'm known to be keen to earn extra money on overtime, so I volunteer for everything and I get most of it because – wait for it – I am prized! I am good-humoured, adaptable and I can understand instructions. I am therefore bliss for poor old Gooseneck, who this week has already suffered five losses. Elsa departed because she couldn't take Fagg's oft-repeated loud muttering of "Swiss maybe, but Swiss-Kraut certainly"; two male Chinese took umbrage when he denounced them as Nips; an observing Hindu became revolted when Mauleverer, an occasional resident, subjected him to intense cross-questioning about whether the liver was from a Dutch calf and was being served sufficiently rare; and a delicious-looking Filipino, who strayed too close to Fishbane at breakfast, received a pinch which made her hysterical. Never a dull moment in this establishment. Despite my many and varied duties I have quite a lot of free time and this is where the ritual sets in. Nine-thirty to ten-thirty, stroll in St James's Park, having, I hasten to say, changed out of my uniform. I may not suffer much from *amour propre*, but I'm fucked if I'm prepared to run the risk of running into people from my past life while clad as a bellhop. Return and change into uniform. Ten-thirty to eleven-thirty, read in the Card Room, and then off to staff lunch and work.

'Afternoon duty is quite pleasant: I can usually get quite a lot of reading done in the library because there's little activity on the gallery after three o'clock. Glastonbury is usually asleep – in fact, apart from mealtimes, he seems to be rarely awake. Fagg and Blenkinsop gossip and doze, sometimes joined by Fishbane, and the occasional non-resident looks in for afternoon tea. I'm off duty at five and staff supper is at seven.

'On the nights I'm on duty I work from seven-thirty to nine-thirty. I turn up for staff meals but I don't really eat at them because young Pooley is so guilty about what he's condemned me to that he keeps on having parcels of goodies delivered. I share the spoils with Sunil, to whom I've spoken vaguely about an eccentric rich friend.

We are waxing fat on a diet of Fortnum & Mason's cold meats, game pies, smoked fish and cheese. It's amazing the difference it makes. He even puts in the occasional bottle of claret. I have absolutely no conscience about taking this stuff from Ellis, who incidentally has shunted Plutarch off to a luxurious cattery and is still wrestling at getting the hairs out of the carpets. We're meeting tomorrow. I've got a lot to tell him and Jim and by then they should have seen our chairman.

'When I have evenings off, I tend to stay in the club lurking in the shadows reading: I am disinclined to meet friends. It's too difficult to explain what I'm doing and I can't face lying. Nor do I really want to go home. I only get depressed when I'm there, thinking that you should be there too. "Self-pity", I hear you cry, all the way from New Delhi, so I won't indulge in that any more. Oh yes. Speaking of not indulging, you'll be pleased to hear that this place is conducive to staying off the ciggies. Lots of the old boys smoke and nobody objects, so I don't get into my anti-anti-smoking mood.

'There is another unexpected bonus with this job. I had decided when in Rome to do as the Romans or in this case, more appropriately, when in Babylon do as the Babylonians – no, I don't mean I'm having orgies in the servants' quarters, or letting Gooseneck have his way with me. What I'm doing is getting stuck into erotic literature and pornography: the club has a fascinating, not to say incredible, collection, and I can't imagine the opportunity is likely to arise again. I haven't quite grasped what the acquisitions policy is here. Ffeatherstonehaugh's does not have a librarian. Mr Fishbane, he whom no woman should approach before he has had his breakfast, is the driving force behind the library committee. He is not a man of esoteric tastes: his seem to accord with those one would associate with a long-distance lorry driver: lots of straight girlie magazines, only the more common perversions, e.g., mild S & M. If my deductions are correct, Fishbane has been in charge of buying only for about three years, because for the previous three the magazines being ordered were very rum indeed. I can't quite imagine where they were getting them from. Job lots from Amsterdam by the look of them. They're what you might call a very catholic collection: flagellation, paedophilia, coprophilia (sorry, I forget you're not an *aficionado* – the sexual dimension of shit – J. Joyce had leanings that way), along with the usual nuns-and-donkeys sort of stuff. In fact, a police raid on ffeatherstonehaugh's would lead to a great deal of embarrassment. However, that buying policy seems to have existed for only a very short period and to have been an aberration, as indeed is Fishbane's reign. For up to then, even if the old buggers in the club were lewd, they had a certain style. The erotic material they bought in had literary pretensions. Indeed, the club's collection of erotica is very fine indeed. Probably the most extensive in this country outside the British Library.

'I'm zapping through old classics from de Sade and Fanny Hill right through to William Burroughs and Henry Miller – all the dirty books one has heard of but never read. Though most of them are to my boring straight tastes profoundly unerotic, the process is interesting none the less and I have a new hero: the Earl of Rochester. Have you come across him? A seventeenth-century libertine who wrote excellent satirical verse (he's the author of the famous epigram about Charles II: "God bless our good and gracious king/Whose promise none relies on;/Who never said a foolish thing,/Nor ever did a wise one" – one of the reasons I like him so much is that allegedly he recited it extempore to the king) and some great, great poems about sex. How about this?

> Naked she lay, clasped in my longing arms,
> I filled with love, and she all over charms;
> Both equally inspired with eager fire,
> Melting through kindness, flaming in desire;
> With arms, legs, lips, close clinging in embrace,
> She clings me to her breast, and sucks me to her face.
> The nimble tongue (Love's lesser lightning) played
> Within my mouth, and to my thoughts conveyed
> Swift orders that I should prepare to throw
> The all-dissolving thunderbolt below.

'Good, eh? That's one of the polite ones. Lots of them are seriously lewd. I must learn some to shock Ellis with.

'What does amuse me is that although all the erotica and pornography are readily available, hypocrisy triumphs in the way they are stored. The pornographic magazines are all in narrow drawers in the library, the erotic classics are in grave bindings, and the drawings are never put on display. Indeed the magazine tables proffer *The Economist*, the *Spectator* and a clutch of literary magazines, although I've never seen any of them being read. If what you want is to peruse a publication like *Big Women*, you'll find it in a discreet magazine rack in a corner of the Smoking Room. Oh, and before I leave the matter of ffeatherstonehaugh's and pass on to more general issues, I've at last cracked the surname problem. You will remember that when we last spoke you said the Ramsbum, Gooseneck business was impossible, and that was even before I had met my colleague Blitherdick, the wine waiter who had been on holiday when I arrived. It was at that stage that I too decided that it was beyond any rational explanation. I happened to find myself with the Commander on the gallery one afternoon: the other usual suspects were missing. He was in highly sociable mood and, bereft of any equals, was addressing me on the subject of the decline of western civilisation and the loss of old standards. When he'd been banging on for several minutes about immigration, infiltration, dilution of the great Anglo-Saxon race and a lot more of the same, I seized the opportunity, rather neatly I thought, to observe that indeed things had come to a pretty pass when the name Patel was as common as Smith in England.

'"One of the reasons I like this club, sir," I said, "is all these extraordinary old Anglo-Saxon names that one rarely comes across any more. I never thought to find in the same establishment a Gooseneck, a Ramsbum and a Blitherdick."

'This observation caused the Commander to fall into roars of drunken laughter at the innocence of this poor poltroon of a servant. "It takes an egghead," he cried, wiping the tears from his eyes. "Anglo-Saxon, my arse. They're jokes. Way back at the beginning of the club's history there was a Ramsbottom as hall porter, and the wags in the club shortened it to Ramsbum. Ever since, the hall porter is always called Ramsbum. Same thing with Gooseneck. The first head waiter had the silliest name of any applicant: Goosen, not very silly I grant you, but enough. So because he had a scraggy neck he was christened Gooseneck."

'"So Blitherdick?" I enquired.

'"Blatherwick originally. Quite a distinguished name."

'"Excuse me, sir," I said, "but don't people mind being given these names?"

'"Mind? Mind?" he said. "Bloody cheek they'd have to mind. Should be honoured bearing the names of their distinguished forebears. You young people, no idea have you? No sense of history. Don't know what the . . . " And then mercifully he lost interest and fell asleep and I was able to go back to my researches in the library.

'I must pause in a minute. It is almost half-past six and I am due to meet Sunil in our room for a quick snack. Ellis has sent us some veal and ham pie and a few half-bottles of champagne: I must keep playing on his guilt. Sunil won't drink the champagne of course. He spends all his free time studying and he doesn't cloud his brain. He may be a secular Indian, but by Christ, sorry, by Ganesh, he's got an Indian attitude to work. He says he will have time enough to relax and carouse when he's had a smash hit with his first novel. I said I hoped it wouldn't involve him in being menaced by hoards of vengeful Hindu fundamentalists. He said if I thought he was going to be the Hindu Salman Rushdie, I was mistaken: he saw himself more as a Hindu P. G. Wodehouse. Anyway, he pointed out, by and large Hindus have a sense of humour. So have I, but sometimes it gets sorely strained. Yesterday, I incautiously sat down in the library in a chair just vacated by Colonel Fagg, and discovered later that the back of my entire uniform was covered in snuff. I had to go upstairs and take the uniform off to brush it, as otherwise it would have been deduced that I had sat in the chair of a gentleman. Perhaps when I leave here I'll join the Class War party, though I'll have to insist they spare Ellis when the revolution comes . . . '

9

'The Vice-Admiral's back, sir.' Pooley was so excited he was almost squeaking. 'He says he's free any time this afternoon.'

'Vice-admiral? What vice-admiral?'

'Vice-Admiral Sir Conrad Meredith-Lee, sir. Don't you remember? The chairman of ffeatherstonehaugh's general committee?'

'Oh Lord, yes. That again. All right, Ellis, I expect I can find time this afternoon. Let's say three o'clock. I presume you want to come?'

Pooley nodded wordlessly.

'Where does he live?'

'Albany, sir.'

'Mmmm,' said Milton. 'Very nice too. Pick me up at two forty-five.' He bent his head once more to the pile of paper in his in-tray.

'I'm afraid Colonel Fagg has taken an objection to you, dear boy,' said Gooseneck to Amiss that lunch-time. 'He claims you look as if you have Itie blood.'

'Because I've got dark hair, Mr Gooseneck?'

'That's a good enough reason if he's taken an objection to you. Has there been an incident of any kind? He said something about an insolent pup.'

'It wasn't anything I said, Mr Gooseneck, but I suppose I don't always keep my face impassive when the snuff takes over, as it were.'

'You mean when it starts dribbling down his chin?' asked Gooseneck.

'And when he smears it on his shirt.'

'Or rubs it on his ear?'

'Or a gobbet sticks in his nose.'

'In any event, you should exercise self-control,' said Gooseneck. 'You don't want to lose your job, do you?'

'Oh, no. I can't afford to.'

'Well, if I were you I would cutivate the *gravitas* of Jeeves. Fagg's already muttering threats and he's a very powerful figure in this club. If he wants you out I can't save you.'

At this moment Fagg entered the dining-room and marched straight to his usual table. With a sinking heart Amiss went over to take his order. A ray of sunlight came through the window and lit up the specks of snuff that had wafted from Fagg's clothing as he sat down.

'What are you gaping at, boy? You look like a damned wop. Can't keep your eyes to yourself.'

Amiss thought of the indignities he had so far endured and surmounted; this was a mere pin-prick.

'I beg your pardon, sir. Just for a moment the sun was in my eyes and I couldn't see properly. And for the record, sir, my father fought under Monty at Alamein.'

The red glare left Fagg's eyes: the floating snuff seemed to settle snugly into the folds of his suit.

'Desert Rat, eh? They were a fine body of men. All right, then. All right. But get your hair cut and look like a proper Englishman. Now get me the turtle soup.'

Milton and Pooley entered Albany, the great eighteenth-century house off Piccadilly that contains the most exclusive and convenient apartments in London. The Vice-Admiral lived at the back, and he opened his front door a few seconds after Pooley rang the bell. *Who's Who* had revealed him to be seventy-four: in the flesh he could have passed for ten years younger, despite having a head entirely free of hair. As he led them into his large and sunny sitting-room, his scalp gleamed in the light.

Lining the walls were a couple of hundred maritime paintings, ranging in size from tiny to huge and in subject from peaceful rowing boats to titanic struggles between enemy fleets. The theme was picked up in the ornaments, which in their turn ranged from the kind of small plaster ship one won at a fairground, to a vast silver centrepiece of a battle cruiser. The books on the coffee-table concerned naval battles, and many of the photographs on the occasional tables featured men in naval uniform.

'Sit down, sit down.' Meredith-Lee waved them to a comfortable sofa and sat down in an armchair opposite.

'You're looking overwhelmed and I'm not surprised. I have to explain to everyone that I'm not so much of a monomaniac as this collection makes me seem, but when my old man died, thirty years ago, he left me his paintings. Somehow the word got round that I was mad about maritime art. Ever since then, whenever I left a job or anyone gave me a present, I was given more of the same. Tell you the truth, I'm sick to death of the lot of it, but I can't think of anything to do with it that won't have my old man haunting me and have other people's feelings hurt. However, that's not your problem. What is?'

'Ffeatherstonehaugh's, Sir Conrad,' said Milton. 'Particularly the death of Mr Trueman.'

'Mmmm,' said the Admiral. 'So you don't think it's a clear case of suicide do you? I've been brooding about that myself ever since I heard. Didn't somehow seem to tie in with Trueman. As for ffeatherstonehaugh's, well, what d'you want to know? Damned if I could make out quite what's going on and I've been trying hard enough.'

'But you're the chairman,' said Milton.

The Admiral reached for the pipe that lay on the table beside him, took out a tobacco pouch, filled the pipe carefully, lit it, sucked in the smoke and blew it out luxuriously. 'I think I'd better tell you the whole story right from the beginning.'

He settled back in his armchair and put his feet on the coffee-table. 'I was very fond of ffeatherstonehaugh's from the time I was introduced to it by a pal of mine in the late 1940s. I'd been to sea for a few years. I was in my late twenties and, like any sailor, I liked a good time when I was on leave. You're too young to remember, but that was the time of austerity. There was still rationing, it was nearly impossible to get a decent meal in London, and the whole atmosphere was very puritanical. My pal Pinkie Blenkinsop took me one night to ffeatherstonehaugh's.'

'This is Commander Blenkinsop?'

'That's right,' said the Admiral, 'but he was fun in those days. Not the opinionated old soak he's become. Anyway, I'd never come across a place like it. The food was magnificent, because it was supplied from members' country estates; the service was marvell-ous, because the staff were so well treated.' Milton and Pooley caught each other's eyes and tried not to register disbelief. 'They were so well paid too, that even at a time of servant shortage people were queuing up to work there. The building hadn't been touched in the war, the wine-cellar was intact and the whole atmosphere was one of joyousness and laughter. It could be a bit vulgar, I grant you, but Rabelaisian, nothing nasty.' He puffed furiously on his pipe and gazed dreamily at the ceiling. 'The first night was better fun than I think I'd ever had. We had a great feast and lots to drink and afterwards there were recitations and a great singsong, and those that wanted to played poker. It wasn't like one of those stuffy clubs where the only card game you're allowed to play is bridge, and it's threepence a hundred. And although women weren't provided – it wasn't a brothel or anything – you could bring them in if they were good fun, and if they stayed over, a blind eye was turned. It was not like most gentlemen's clubs, if you know what I mean. It seemed to be run for the benefit of chaps who wanted a good time – not chaps who wanted to re-create their public schools. No silly rules. You could wear what you liked and the only bans were on people being boring or obnoxious. It was fun, it had style: I thought it was paradise. I joined that night. That was another thing about ffeatherstonehaugh's. Most clubs, you have to go through a long rigmarole of being proposed and seconded and vouched for by other members and having your background scrutinised, and weeks and months go by before you're elected. With ffeatherstonehaugh's, if you came in as a guest and they liked you, you could be elected by acclamation on the spot.' He fell into a reverie.

After a few moments Milton remarked, 'It sounds extremely pleasant, sir. Rather more lively than it would appear to be nowadays.'

The Admiral jerked himself back into consciousness of his surroundings. 'By God, you're telling me,' he said. 'Bloody place is like a morgue nowadays.' He stood up and went over to an escritoire and took a piece of paper out of a drawer. 'I photocopied this a few weeks ago. It's a poem by a fellow called the Earl of Rochester that used to be recited when someone was elected. It's a bit rude, but it'll give you an idea of the club ethos then: it's called "The Debauchee".' He handed the sheet to Milton.

> I rise at eleven, I dine about two,
> I get drunk before seven, and the next thing I do
> I send for my whore, when for fear of a *clap*
> I dally about her, and spew in her lap;
> There we quarrel and scold, till I fall asleep,
> When the bitch growing bold, to my pocket does creep;
> Then slyly she leaves me, and, to revenge the affront
> At once she bereaves me to money and cunt.
> If by chance then I wake, hot-headed and drunk
> What a coil do I make for the loss of my punk
> I storm, and I roar, and I fall in a rage
> And missing my lass, I fall on my page:
> Then crop-sick all morning, I rail at my men,
> And in bed I lie yawning till eleven again.

Milton laughed and passed the poem to Pooley. 'I presume I shouldn't take this as a literal record of members' behaviour, sir.'

'No. But you get the tone.'

'Indeed I do. When did the change begin to occur?'

'Hard to tell,' said the Admiral. 'It's all very mysterious. I went there pretty regularly on and off on shore-leave during the early and middle fifties. Then I was attached to the Foreign Office in various postings as a defence attaché. I had years in Latin America, the Far East, all over the place, and any time I came back to London, well, there was too much to do to have much time for somewhere like ffeatherstonehaugh's, and anyway I was married by then and my wife wouldn't have approved. Any entertaining I had to do in London was in the United Services Club. I saw ffeatherstone-haugh's as a young man's club, and kept up my subscription purely for sentimental reasons. Inflation made it a negligible amount, in any case.'

'Sorry, sir. I don't quite follow that.'

'There was a rule that one's subscription never went up from whatever it was the year you joined. Of course that should have been altered when inflation became serious, but it wasn't. I pay forty pounds a year, about a twelfth of a normal club subscription.' He sucked fruitlessly on his now extinct pipe, laid it down on the table beside him, got up, and turning his back on his visitors, wandered over to the window. 'A couple of years ago I thought I might get involved again. I'd retired by this time. I'd been living in the country with my wife when she died unexpectedly. As you can imagine I was at a bit of a loose end. Decided to move up to town. Didn't really fancy staying in the country on my own. Got these chambers, looked round for something to do. I've always been a bit of an organiser, so when I looked in on ffeatherstonehaugh's, started to go regularly and saw that things seemed to be in a bit of a mess, it seemed to me I might usefully give it some of my time.'

'When you say "a bit of a mess"?'

'Come on, Chief Superintendent. You've seen what it's like. There aren't a quarter of the members there are supposed to be. Do you know why? It's because subscriptions for new members are set at fifteen hundred pounds to make sure no one joins. The servants are treated like slaves. There's no life in the club any more. It's more like a luxurious rest-home for geriatrics, except rather than them paying the club, the club is essentially paying them. There's actually a rule that members of the general committee don't have to pay for meals. I smelled several rats immediately.'

'Commander Blenkinsop? Was he able to help you?'

The Admiral wheeled round and emitted a loud snort. 'Pinkie? That bollocks.' He threw up his hands. 'He'd gone to pot. Sold out. Secretary indeed. He should have been put up against a wall and shot, if you ask me, for dereliction of duty. I was ashamed that I'd written a reference for him when he applied for that job. It's always a bit of a shock when you find your friends lack moral fibre.'

'But was he not pleased to see you back?'

'He was, until he got a whiff of what I was planning to do. But at least he didn't spot that until he'd got me on the committee.'

'How does the system work?'

'It's a travesty,' said the Admiral. 'The old system was fine. Just the way Lord ffeatherstonehaugh wanted it. With a good, happy and well-looked-after staff and a first-class butler in charge of everything, all you needed was a committee of half a dozen blokes who were elected by popular vote to keep an eye on things and keep things lively, come up with new ideas, that sort of stuff. That's how it was when I joined first. Now they've managed to get round the popular vote. There's a new system. Any vacancies on the committee, they co-opt somebody new – someone like themselves of course. Elections happen every year, yes, but it's always the standing committee that gets elected. Not surprising really. It's the club secretary that counts the votes under the supervision of the committee.'

'So they fiddle the results?'

'Certainly. How else could a crowd of deadbeats like that have kept control all these years?' He sat down again and began to refill his pipe.

'And for some reason they thought you were a fellow deadbeat?'

'I enjoyed playing that role. Always had a penchant for amateur dramatics.' The Admiral set fire to his tobacco. 'That was easy enough. All you did was sit round like some old colonel in an Agatha Christie book, bellowing about the country going to the dogs. I didn't show my true colours until they made me chairman. That was what I'd had my eye on. Suppose it was a bit sneaky really.' He seemed unabashed.

'But how did you get to be chairman? What happened to your predecessor?' asked Milton.

'Glastonbury? He was pushed out. Not that he's the worst of them, poor old devil. Just not in touch with it half the time. For a long time it suited the others to have him in that job. You see, they all run their own little fiefdoms. Fagg has provender, fattening the members and starving the staff. Fishbane buys the dirty books for the library. We don't need a wine committee. Nobody's interested in laying down wine for the future, when they're dead: instead they're all drinking up what's been in the cellar for decades. But we do have a committee nevertheless. It's run by that old ruffian, Chatterton. My guess is he's been selling off some of the better vintages over the past few years.'

'I haven't come across him.' Milton looked puzzled.

'He's probably not back from his latest gambling trip. Monte Carlo I think he was going to this time. Quite impressive to afford that on an academic's pension.'

'Why did they make you chairman?' asked Milton.

'Mainly because they are (a) too idle, too stupid, too drunk or too arrogant to see through me and (b) because there was a bit of work to be done. I tipped the wink to a pal of mine who's big in local government, and he managed to fix it for someone from the public health authority to write a letter full of threats and demands and legal gobbledegook. The committee became so unnerved at the thought that the club premises might be under threat that when I said I knew how to deal with these bounders, but it could only be as chairman, they swallowed it hook, line and sinker. Glastonbury was out. I don't think he even noticed. I was in. They'd made a mistake. Once I was in that job, I started looking to see where the bodies were buried.'

He sat upright. 'I left the committee alone. My first objective was to get rid of Blenkinsop. I did that by straightforward blackmail. He'd been fiddling. Not in a very big way, but I've got an eye for that sort of thing and I told him I wouldn't split on him if he resigned and helped me choose the successor I wanted. That's how we got Trueman. Fagg and company were upset about Blenkinsop going, but since they trusted him utterly they left it to him to choose someone just like himself. So three months ago the club ended up with an efficient and honest chairman and secretary.'

'Must have come as something of a shock to the old brigade,' said Milton.

'Well, we didn't make it too apparent immediately.' The Admiral sat back and blew a few reflective smoke rings. 'The first step is to get the evidence, as you will know yourself. Then you act. So we let them go on in their grubby little greedy ways while we looked at papers and account books and took an inventory of the wine-cellar and just watched how the system operated.'

'And Mr Trueman was a good ally?'

'Very,' said the Admiral. 'A very thorough, honest man. I'm not surprised they killed him.'

10

Amiss was clearing away dirty glasses in the Smoking Room after lunch when he heard the door open and Glastonbury's voice crying, 'No, no, Cully. You must be careful or you'll trip up.'

Glastonbury held the door open while a walking-frame entered at some speed followed by its lean and dapper-looking proprietor. Chatterton made fast progress over to a quartet of comfortable armchairs. He dropped into the nearest one and let the zimmer fall to the ground. Uttering little bleating cries, Glastonbury followed. 'Oh dear, oh dear, let me put that away, Cully. Anyone could fall over it.' Fussily he searched for a safe place, finally leaning the contraption against the wall behind his chair before sitting down. Amiss hovered discreetly, curious to see more of Chatterton, whom he had glimpsed only in the distance but who Gooseneck had told him was one of the liveliest members of the club. He had lunched with Glastonbury, whose comparative vivacity had been remarkable.

'Now, my dear friend, what would you like?' Glastonbury looked up and saw the hovering Amiss. 'Ah . . . Robert, yes, Robert, isn't it, dear boy.'

'Sir?'

'Would you be so kind as to fetch . . . what?'

'A decanter of port,' said Chatterton firmly.

'Oh, are you sure? Don't you think you'd be better off with a soft drink? After all, you've been travelling today. The port might upset your stomach.'

'I haven't had an upset stomach since . . . let me see, it would have been February the twelfth, nineteen fifty-three, the occasion when I crossed to Biarritz during a storm and threw up into the Channel. It would have been a Wednesday afternoon, if I'm not mistaken. Port it is.'

'Well now, should I join you? Oh, dear. What d'you think. I might get a headache later in the afternoon.'

'Get the port,' said Chatterton to Amiss, 'and two glasses.'

With the arrival ten minutes later of Commander Blenkinsop, Fagg and Fishbane, three more glasses and a second decanter were called for. Having supplied them with a fifth chair, Amiss made them generally comfortable and vanished noiselessly through the nearest door. Constructed as a fake bookcase, this could be unobtrusively left sufficiently ajar for a conversation to be overheard. It was his first opportunity to use his listening post.

'So how did you get on in frogland?' enquired Colonel Fagg civilly. 'Don't know how you can stick them. Let us down in nineteen-forty.'

'Trying to take away our sovereignty through the bloody Common Market,' chimed in the Commander.

'Good-looking birds, though,' observed Fishbane. 'And keen.'

'I often feel French food is a trifle rich,' contributed Glastonbury. 'But still, you had a good rest, didn't you, Cully?'

'I didn't go there for a rest, you silly blighter,' said Chatterton affectionately. 'But yes, I enjoyed the change. I could get tired of even roulette if I always played it in the same place.'

'Must have been very expensive though,' observed Fagg. 'I've heard it costs pounds to stay in hotels in places like that.'

There was a lull in the conversation.

'Well, what's been happening here then?' asked Chatterton.

The Commander embarked on one of his monologues on the supineness of the Tory government and the unregenerate socialism of the opposition, interrupted only by murmurs of approval from Fagg, who contributed the insight that rioting yobs in a northern city should have been put down by the Gurkhas.

'Any survivors – put them straight into the army. Give them a short back and sides and give them a taste of the birch. That'd sort them out soon enough. Which reminds me,' he said, his voice rising to a shout. 'Where's that bloody waiter? What's his name?'

'Er . . . em . . . er . . . it's Robert, isn't it?' said Glastonbury. 'He always seems to be very nice.'

'Insubordinate bounder,' said Fagg. The port did not appear to be improving his temper.

The bell was rung several times. Amiss allowed half a minute to pass before he pushed open the door and stood in front of the quintet.

'I thought I told you to get your hair cut,' bellowed Fagg.

'I did, sir. I had it cut yesterday.'

'Doesn't look like it to me,' said Fagg. 'Turn around. Look,' he announced to the others, 'it's over his collar.'

'That's the way intellectuals wear their hair,' said the Commander. To his relief, Amiss detected a genial note in his voice.

'Pinkie, are you telling me this fellow's a bloody intellectual? We don't want his sort here.'

The Commander looked at Amiss and jerked his head towards the door. Amiss departed, leaving the four old men calming down Fagg. After a couple of minutes he heard the familiar clanking sound that indicated that Fagg was taking refuge in the contents of his various pockets and had commenced the process of smearing snuff all over himself and the surrounding furniture.

'Well, what's been happening in the club?' asked Chatterton. 'Wine, women and song, no doubt.'

'Oh no, Cully,' said Glastonbury. 'It's been very dull since you left.'

'Apart from all that hoo-ha about that bloody fellow Trueman,' said Fagg.

'What hoo-ha?' asked Chatterton. 'Boy's already explained what happened and that things were all back to normal since he did himself in. I'm sorry I missed that. It would have been a bit of excitement. I'd have seen it if I'd been coming down the stairs instead of in the lift. This bloody hip . . . '

'We've had all those impertinent jackanapes around the place,' said Fagg, 'implying he might have been pushed.'

'Pity they don't spend their time catching criminals,' observed the Commander, 'instead of wasting their time harassing respectable citizens.'

A general chorus of approving grunts indicated that this view had been approved unanimously.

'There's no question that he jumped, is there?' asked Chatterton.

'Course not,' said Fagg. 'Bloody neurotic fellow. Twitchy. No sense of judgement. Never trusted him from the first moment. Weaselly-looking creature.'

With the exception of Glastonbury, who produced the occasional 'Oh dear, I don't know' sound, those present were also united on the general untrustworthiness of the late Trueman. 'The fact was,' said Fagg, 'that patently he wasn't a gentleman.'

'And he was a killjoy,' said Fishbane.

'Puritan,' said the Commander.

'Well, maybe a bit too enthusiastic,' said Glastonbury: it was the harshest thing Amiss had ever heard him say.

'Fellow was a damn pain in the neck,' said Chatterton, 'and we're all well rid of him.'

'Let's drink to that,' said Fagg.

A squeak of 'Oh, I don't really think we . . . ' was drowned out by Fagg saying 'Hooray!' and a clink of glasses.

'The last suicide on the club premises,' observed Chatterton. 'Let me think. Would that have been Buffy Strangeways?'

'Oh dear! I remember that,' said Glastonbury. 'Some time in the late forties, was it?'

'It would have been August the nineteenth, nineteen fifty-one,' said Chatterton. 'I remember it well. It was the last day of the fifth test between England and Australia. We won by . . . seven . . . no, eight wickets. I came back from the Oval to find that Buffy had blown his brains out because his father had refused to pay his gambling debts. Anyway, surely this Trueman business has all blown over now? Officially, I mean?'

'Haven't seen hair nor hide of a copper for more than a week now,' observed the Commander cheerfully.

'Is Con Meredith-Lee back yet?' asked Chatterton.

'Due back around now,' said the Commander.

'So it'll all be news to him, will it?'

'Suppose so,' said Fagg. 'He'd been gone several days before

Trueman did it. Be interesting to see how he gets on without his precious protégé.' The malice was palpable.

'I dare say he won't have the heart to push on with any changes,' said Fishbane. 'He'll leave us in peace now.'

'Oh, I do hope so,' bleated Glastonbury. 'I didn't like the sound of changes. Everything works so well as it is. We're not doing anyone any harm.'

'Don't underestimate Con,' said the Commander. 'When he's got the bit between his teeth, you can't hold him back. If you ask me, he's got some damn notion in his head that it will be hard to rid him of.'

Silence fell. The bell rang and Amiss went in to find a pair of newcomers in search of tea and toast. Since one of them was the old gourmet Mauleverer, Amiss had to endure a lengthy disquisition on how the toast should be (very hot and dark brown), on how much butter (lots), and why the club should provide hedgerow jam (blackberry, elderberry and rosehip) and a great deal more. By the time he had dealt with all this, the quintet had dissolved: only Glastonbury and Chatterton remained. Glastonbury appeared to be warning his friend to stay well away from the boiled onions that would accompany the mutton at dinner.

'Onions always give one indigestion, Cully.'

'I haven't had indigestion since that occasion in, let me see, it must have been nineteen sixty-one, when I dined with . . . '

Amiss left thankfully and went back to his researches in the library.

'What are you doing this evening, Sunil?'

'The usual. I have an essay on the disintegration of the British Empire. And you?'

'I'm off to dinner with friends. Two other blokes. Just the three of us. My girlfriend's in India. My friend Jim's wife is in America and my other pal's had his heart broken by a hard-hearted woman with a background like yours, who passed him up in favour of an arranged marriage.'

'Bloody women,' said Sunil, producing a passable imitation of the Commander. 'Don't know their place any more, like everyone else. Don't know what civilisation is coming to.'

Amiss finished changing into his outdoor clothes. 'Maybe the Commander could give you a few tips for your essay,' he said.

'No need,' said Sunil. 'Ffeatherstonehaugh's gives me quite enough inspiration as it is. The miracle is that Britain held on to the bloody Empire for so long. D'you think the Raj was like this?'

'Without the sex. We always left that to the natives.' Amiss gestured at Ganesh's attendant ladies.

'Depends on what kind of sex you've got in mind,' said Sunil. He sat on the edge of his bed tucking into the remains of a Pooley-provided Stilton that Amiss had insisted he finish. 'The lovers were in today.'

'Who?'

'Glastonbury and Chatterton. Didn't you know about them?'

'Know what?'

'Oh, Gooseneck told me about them. They used to be lovers. The club was liberal about that sort of thing in the old days apparently. It was well known. Of course all passion is spent now.'

'Just as well,' said Amiss. 'I can't imagine how they'd manage with the zimmer, although there's probably a whole magazine in the library devoted to obscene things you can do with disability aids.' He picked up his raincoat. 'Goodnight, Sunil. See you later.'

'Goodnight, Robert. Enjoy yourself.'

Amiss looked back before he closed the door. The sight of the rather forlorn youth sitting on the uncomfortable bed at the top of a vast, almost empty building touched his heart. He wished he could have invited him to dinner that night.

'Will you come out some evening, Sunil?' he asked. 'We could go to the theatre or out to a restaurant or something.'

'When term is over, Robert, I'd be delighted. But you mustn't feel sorry for me. Now go off and enjoy yourself.'

'Work well.'

A few minutes after Amiss had gone Sunil cleared up the fragments of cheese and biscuits, deposited them neatly in the waste-paper basket, picked up a couple of books and some blank paper and descended to the next storey. He turned right and went half-way along the corridor and knocked at the fourth door.

'Come in,' called Gooseneck.

Sunil closed the door behind him and Gooseneck took his books and papers from him. They embraced and Sunil began to sob.

'My dear boy,' said Gooseneck. 'My dear, dear boy.'

11

Amiss was melancholy. 'It's enough to make you want to top yourself when you get to seventy.'

'You just might be over-reacting, Robert,' said Milton. 'I wouldn't have thought your employers are exactly typical of our senior citizens.'

'Well, damn it, they're more privileged than most of them,' said Amiss. 'You'd think it would make them more sane and agreeable than the norm. At least they're not spending half their lives standing in queues.'

'Adversity never hurt anyone,' said Pooley. 'It's strengthening, if anything.'

'What a load of pompous twaddle,' said Amiss. 'There's a post office around the corner from where I live, and every Thursday morning the pensioners start queuing outside from about half-past eight, whatever the weather. They stand there and moan about being cold or wet, about their ailments, about the inadequacies of the National Health Service, about rising crime levels.'

'How d'you know all this?' interrupted Milton.

'Because it's what they always talk about when they're in queues. I've got caught in the post office once or twice on pension day when I was buying more stamps for my fruitless job applications.'

'And why do they start queuing half an hour before the post office opens?' asked Pooley.

'Christ, don't ask me. Presumably they're afraid it will run out of money before it's their turn. A touch pessimistic, our senior citizens, I find.'

Milton laughed. 'I think you're being just a touch bleak, Robert. More coffee and perhaps a spot of brandy? And let's move into the sitting-room.'

'I'm very pleased to have this competition going between you and Ellis,' remarked Amiss when they were settled in comfortable chairs. 'This meal was quite as good as the one provided by his noble cousin last week. I presume you didn't do it yourself?'

'No, I didn't,' said Milton. 'As you know, I'm an adequate, plain cook, but I've neither the time nor the talent to produce a *coq au vin* like this one: it was produced by my neighbour, Mrs Neville, who is seventy-five years old and runs a thriving emergency cooking, house-sitting and general crisis-management service for the neighbourhood.'

'That's just too neat,' said Amiss. 'You're having me on, Jim.'

'I am not,' said Milton. 'You appear to be familiar with two groups of the old: the wingeing paranoid dimwits who can think of nothing better to do than queue unnecessarily, and the depraved and corrupt denizens of ffeatherstonehaugh's. Well, I happen to know quite a lot of clever, amusing, wise, energetic old people who are excellent company and among whom are several of my friends. So there.'

'I'm on Jim's side,' said Pooley. 'Where I come from is chock-a-block with perfectly useful and agreeable people who happen to be old.'

Amiss arranged himself more comfortably in his armchair and dangled his leg over the arm. 'So how do we avoid turning into those sort of pillocks I've been talking about, Jim?'

'It's self-evident. By and large, old people are what they were when they were young, only more so.'

'Right, so Fagg is just more xenophobic and choleric than he would have been in his prime.'

'Well, he's a classic. He wouldn't have got away with talking to servants that way in his mess or wherever it was he spent his working life. And he'd have had to hold back on some of the madder racist stuff in public. Now he can get away with anything.'

'Of course, Gooseneck did tell me that Fagg suffers from gout and haemorrhoids, which make him behave even more horribly than when symptom-free.'

Pooley was looking thoughtful. 'Wasn't there a judge in the 1950s who had a similar problem? The criminal fraternity knew that if he was shifting uncomfortably in his seat when sentencing time came, they were likely to get a ferocious sentence.'

'In any case,' said Milton, 'the point is that Fagg was obviously never a nice person. He's just got nastier.'

'Glastonbury's nice, but he just has no sort of grip on what's going on.'

'That's pretty straightforward senility. He's just gone to pieces rather early.'

'And from what you say,' said Pooley, consulting the copious notes he had taken throughout their dinner, 'apart from a tendency to sleep most of his life away, his only major problem is that he's a worrier.'

'Yes, I suppose he's OK,' said Amiss. 'There could be worse role models for old age than Glastonbury. His is not a bad life: I could take to it myself.'

'As long as it didn't include sleeping with Chatterton,' proffered Milton.

'A *sine qua non* for a happy old age,' said Amiss.

'Fishbane's an interesting case,' said Pooley. 'It must be embarrassing to be like that.'

'I detect no embarrassment in that libidinous old bastard,' said Amiss. 'I think what happened to Fishbane was that years ago people told him he was a bit of a dog and he therefore confuses licentiousness with lustiness.'

'What does he do with himself when he's not pinching waitresses?' asked Milton.

'Well, of course, there are his heavy duties as librarian – checking through all those magazines to make sure they're intact takes a fair bit of time. Otherwise, he goes out quite a lot and he occasionally, according to Gooseneck, entertains ladies in his bedroom.'

'I'd formed the impression,' said Pooley, 'that they all had spartan bedrooms.'

'Well, not our Fishbane. It's only the monastic types who like their bedrooms uncomfortable. Fishbane has something on a grander scale altogether. He sent me there the other day to pick up his reading glasses. No, sorry, not quite reading glasses in the normal sense – pince-nez. I think the reason he dresses as an Edwardian is because he wants to see himself as a dashing young stage door Johnny.'

'So what was the room like?' Milton was fascinated.

'Huge. Vulgar 1930s. Quite a large collection of rather amusing French prints by Toulouse-Lautrec and some more obscure colleagues. You know the kind of thing. Ladies of the night dancing on tables among the champagne bottles while watched lecherously by older, affluent-looking chaps. The room is naturally big on mirrors, with a large sofa for dalliance and, of course, a four-poster bed. Oh, and, of course, red velvet curtains and brothel wallpaper.'

'And he's allowed to entertain?'

'The committee make the rules. You know that. And they seem to work on the principle of allowing each other to do anything they like. Fishbane's bedroom is somewhat out of the way and near the lift, so that the ladies can be discreetly smuggled up there by Ramsbum. So whatever noises he and his friends make don't disturb his colleagues, and the ferocious snoring of the Commander doesn't penetrate the love-nest.'

'Well, full marks for single-mindedness,' said Milton. 'Short of having an operation, I think he's dealt with his condition reasonably well.'

'Unlike the Commander.' Pooley was sounding condemnatory. 'It's a sad thing to see someone who had an important job in the navy becoming such an irresponsible old soak.'

'Sometimes you really are incredibly stuffy, Ellis,' said Amiss. 'I'm surprised you didn't say Her Majesty's navy. As far as I understand it, commanders were ten a penny and the whole cultural ethos of the navy was based on drink.'

'You're surely not defending him.' Pooley looked shocked.

'Oh, I'm sorry, Ellis. Of course I'm not. He's obviously neglected his job and let the club go to pot and is generally a frightful old bugger and an excrescence. It's just that sometimes you sound like someone straight out of a Second World War movie and it gets on my lower-middle-class nerves.'

'Lower-middle-class, my ass,' said Pooley.

Amiss looked surprised.

'You're an Oxford graduate and a high flier. Well, a retired high flier in the Civil Service. Don't give me that crap about being lower-middle-class: it really annoys me.'

'Now chaps, now chaps,' said Milton hastily. 'Let's drop the class warfare and get back to business. I know what you're going to be like when you're old, Robert.'

'Provoking, I suppose,' said Amiss.

'Too damn right,' said Pooley, grinning. 'You'll sit in the corner in your club making barbed comments to all who come within your ken.'

'They'll all avoid you,' said Milton. 'They'll be terrified of hearing you say something about them that they can't bear.'

'You'll be a pariah,' said Pooley.

'Oh, I don't know,' said Amiss, 'I think I might become a popular pet of the young. I'll tell them malicious gossip about the rest of the club and I'll become a kind of mascot. "Old Amiss, tongue like an asp, but not a bad fellow really and generous with the whisky."'

Pooley was looking again at his notes. 'We haven't talked about Chatterton.'

'Well, what more is there to say?' asked Amiss. 'He's pretty lively as they go. A fellow whose hip operation and general physical incapacity doesn't stop him going off to gaming-houses gets my vote, even if he does have a tendency to gurn on endlessly about obscure dates in the past of no interest to anyone.'

'Comes of having a mathematical mind I expect,' observed Milton.

'If you ask me, it comes of hanging around too long with Glastonbury, who regards his every word as wise or witty. I've never seen anyone so besotted.'

'So which of them is the murderer?' asked Pooley.

'I think you are slightly jumping to conclusions, Ellis,' observed Milton. 'The Admiral wasn't able to adduce anything new in evidence when he made that allegation. He was basing it only on a recent knowledge of Trueman and the belief that his committee colleagues are capable of doing whatever it takes to preserve their ill-gotten privileges.'

'Anyway, why should they think that getting rid of Trueman was going to solve anything?' asked Amiss. 'The Admiral's still in charge.'

'Well,' said Milton, 'I have to admit that if you're very old, short-term solutions must carry more weight than they would for the middle-aged. It might be just a matter of buying time and hoping the Admiral dropped dead of a stroke or something.'

'Maybe they'll kill him too,' said Pooley, 'once he mounts his grand plan.'

'That's going to take time,' said Milton. 'He said he was going softly and that he was much hampered by having Trueman replaced by the Commander.'

'Anyway,' said Amiss, 'from what you say, it's not as if he could bring in the police and have the club cleansed of sin. Didn't he say they weren't technically fraudulent.'

'Oh, exactly. That's it.' said Pooley. 'That's the brilliance of it all. Some of these guys had brains once, even if not that much sign remains. Lord ffeatherstonehaugh left the money in trust for the good of the club, but it is absolutely up to the committee to determine priorities. If Chatterton chooses to flog, with the agreement of the committee, priceless port from the cellar, so long as the money is laundered through the entertainment account it allows him to be subsidised for a jaunt to Monte Carlo and no doubt Fishbane for nights of bliss with ladies from a call-girl agency.'

'But why have disaffected members never revolted?' asked Amiss.

'Because the town members get an excellent deal and the residents get paradise. The only people who really know how rotten the whole set-up is are servants or residents, and servants are powerless and residents are enthusiastically in favour of the *status quo*. It takes a crusading type like the Admiral to find out what's going on and retain the desire to do something about it.' Milton got up and refilled their coffee cups and brandy glasses.

'Well, what are you going to do now?' asked Amiss. 'Does the interview with the Admiral make any difference to anything?'

'It strengthens my case,' said Pooley.

'Hold on, Ellis,' said Milton. 'It doesn't on paper. There is no new evidence that entitles us to start pulling ffeatherstonehaugh's apart. I had hoped that the allegations of fraud might make our path easier on this one, but the Admiral himself admits that there really is no legal transgression that he can yet point to. I've got to have some new official piece of evidence before I can go in and start interrogating those old sods. The only good news I can tell you is that I would very much like to have the opportunity. I'm much less agnostic than I was, Ellis, when you first started to make an issue of this. Between you, the Admiral and Robert, I have become convinced that the timing of Trueman's death was a mite convenient.'

'I expect things will get stirred up pretty soon now that the Admiral's back in town,' observed Amiss. 'I hope you've warned him that he's the obvious next target.'

'He knows that perfectly well,' said Milton. 'The one thing that worries me is that I don't think he cares. He's got his teeth into this, he's angry and he doesn't seem to have a lot to live for really. If you ask me, he's one of those chaps whose marriage was so close and idyllic that he'll never get over his wife's death: he's just passing the time as usefully as he can. Except when he had to go to sea, they were never apart during their whole thirty-five years together. She went everywhere with him unless forbidden by regulations and never went away on her own.'

'How unlike the modern woman,' said Amiss. 'Take our advice, Ellis. When you decide to get married, fix yourself up with someone of the old school, not one of those feminist flibbertigibbets of the kind Jim and I have landed ourselves with – undomesticated, never there, eyes set on further career mountains to be climbed. I don't know what the world's coming to.'

'Quite right, Commander,' said Milton. He topped up Amiss's drink.

The doorbell rang at midnight.

'Ah!' said Pooley. 'That'll be my taxi. I ordered it in advance to stop Robert trying to persuade me to stay on.'

'You doubt your own will-power?' asked Amiss.

'I remember the hangover I had the last time I went on the tiles with you, and tomorrow I have to play squash at nine. D'you want me to give you a lift back to the club?'

'Drop me at home instead,' said Amiss. 'I've been rather avoiding the flat except to call in once or twice to pick up mail, but I'd a letter this morning from Rachel. I must say, the diplomatic bag works extremely fast in both directions, so we are managing to keep up some kind of dialogue: she was insistent that I get out of ffeatherstonehaugh's as much as possible. I suppose she's afraid I'll get as dotty as everybody there. So I thought I'd spend tomorrow at home clearing up and reading the newspapers and engaging in some spiritually uplifting reading. What d'you suggest? *The Vanity of Human Wishes*? A bit of Milton? Pope?'

'I told the chap two minutes,' said Pooley, returning from the front door. 'Maybe you could go to church.'

'I only ever go to church when I have to go to funerals,' said Amiss gloomily. 'Latterly that takes me there quite often enough for a member of the Church of England, let alone an atheist. I suppose you have a family pew in your local?'

'Well, when I'm at home one has to show the flag.' Pooley had adopted the embarrassed tone he reserved for all conversations about the family estate.

'I have an alternative suggestion,' said Milton. 'I've nothing to do until Monday, so why don't you stay over, Robert? We can stay up late and drink too much, not play squash in the morning, go to the pub at lunch-time via the newspaper shop, and stuff ourselves with roast beef and beer. Then if the weather's OK we can have a walk in the afternoon and reminisce about the days when women stayed at home and looked after their menfolk.'

'You're on,' said Amiss. 'And before I go tomorrow we'll compose a joint letter to the two of them, pointing out how well we get on without them and urging them not to hurry back. We will include this poem: I've been saving it up for the right occasion.' He pulled a piece of paper out of his pocket and declaimed:

> 'Love a woman? You're an ass!
> 'Tis a most insipid passion
> To choose out for your happiness
> The silliest part of God's creation.
>
> Let the porter and the groom,
> Things designed for duty slaves,
> Drudge in fair Aurelia's womb
> To get supplies for age and graves.
>
> Farewell, woman! I intend
> Henceforth every night to sit
> With my lewd, well-natured friend,
> Drinking to engender wit.
>
> Then give me health, wealth, mirth, and wine,
> And, if busy love entrenches,
> There's a sweet, soft page of mine
> Does the trick worth forty wenches.

Maybe that'll bring them back on the next plane.'

'That would only be a distraction now,' said Pooley. 'Goodnight and thank you very much, Jim. Don't let him keep you up too late. I'll let myself out.'

'D'you think he felt left out?' asked Milton as he topped up Amiss's outstretched glass.

'I don't give a fuck if he did or didn't. I've become very fond of

Ellis and I'm prepared on occasion to be tempted into his latest hare-brained scheme, but I'm buggered if I'll carry on like Richard Hannay and his chums in a John Buchan novel. The trouble about Ellis's preoccupation with crime fiction is that it's a genre that sits most comfortably in an England that is dead and gone.'

'Like ffeatherstonehaugh's?' said Milton.

'Precisely,' said Amiss. 'It's enough to make one feel one should go into the West End to a Heavy Metal disco or something.'

'Why don't we watch the re-run of today's "Match of the Day" instead?' suggested Milton. 'There won't be anybody in it over thirty.'

'Perfect. And let's make a vow. We won't talk about anything earnest, serious, or in any way related to ffeatherstonehaugh's between now and my departure.'

'Done,' said Milton.

12

'There's something peculiar going on,' said Sunil on Monday morning, during their private morning snack. 'Mmmm. I've never had gulls' eggs before, Robert. Very nice.'

'Good. Pass the pâté,' said Amiss. 'What d'you mean, peculiar? How can anything that happens here be called peculiar?'

'I mean abnormal,' said Sunil. 'You can be a frightful pedant, Robert.'

'Sorry. Go on.'

'Well, the Admiral came in yesterday afternoon.'

'On a Sunday. That's very unusual, isn't it?'

'For a non-resident it is, though I suppose he's got a perfect right, being chairman and everything. He wandered around for a couple of hours having chats with any of the old fellows who were around the place.'

'Like who?'

'Mainly the hard core. You know – Fagg, Fishbane, Glastonbury, Chatterton and the Commander. There's hardly ever anyone else staying at weekends.'

'Ah! The dear Commander. Slaving away at his job, even on a Sunday. Heroic.'

'An example to us all, I think.'

'Was he just being sociable?' Amiss tried to sound no more than mildly interested.

'Don't think so. He upset Glastonbury. Poor old boy looked a bit tearful after they'd talked. Fagg was in an absolute rage.'

'Fagg's always in a rage. Here, have the last of the eggs. I've had most of the pâté.'

'Thanks, I will. Today's lunch in the servants' hall consists of tripe and onions, followed by tapioca pudding.'

'Some people like tripe, you know,' said Amiss wonderingly. 'In fact I've heard Mauleverer going on about a tripe restaurant in Paris.'

'Even if I weren't of Hindu stock, I doubt if I would ever have been attracted by the notion of eating a cow's stomach.'

'Shall we give it a miss then?'

'Oh, I'll look in. I have to have a word with Gooseneck about my timetable for this week.'

'So what d'you think the Admiral was up to? You didn't hear anything that was said?'

'Just the odd sentence here or there. But none of his encounters seemed to be convivial, so they weren't calling for drinks while he was there. I just heard Fagg shouting, "How dare you, sir?" and the Commander wailing something about old times. Honestly, it sounded to me as if he was giving them all some kind of ultimatum.'

'Did they get together afterwards or anything?'

'No. The Commander was going out anyway. He always goes to his married daughter on Sunday evening. And Glastonbury goes to his mother's grave to do a bit of gardening. Anyway, Fagg looked too furious to speak to anyone.'

'Well, it'll be interesting to see if they go into conference this afternoon,' said Amiss. 'It would make a nice change to have something happening in this place for once. Maybe they'll launch a *putsch* and get themselves a new chairman.'

'Maybe,' said Sunil. 'But my feeling is that the winds of change are blowing through this club and that the old guard's days are numbered.'

'And which side will you be on, Sunil?'

'I shall be neutral. I've got two essays to write in the next fortnight. And you?'

'Oh, I shall compose an elegy when the time is right.'

'What's the Admiral up to, Ellis?' Amiss shovelled some more change into the slot.

'Nothing that I've heard. I mean, we told you that he was planning what he called a tactful chat with the main protagonists, but I thought the idea was to lull them into a sense of false security. Sunil's evidence suggests that he upset some of them.'

'Well, if you hear anything, ring me. Pretend to be from the employment agency.'

'What's it called?'

'It's called Service With A Smile,' said Amiss through clenched teeth. 'And the motto on its letterhead reads: "We also serve who only stand and wait". Now if you'll excuse me, I have to go and do that very thing.'

The group in the Smoking Room that afternoon resembled rather more the Angry Brigade than the Gang of Five. Amiss was fascinated by the range of inarticulate sounds they could produce. Gaggings and chokings and wailings and grumbles and mumbles and expostulations and curses and oaths followed each other in rapid sequence in response to the fluent introductory speech by Fishbane, who appeared to have appointed himself master of ceremonies. Much to Amiss's chagrin, his eavesdropping was greatly hampered by a new cleaner, who had arrived to do a serious job on the upstairs kitchen. Amiss spent a deeply frustrating hour rushing to his post any time the cleaner left or appeared to be absorbed in his job, frequently having the conversation drowned out by the sound of a vacuum cleaner and in between having to exchange inane pleasantries. He spent as long as he could going round the Smoking Room at a snail's pace, cleaning clean ashtrays and polishing polished tables, and when summoned once or twice to wait on other members he dragged out the process of serving them for an inordinate length of time. Nevertheless, he could pick up very little. Glastonbury was certainly upset, although that didn't stop him nodding off on several occasions; Fagg was enraged – the term 'bloody fellow' came up frequently; Fishbane was considered; the Commander spluttered a lot and Chatterton said very little except to draw on his memory of some committee problem that had arisen in 1964. Chatterton thought this event had occurred on the afternoon of the tenth of January, although he did concede that it might have been the eleventh. He remembered this because it was the day on which the BBC Home Service had announced the news that Her Majesty the Queen had given birth to what would become known as Prince Edward. Chatterton declared himself slightly worried that he could forget such a momentous date.

When Pooley rang around six o'clock, Amiss's frustration had still not been dispelled.

'Jim had a word with the Admiral, Robert. Sunil was right. It didn't go too well yesterday. He said he got angry at the absolute resistance to any kind of moderate reform and at the dismissive way some of them spoke about poor old Trueman. Anyway, the upshot was that he demanded there be a committee meeting this Thursday to work out a club strategy.'

'They won't like that: it sounds ominous and modern and dangerous.'

'Well, he did say he'd try to cool things down in advance of the meeting,' said Pooley. 'He's intending to drop in and have a social drink with a few of them in the next day or so, have lunch or dinner, participate in old boys' chat, that sort of thing.'

'I wish him luck. It's hard to be one of the boys when the boys unite only against a common enemy and at the moment that is oneself. Tell him to stay well away from the balustrade.'

Though Amiss was not entirely convinced that Trueman had been murdered, he did feel a sense of unease about the Admiral's safety, so he was relieved to see that he seemed to be getting on rather better with his committee colleagues than the Sunday experiences had promised. He lunched amicably with Glastonbury and Chatterton, dined civilly with Fagg and Fishbane, and even had a seemingly friendly tête-à-tête with the Commander on Wednesday afternoon. Yet Amiss felt that to a group of paranoid old men the Admiral's conduct must have appeared worrying. He refused three of the courses at lunch, four at dinner; he skipped the Madeira and champagne; his consumption of port was derisory. He tended to bow out when the other old codgers were getting stuck into tedious reminiscence, clearly lacking the high boredom threshold necessary to keep these dissidents happy.

Amiss wondered what a management consultant would do, faced with the Admiral's problem. He had explained to Milton and Pooley that he had to carry the body of members with him. History suggested that *anciens régimes* tended to resist modernisation. The Admiral was going to have quite a job persuading even the ordinary bloated members to pay more, and to eat and drink less. None the less, Milton believed that he had a fair chance, if one believed that the English gentleman normally had some good in him, and that an appeal to decency and tradition could work. What was pretty clear was that Colonel Fagg would not be in the vanguard of modernisation.

'Bloody fellow says he can't manage fish and meat at the same meal,' Amiss overheard him saying, as globules of congealed snuff quivered in his nostrils. 'It'll be austerity packages and spam fritters if we're not careful.'

'Never mind,' he heard Fishbane offer, 'we'll sort him out tomorrow.'

The committee never got the chance to remonstrate with their persecutor. On Wednesday evening, the Admiral looked in on the club after dinner and Amiss heard him say goodnight to the five, remarking that he had a little work to do in the office, after which he would get back home and turn in: he looked forward to seeing them the following day.

Among the many fictions maintained in ffeatherstonehaugh's was that committee members were busy men. Meetings therefore always took place at five-thirty in the evening, a time when a politician, a lawyer or a captain of industry might be expected to be able to get away from his office for an important private occasion. Gooseneck deputed Amiss that Thursday afternoon to provide refreshments. At five-fifteen he was to take tea and Dundee cake to the committee room. At six-thirty he would turn up with a large jug of the club cocktail, for it was a tradition that committee meetings ended with a toast to the club in its own tipple.

*

Punctually, Amiss descended the staircase with a laden tray: the Admiral was a hundred yards ahead of him. As Amiss entered the room the blast went off: he was flung across the room unconscious. The Admiral, who had unwittingly detonated the explosive, never had a chance.

13

The call came first to the anti-terrorist squad, so it took an hour before Milton heard the news on the grapevine. By then the press had already been told that the likelihood was that this was a terrorist act: the media were already speculating on whether the perpetrators were Arab or Irish. While Milton explained the background and tried to wrest the case back to his jurisdiction, Pooley, who had gone with him to ffeatherstonehaugh's, was white-faced with fear at Ramsbum's gleeful account of the state of the two victims.

'Course the Admiral, 'e was a goner. His own mother wouldn't have recognised him. Lost a fair bit of his 'ead.'

'And the waiter? D'you know which one it was?'

'Oh, yeah. It was young Robert. Can't remember his second name, but he was an English chap.'

'Was?' Pooley was overwhelmed with horror. 'But he's still alive, isn't he?'

'Can't see 'e'd be able to hang on. 'E was covered in blood. They couldn't 'ave caught him in time. Must 'a lost gallons.'

Without another word Pooley tore into the club and found Milton. 'I must speak to you, sir. It's urgent.'

Milton apologised to the chief of the anti-terrorist squad and took Pooley into a corner.

'Ramsbum says the injured waiter was Robert and that he's in a serious condition.' Pooley was gabbling.

'I've just been told the same. Apparently there's no word from the hospital yet.'

'Can I go along there please, sir?'

'No, I'm afraid you can't. We're taking over here now and you've got to stay. We can't let personal feelings interfere with duty: you know that.'

Pooley straightened himself. 'Yes,' he said. 'I know that, sir.'

'Good man, Ellis. Now here's what I want you to do.'

The switching on of a harsh electric light woke Amiss at 6 a.m. He stayed immobile, trying desperately to identify where he was and to recall how he had got there. He raised his head slightly and took cautious stock. He was in an iron bed which resembled that on which he slept in ffeatherstonehaugh's, but it had on one side a sad leatherette-and-wooden armchair and on the other a small white cabinet. Enclosing these three items were murky yellow-and-green curtains. There was a strong smell of disinfectant. He was wearing winceyette pyjamas like those he had had as a child. Enlightenment dawned: he was in hospital.

'Morning, Bert,' called a loud, high-pitched, trembling voice from his left.

'Morning, Alf,' came the shouted response from opposite. 'How did you sleep?'

'Oh, not too bad. Mustn't grumble. Much better than the other night when my leg was so bad. I think that cup of tea last thing at night really helps. How about you?'

'Pardon?'

Alf turned up the volume. 'I said, how about you? How did you sleep?'

'Oh, not bad. Mustn't grumble, mustn't grumble. Wonder what's for breakfast this morning. Think it will be cornflakes or rice crispies?'

'It's Friday. Probably rice crispies. Don't like them as much as cornflakes.' Alf's voice had dropped a decibel.

'Don't like what?'

'I don't like rice crispies as much as cornflakes,' roared Alf.

'Nor do I. Still, mustn't grumble. And there might be strawberry jam today.'

'Hope so.'

'All right, Alf?'

'All right, Bert.'

The conversationalists relapsed into silence, broken by intermittent spitting and coughing. Amiss stayed hidden in his enclosure, nervously examining his body for signs of damage. He could find only a small cut and bruise on the back of his head. Confused and agitated, he pressed the call button.

Three or four minutes later he heard a female with an Irish accent enquiring who wanted her: after a few cheery exchanges with the other inmates, she arrived at his pen. She pulled back the front curtain vigorously and revealed herself to be young and jolly-looking. 'Hello there, I'm Bernadette. You're Robert, aren't you? And what can I do for you?'

'Why am I here, Bernadette?'

'Bit of an accident. Nothing serious. You're grand now, thank God. Sister'll tell you all about it in a minute.'

'Can't you?'

'Sorry. Robert. Sister knows the details. Now don't you worry your head. You're in fine fettle.'

'I can't find my watch. What time is it?'

'Ten past six.'

'Christ.'

'We have to get an early start in hospital, you know.' She began to draw the other curtains back. 'No, no, please,' squealed Amiss. 'I want the curtains closed.'

'Closed. Why?'

'Because I want to be alone.'

'What for, for heaven's sake? Who do you think you are? Greta Garbo?'

From his period of employment in an Irish pub, Amiss was well accustomed to its denizens' congenital gregariousness; this went hand in hand with a complete inability to understand anyone else's need for peace. Unable to explain, he fell back on charm. 'Oh, go on, Bernadette. Humour me.' He spoke as flirtatiously as was humanly possible in his anxious state.

'Oh, all right. Fair enough. If that's what you want. Be seeing you.' Shaking her head with mystification, she drew the curtains to.

After a few minutes they were half opened and a middle-aged woman came and sat on the chair by his bed. Her uniform was festooned with epaulettes, badges and stripes: Amiss wondered why a profession so given to the trappings of power stopped short of medals.

'Good morning, Robert,' she said. 'You gave everyone quite a fright.'

'What did I do?'

'You got yourself involved in an explosion. Don't you remember?'

'I don't remember anything except carrying a tray of tea and cake down a long corridor.'

She looked at him sympathetically: her crisp, rather school-mistressy manner gave way to something more gentle. 'You've been very lucky. Some kind of bomb went off. I'm afraid it killed Sir Conrad Meredith-Lee.'

'Oh, Jesus Christ!' said Amiss. 'The bastards got him.'

'What are you talking about?'

'Sorry.' Amiss recollected where he was. 'Pay no attention. I'm rambling. Was anyone else hurt?'

'No. You're the only other casualty.'

'Well, I seem to be all in one piece, Nurse – sorry, Sister. What should I call you?'

'Sister.' Amiss speculated about why she felt entitled to call him by his first name. His conclusion that it was simply an old-fashioned recognition of his comparative youth was to be torpedoed a few minutes later when he heard her addressing his neighbour as Alf. 'Yes,' she said, 'you are in one piece, but you have had slight concussion. Have you a headache?'

'Just a mild throbbing – rather reminiscent of a hangover.'

'Anything else?'

'No.'

She looked at him and began to smile.

'What's the joke?'

'Well, it does have its funny side,' she said. 'When you arrived in casualty last night you were covered with blood and they started hunting for the wounds and getting the blood transfusion supplies ready. But apart from a small cut on the back of your head you were fine. It wasn't blood. It was red ink.'

'Red ink?'

'Red ink.'

Amiss closed his eyes tightly for a moment, as an aid to thought. 'So the bomb must have gone off in the committee room. They have ink-wells on the table. Three of them. Three metal ink-wells for blue, black and red ink, respectively.'

'Well, you were a lucky man to have got the ink and not the ink-wells. But I can tell you it gave them all a good laugh in casualty when they discovered what had happened.'

'Just as long as I can spread a little happiness at whatever cost to my dignity, I will not have lived in vain. Thank you, Sister. You've been most helpful. Now I'd like to leave, please.'

'You can't leave.' She appeared outraged. 'You've got to wait for Doctor to come along and give you permission. You might be suffering from all sorts of delayed effects. Shock does funny things to people.'

'Well, when is he coming round?'

'He'll be along by midday. Now you just lie here and enjoy the rest. I'll pull back the curtains so you can have some company.'

'I don't want company, Sister.'

'Now, now,' she chided, 'don't be so miserable.'

'Please,' he begged. 'Get me something to read and keep the curtains drawn.'

She stood up and looked at him unyieldingly. 'Now, now, Robert, when you're here you must do what you're told. You shouldn't be reading until Doctor's seen you and you need company to take you out of yourself. We don't want you brooding.' She pulled back the curtains with a dramatic flourish. 'Now sit up.' She shook his pillows and propped him against them. 'Now you're all comfy and ready for your breakfast.'

'Bossy bitch,' muttered Amiss under his breath as she turned to Alf. 'This is Robert,' she announced, 'and, Robert, this is Alf. Now you'll be able to have a nice chat.' And with her hostessly duties completed, she strode triumphantly out of the room without a backward glance.

Alf pounced immediately. 'That's me all right – Alf Bundy. What are you in for then, young fellow?'

Amiss turned and looked at him. He was shrivelled, wispy-haired and had a pronounced squint. By now a connoisseur of age, Amiss placed Alf in his late seventies.

'I had an accident,' said Amiss grudgingly. 'Nothing important. I'll be going shortly.' Innate politeness drove him to add, 'And you?' He bitterly regretted the question as soon as it was out of his mouth.

Alf opened his monologue inauspiciously. 'Oh, I couldn't begin to tell you all that's wrong with me.' He shook his head, but gamely decided to make a stab at it. 'What I suffer from most are my bowels.

I'm a martyr to my bowels. I've been in and out, and in and out, and in and out and had all those tests and can they tell me what's wrong? They can not. Do my bowels get any better.? They do not. And as if that wasn't enough . . . '

He didn't stop until breakfast arrived at seven. Amiss directed ferocious attention towards his tray, giving a spirited impression of a man who couldn't eat and listen at the same time. He hacked his way through his cereal – Alf had been right – or had it been Bert? It was indeed rice crispies, a substance for which Amiss had always felt a dislike verging on contempt. His hunger was however strong enough to get him through that, along with the slice of ersatz brown bread.

What riled Amiss more than the rottenness of the food were the cries of appreciation from Alf and Bert at the fact that strawberry jam had been provided. They believed its flavour to be much superior to the raspberry which they were given frequently, although as Bert remarked sapiently, it would be wrong to grumble. The duo were clearly foodies – either could be a poor man's Mauleverer. They moved from analysing breakfast to an anticipatory conversation about lunch. Alf opined that it would probably be a choice between fish cakes and cheese pie. Bert had a feeling in his bones that beefburgers might feature. Would it be peas or beans? Alf hoped for beans, Bert, for once dissenting, favoured peas.

'Now that was a nice cup of tea,' confided Alf. 'I like a nice cup of tea. What about you, Robert?'

'Yes,' said Amiss bleakly.

'You haven't drunk yours.' Squint or no squint he had excellent eyesight, thought Amiss resentfully. 'What's wrong with it?'

Amiss thought of mentioning that it had tasted like condensed milk with a tea bag waved at it, but felt that might be a slur on Alf's taste-buds.

'I wasn't thirsty,' he said. It sounded lame, but it seemed to do for Alf, who took the conversation in a new direction. He pointed across the room. 'That's my friend Bert over there,' he confided. 'Burlington Bertie from Bow I call him.'

Amiss wondered how long he could last without murdering this old fool: the ffeatherstonehaugh crew were sparkling wits by comparison. He pushed his mobile tray away from him, mumbled non-committally, lay down and turned on his right side, determined not to be trapped again. The man on the right had been reading while the scintillating cut and thrust of Alf and Bert had dominated the ward: Amiss thought that a good sign. As he looked to be of West Indian extraction, Amiss thought they might have a sensible chat about cricket.

'What did you think of the Test series, then?' he asked jovially. 'Exciting, wasn't it?'

The man looked at him solemnly. 'I have put such childish things behind me,' he intoned, 'since I discovered the word of the Lord. For the way is the light and we can all be saved if we trust in Jesus.'

'How interesting,' said Amiss. He got out of bed and looked in his cabinet for his clothes: it was empty. He marched purposefully down the central aisle of the ward until he found the sister.

'Excuse me, Sister. Where are my clothes?'

'Well, if they're not in your cabinet, they've had to be thrown away,' she said. 'Anyway, what are you doing up? You've got to stay in bed till Doctor comes.'

'I need to make an urgent telephone call.'

'You shouldn't be bothering with that sort of thing now,' she said. 'You should be having a rest.'

Amiss kept his temper. 'I quite understand, but I won't be able to rest peacefully until I've made the call.'

'Well, there's a public phone in the recreation room down there on the right – if you must.'

'I don't seem to have any money. D'you think I could use the hospital phone? It's just a local call.'

'Afraid not. It's against regulations. Where would we be if every patient did that? You'll have to reverse charges.'

'Thank you,' he said through gritted teeth as he set off down the corridor.

The recreation room was reminiscent of the dole office. The walls had once been beige; the chairs were like the nasty one beside his bed; the tables were formica. Half a dozen silent men and women sat around smoking: old tins served as ashtrays. Their wickedness was emphasised by several large posters detailing the dangers of both active and passive smoking. Amiss had an almost overwhelming desire to cadge a cigarette in order to demonstrate solidarity, but he repressed it. First he rang directory enquiries and then the operator. A few minutes later he was talking to Pooley.

'I've told you before that you can't leave without seeing Doctor,' said the Sister, arms akimbo as she stood in the middle of the ward.

'Watch me,' said Amiss, as at high speed he put on the clothes Pooley had just brought him.

'You should be ashamed of yourself,' she said to Pooley, 'aiding and abetting him like this. Completely irresponsible.' She glared at Amiss. 'Stop this nonsense, Robert. I'm not going to let you go.'

'Listen, sunshine,' said Amiss, 'I am thirty years old and a citizen of a free country. I am leaving. Thank you for your care and concern. I will take it easy and I will have myself checked by a doctor. Thank you and good day.' And nodding politely to Alf, Bert and the religious maniac, he stormed out, followed by his embarrassed friend.

'Thank you for springing me, Ellis.'

'Well, I'm sure I shouldn't have, but I was feeling so guilty about you that I would have agreed to do anything you asked.' Pooley negotiated his car into the line of traffic outside the hospital gates. 'Have you any firm ideas on what you want to do next, Robert?'

'Not really. Go back to work. Go home for a few hours. I was just concentrating on getting out.'

'Right. My proposal is as follows. I drop you off at my flat where you do what you like. Sleep, have a bath. There's coffee and food. I'll have my doctor call on you and you can ring Rachel. I spoke to her last night as soon as I knew you were OK, but she'll need to hear from you. And what about your parents?'

'They don't know anything about ffeatherstonehaugh's. Oh, Christ! My name isn't going to be in the newspapers is it?'

'Well, yes and no. I've got a complete set of them here for you. But I think you're probably safe. Jim deliberately gave out your name to the press as John Amiss when I reminded him that that was your second name. They're not interested in waiters really, especially waiters who haven't been badly hurt. All guns are trained on the Admiral and the club, so with a bit of luck, you'll be able to preserve your anonymity.'

'Hope to God I can. My parents will go crazy if they find I'm tied up in yet another messy murder. They already wonder where they went wrong.'

'So do mine,' said Pooley cheerfully. 'It's worse for them because they blame themselves for having provided me with the financial means to take a plebeian job.'

For several minutes a companionable silence reigned. Pooley pulled up in front of his apartment building and handed Amiss the keys and the newspapers. 'I'll ring you later on. With a bit of luck the three of us should be able to get together tonight.'

'I would appreciate that.'

'Oh, by the way, Robert.'

'Yes.'

'I'm glad you're alive.'

'Just make sure I stay that way,' said Amiss.

14

Amiss was as insulted as he was relieved at how little space was given in the newspapers to the injury sustained by J. Amiss, waiter: only two of the papers mentioned his name at all and one of them misspelt it. Vice-Admiral Sir Conrad Meredith-Lee, DSO, DSC, KCMG got an enormous spread as a defender of his country, a great patriot and a fine sailor.

Amiss detected a note of crossness in the press that it was impossible to pin this murder definitely on the IRA. What the tabloids were seeking was the opportunity to juxtapose a patriot with a traitor. Instead, they were faced with a statement from a Scotland Yard spokesman that there was no indication that this was terrorist activity, while the IRA had denied all involvement. The hacks had therefore turned their attention to ffeatherstone-haugh's and the resultant crop of colour articles gave Amiss a great deal of amusement. None of the papers was well informed, unable, it would seem, to find among their staff any ffeatherstonehaugh members. The quality papers had therefore commissioned rather feline pieces from frequenters of the more gossipy clubs. Much emphasis was placed on the raffish past, with roll-calls of distinguished libertines. One source gave a graphic description of an 1850s party in the club where an attempt was made to emulate some of the wickeder deeds of the Hell-Fire Club, black masses and all. These pieces all ended with phrases like 'a shadow of its former self', 'the sad decline of a great eccentric institution', 'no role in the new permissive Britain' or other euphemisms for 'let go to pot'.

For the tabloids though, ffeatherstonehaugh's was a gift, allowing them to devote dozens of column inches to the sexual misdeeds of aristocrats. There were close-up photographs of the Hindu erotic frieze, graphic accounts of the doings of the founder, and even a number of verses from a Rochester poem with the four-letter words blanked out. An unusually educational day for the common reader, reflected Amiss. The most disreputable of all the tabloids had got itself a scoop. 'LADY JANE BARES ALL IN TOP NOBS' SEX CLUB' was the headline of the article that followed the murder report. There were several photographs of a woman in a state of total or semi-undress (obscured where necessary, as this rag liked to refer to itself as a 'family newspaper') disporting herself around the club premises. In one she lay spreadeagled on the tiled floor on which Trueman had met his death, with the playful nymphs and shepherds entwining themselves around her. Another showed her on top of a mantelpiece with Lord Byron's bust tucked cosily between her legs. And rather alarmingly in a third, she lay flat on the balustrade of the gallery with one leg pointing towards a portrait of the Duke of Wellington who, with Lord Palmerston, was one of the few statesmen whose private life had been sufficiently scandalous to qualify him to be a ffeatherstonehaugh hero. She ogled the portrait of Beau Brummell, and intimately massaged the full-length marble statue of George IV. The lady, the readers were informed, was Lady Jane, an upper-class stripper, and these photographs had been printed in a soft porn magazine several years earlier. To Amiss, it was clear from studying the small print that Lady Jane was no earl's daughter, merely an enterprising working girl. He laid a small bet with himself that Fishbane had been responsible for giving her this photo-opportunity.

Amiss wondered what the average reader would make of the club. Nothing much, he suspected. The tabloids presented two views of the aristocracy. Either they were decadent, champagne-swilling, cocaine-sniffing sex maniacs, or they were stuck-up, toffee-nosed, pompous and out of touch with ordinary people. Quite often individuals were represented as being both, therefore presumably the tabloid reader would regard ffeatherstonehaugh's as an absolutely typical haunt of nobs – being simultaneously decadent, exclusive and run-down.

He looked at the watch that Pooley had provided. It was an hour since he had left a message for Rachel: surely her meeting was over by now. He was getting desperate to hear her voice. At that moment the front door bell rang and the voice on the intercom declared itself to be Doctor Hawkes. A brisk antipodean, she moved with speed and efficiency, despite being weighed down by the most magnificent chest Amiss could remember ever seeing in real life. He tried to keep his eyes on her face as she examined him thoroughly, declared him fit, warned him to take it easy for a day or two and to drink sparingly because of the risk of delayed shock. It was a relief when she dashed off to her next call. As the door closed behind her the telephone rang and Amiss and Rachel spent several minutes in near-inarticulate exchanges of endearments and expressions of relief.

'I suppose you'll go back,' she said.

'I can't leave it half-way. You know that.'

'You wouldn't come out here if I sent you the money for the air ticket, would you?'

'When this is over I might. But don't worry. Nobody wants to kill me. It was a pure accident.'

'If they succeed as well as they did when they're not trying to kill you, what mightn't they achieve if they decide they do want to? I shall be worried sick until you're out of that madhouse.'

'Be reasonable, Rachel. I may be in a murderous place, but I am in a sensible country. It's the opposite of you really. How d'you think I feel about you spending your days in a country full of sectarian murders, riots, corruption and all the rest of it?'

'I feel very safe here,' said Rachel. 'Everybody tries to rip one off, but not in any violent way. Keeps your brains ticking over. But it's very safe if you're an outsider. I love it. I just miss you. D'you think it's very perverse of us to want to be together and yet keep finding ourselves apart?'

'You mean, on the theory that there are no accidents?'

'Yes. Maybe we both have a deep-seated objection to marriage which makes us embrace all obstacles placed in our way. It's a good Hindu position – passive acceptance of one's lot.'

'Perhaps we'll convert when this is all over. However, we'll have a caste problem. If I remember Sunil correctly, administrators rank at number two. What are they called?'

'*Kshatriyas.*'

'I reckon I'm an untouchable.'

'No, you're artisan, so *Vaisyan*. That's not too bad. Only one down from me.'

'But surely I'm defiled simply by being in ffeatherstonehaugh's.'

'Mmmm. You have a point. I'd better rethink our relationship.'

'Now to look on the bright side of ffeatherstonehaugh's, I've a few more lines of Rochester for you:

> Poets and women have an equal right
> To hate the dull, who dead to all delight
> Feel pain alone, and have no joy but spite.'

'I don't see the relevance of that to your employers. No one could accuse them of being dead to all delight. Even your friend Fagg enjoys his grub, doesn't he?'

'I was thinking more of some of your colleagues.'

'Ah, now you're talking. Let me tell you about the fax we got from London yesterday . . .'

He had great difficulty in getting through to the club. The lines seemed permanently engaged. And when at last he got a ringing tone, it was several minutes before it was answered.

'What d'you want?' said Ramsbum's voice, his normal veneer of deference a thing of the past.

'Good morning, Mr Ramsbum. This is Robert Amiss. May I speak to the Commander, please?'

'Well, fuck me, Robert. I thought you was dead. 'Oo's a lucky lad then? Not like 'is nibs.'

'Indeed,' said Amiss faintly. 'Is the Commander about?'

'I'll see.'

It took a further five minutes before Blenkinsop made it to the phone, but to Amiss's relief, he appeared to be both sober and reasonable: indeed he was giving a rather creditable imitation of a normal club secretary. He exuded sympathy and concern, urged Amiss to take as much time off as he felt necessary, assured him he would be given sick pay and that his job would be secure, and only after a long argument agreed very reluctantly that he could come back on duty the following day.

'Very well then,' he said, 'if you insist. I must say, I'm very impressed by your grit. Not the sort of thing one expects of this generation, so all the more pleasing when one comes across it. What?'

Amiss mumbled a banality.

'Good. Right. I'll see you then. Got to be off now. Lot of work on my plate.'

It sounded to Amiss as if he might even be speaking the truth.

It was a long day. Amiss felt a mixture of lassitude and restlessness. He wandered aimlessly around Pooley's flat, glancing at magazines, pulling books out of the huge collection of crime fiction, reading a page or two and replacing them. At lunch-time he addressed himself to the kitchen cupboards and the refrigerator and was touched, though not surprised, at how spartan was the fare that Pooley allowed himself. Stores were ample but plain: cans of soup in abundance; simple, frozen meals for one; large stocks of beefburgers and frozen peas; and of course – Pooley being Pooley – a great deal of muesli, yoghurt and fresh fruit. Feeling a strong need for nursery food, Amiss shoved a shepherd's pie in the microwave, cooked himself some peas and washed the lot down with a pint of milk.

His spirits were raised by a phone call from his absent host, promising that he and Milton would be along mid-evening with a take-away.

'Now go and lie down, Robert,' Pooley said solicitously.

'I don't really feel sleepy.'

'Then have a large whisky and collapse.'

Amiss was so amazed at being urged to drink by Pooley that he obeyed orders and then repaired to the spare bedroom. He lay there for several hours, sleeping fitfully, having occasional nightmares, trying to galvanise himself into getting up, and failing because of the absolute exhaustion that appeared to have gripped his limbs. He woke up finally from a nightmare of dismembered bodies and prison guards to find himself bathed in sweat and sobbing uncontrollably. When he pulled himself together he rang Rachel, in search of that mixture of common sense and warmth that she applied to all emotional crises.

She listened sympathetically, murmured the right endearments and then said, 'The only thing to do now is to get up, have a shower, go out for a brisk walk and come back and have a nice soothing gin and tonic.'

'This has got to be a first. A day in which both you and Pooley are urging me to drink. D'you know who you remind me of?'

'That sister who annoyed you so much this morning?'

'No. Mr Dick. You remember when David Copperfield turned up on his Aunt Betsy Trotwood's doorstep ragged and starved and she asked Mr Dick what to do? He said, "Why, wash him." And when she asked, "But then, what?" he said, "Why, feed him, of course."'

'Well, I hope he didn't advocate gin,' said Rachel. 'Now get to it. You'll be fine by the time Jim and Ellis turn up and you'll have a nice evening poring over clues. I wish I were with you.'

'What's ahead of you?'

'Sleep, it being eleven o'clock. The next few days are going to be a mad whirl of a lot of strained socialising. We've got a junior minister from Trade and Industry arriving on a goodwill mission in the interests of better Anglo-Indian business co-operation.'

'These guys certainly like marching over well-trodden ground, don't they?'

'Well, they like going on junkets to exotic places.'

'Don't we all? Chance would indeed be a fine thing,' said Amiss. 'Maybe next time Ellis will find me an undercover job that takes me to opium dens in Hong Kong, dusky maidens in Peru and shark-fishing amongst the coral reefs, or whatever it is they do there.'

'I wouldn't bank on it,' said Rachel. 'He's more likely to set you up as a courier on an over-sixties package holiday to Majorca.'

15

Amiss was feeling fully human again by the time his friends arrived. They looked at him anxiously.

'You're too cheerful,' said Milton. 'I don't like it.'

'In that case you should have been here a few hours ago,' said Amiss. 'You'd have liked that very much.' Milton looked puzzled. 'It's OK, Jim. I've done all the New Man stuff. I have wept copiously and shared my feelings with a woman, that is, my intended. Sorry about the telephone bill, Ellis.'

'Don't worry about that,' mumbled Pooley in deep embarrassment. 'You're sure you're all right now?'

'In the pink, tickety-boo, right as rain and ready for action. I don't think I'll be going in for one of those prolonged periods of Post Traumatic Stress Disorder or whatever it's called. Spare me the bevy of counsellors. When you come right down to it, I didn't actually see anything unpleasant. And physically it wasn't any worse than when I fell off my bike as a kid and was concussed for an hour or two. Also, fortunately, I barely knew the Admiral. So horrid as it all is, it's not that much worse than reading about it in the newspapers. Now, what goodies have you brought? Edible, I mean. I'll wait for the dirt-digging till we're eating. I'm absolutely starving. More post-trauma symptoms, no doubt. What are we eating?'

'Indian,' said Pooley.

'I can't get away from it these days,' said Amiss cheerfully. 'Right! Let's go for it.'

They retired to the kitchen and unpacked the food, opened the cans of lager and carried the lot into the dining-room. When he had wolfed down a few chapattis and an onion bhaji, Amiss took a slurp of lager and then leaned back.

'OK,' he said. 'Shoot. How have you been justifying your existence in the last twenty-four hours and can you name the guilty man?'

'D'you want to, Ellis?' Milton sounded tired.

'Oh, yes please, sir. Sorry – Jim. Sometimes I get confused between work and socialising, especially when we spend our off-duty time discussing what we did on duty. Right, Robert. Now according to forensic it looks as if the explosion was set off by two sticks of gelignite and a couple of detonators trapped under the table and wired into the lamp that stood, as it were, beside the chairman's right hand. It's a dark room, so at any time of the day that light would be switched on by anyone wanting to read.'

'So it was set off by the simple act of turning on the lamp?'

'That's right.'

'Well, how did they know they'd get the Admiral? Surely they might have got a cleaner, or a waiter, or even some other member of the committee.'

'Unlikely. It wasn't set up until the afternoon. That we know because the room was cleaned at lunch-time and the cleaner actually switched on the light to help her see the condition of the table she was polishing.'

'It took hours to sort that out,' said Milton wearily. 'She was a new, temporary cleaner.'

'They all are,' said Amiss. 'They never seem to last more than about a week.'

'She'd come from an agency. By the time we got her address and tracked her down to some miserable tower block in Hackney, discovered she didn't know any English and found someone who could speak Gujarati, it was late afternoon.'

'How does she manage a job if she can't speak any English?' asked Amiss.

'She works with someone else who has a basic knowledge and translates for her,' said Pooley. 'It's incredible really. She's been in the country for about fifteen years.'

'Her husband probably discourages her from learning English in case it gives her ideas beyond what he perceives to be her station,' said Amiss. 'Sunil waxes eloquent on the desire of a lot of men in his community to keep their wives in perfect ignorance.'

'Anyway,' said Pooley, 'if her evidence is to be believed, and I can't think of any reason why it shouldn't be, the lamp was quite safe at two-thirty that afternoon. So the mischief occurred some time between then and five-fifteen.'

'Earlier rather than later, I should have thought,' said Amiss. 'Latterly, the Admiral had a habit of working down there on papers and one might have expected him to have arrived earlier than indeed he did, in order to do his homework for the committee meeting.' He helped himself to some more lamb tikka masala. 'So who are the suspects? Definitely insiders?'

'Well, we have pretty well absolutely ruled out any notion of terrorists,' said Milton. 'This is precisely the kind of job the IRA would have been falling over themselves to claim as their own, and it would be a ludicrous target for any other international loonies we can think of.'

'So it's a family affair?'

'So it would seem,' said Milton.

'Of course,' said Pooley, 'it is conceivable that it was the work of some servant or ex-servant with a grudge against the committee, but it seems so unlikely as to be hardly worth considering. And the same goes for most of the members of the club.'

'You're focusing on the Angry Brigade, then?' said Amiss.

'Well, the motive at least seems clear in their case. Besides, very few others had the opportunity. We haven't finished the process of elimination, but there was hardly anybody in the club in the afternoon except the residents and a few servants, and why the servants should try to blow up someone who was trying to improve their conditions is beyond me.'

'Well, Ramsbum didn't approve of change,' remarked Amiss.

'Yes, but all that "good old days" twaddle is hardly a sufficient reason to murder a man who's trying to raise your wages and give you something decent to eat. Anyway, for the moment we have to make that assumption. There are five people with a pretty clear motive, all of whom had the opportunity. There's a handful of other people with absolutely no motive who had the opportunity. We're ignoring them for the moment.'

'So I'm not a prime suspect?' said Amiss.

'Not yet,' said Milton.

Pooley was looking impatient. 'The first job, of course, was to try to find any traces of nitroglycerine on anybody in the club or in their rooms. Obviously, at the moment we're not publicly pointing the finger at your five chums, so we went in for blanket forensic tests on everyone and examination of everyone's quarters.'

'And found nothing, no doubt,' said Amiss.

'Zilch.'

'But surely no one would be mad enough to hide gelignite in his room?' said Amiss. 'Apart from the danger, there are all sorts of places in that mausoleum where you could hide a small elephant.'

'We know that,' said Pooley, 'and we've been as thorough as we could be without much hope of finding anything.'

'We have, of course, put out feelers to the usual quarters about where the supplies came from,' said Milton, 'but the chances of finding the source of such a small supply are very slim indeed.'

'I thought forensic methods had become so refined that it would be impossible to touch gelignite without some traces lingering about one's person. Indeed didn't some of those unfortunate Micks you buggers kept framing get done for handling gelignite when they'd only played cards or struck matches or something?'

'You can avoid being contaminated if you have the right protective cover and use protective gloves,' said Pooley. 'No. No leads there, I'm afraid.'

He got up and went into the kitchen and came back with three more cans.

'What's baffling me,' said Amiss, 'is the notion of any one of those five having the physical capacity to do this. I mean, look at them, for God's sake. The ones that aren't crippled are paralytic all the time. Ah! No! But of course. I have the answer. Glastonbury does it in his sleep under orders from Nanny.'

'You're reverting to your old assumptions about the elderly,' said Milton. 'Age doesn't stop you being dangerous.'

'Yes, but physical incapacity surely does. Trembling hands and booze stops you doing delicate manoeuvres with dynamite, for Christ's sake,' said Amiss. 'Which reminds me, did you check to see if by any chance Chatterton has more stocks hidden in his zimmer?'

'Oh, shut up, Robert,' said Pooley. 'This is serious.' Milton grinned covertly at Amiss.

'Sorry, Ellis,' said Amiss meekly.

'Apart from anything else,' said Pooley, 'none of them were drunk yesterday.'

'Was drunk.'

'Pedant.'

'Just getting my own back. Of course you're quite right. It comes back to me now. Individually or collectively, they must have made a decision to keep their wits about them for the committee meeting. Goodness, I must be in a state of trauma to have forgotten that none of them had drunk either at lunch-time or in the afternoon.'

'Which makes it more difficult for us,' said Pooley, 'since they didn't hang around for as long as usual, and therefore every single one of them was unobserved by the others for a minimum of half an hour.'

'So where do you go from here?' asked Amiss.

'Interviews,' said Milton. 'I'll be talking to them all individually and in some detail tomorrow. Initially just trying to get to know them.' Pooley shot him an anxious look. 'Yes, of course you'll be coming too, Ellis. I am not a sadist.'

'And where does this leave the Trueman investigation?' asked Amiss.

'Ellis's case is strengthened, obviously, but we've no more evidence. Tomorrow's going to be a long, hard day and God knows if it will yield anything.'

'I'll see you around. I'm going back to work.'

'Should you?' Pooley looked concerned.

'Yes, of course. Come on, you can't seriously expect me to keep my nose out of things at this stage, Ellis. Don't worry. I've recovered. And as long as you keep producing the champagne and caviar, I won't hold it against you that you nearly had me exterminated by an octogenarian.'

'Right!' said Milton. 'Now we'd better have a formal interview with you, which I will allege took place in your flat.'

'Good. So that means that tomorrow we'll be able to acknowledge that we met. Goodness me, deceit is very wearing on the nerves. Still, I suppose it keeps the brain cells ticking over. OK. What d'you want to know? And don't try to extract a confession: I'm as English as you are.'

16

As arranged with the Commander, Milton and Pooley arrived at ffeatherstonehaugh's at ten o'clock the following morning. He was waiting for them, alert, smartly turned-out and radiating helpfulness.

'You are welcome again, gentlemen,' he said. 'The circumstances are regrettable, but it is my pleasure to make you as comfortable as possible. Please follow me.'

He led them across the hall and through the dining-room, down a corridor and into what he explained was a private dining-room where members could entertain groups of friends or associates. 'We call it the Rochester Room,' said the Commander, without further explanation. 'It's not much used these days, but I think you'll find it comfortable for your purposes. I've had some armchairs brought in and put there at the window in case you want to talk to people more informally than around the table.'

He had done more than that. The room had several unexpected creature comforts: mineral water and glasses were on the table, along with a coffee tray, ashtrays and even a vase of fresh flowers.

'Is there anything else you need, gentlemen?'

'No, no,' said Milton. 'Thank you very much indeed, Commander Blenkinsop. You've been extremely hospitable.'

'I'll assign a waiter to you to make sure you have coffee when you need it and, of course, lunch. I've instructed all those you wish to see to be available today, but it would be helpful if I could give them some idea of the order in which you wish to see them.'

'Alphabetical, I think,' said Milton.

'Very good. So you'll want to see me first. Can you excuse me for a few minutes while I have a word with the others and then I'll be straight back to you?' Milton nodded and Blenkinsop left the room briskly.

'Coffee, sir?'

'Yes please, Ellis. Good grief! If we hadn't heard so much about him from Robert, we'd find it impossible to imagine that this bloke was anything but the most upright of citizens.'

The paragon was back within five minutes. 'Now where would you like me to sit, Detective Chief Superintendent?'

'At the table, if you don't mind, Commander. It makes it easier for us to take notes.'.

'Would you care for some coffee?'

'Kind of you. Yes. Black please. No sugar.'

While Pooley poured the coffee, Milton waited for Blenkinsop to seat himself comfortably. Then he asked, 'Would you be kind enough, Commander, to describe to us your relationship with the Admiral?'

'We were old friends. Knew each other for more than forty years. Young shipmates together. He was a fine man, Con Meredith-Lee. A brave sailor and a good friend.'

Milton repressed a familiar urge to tell an interviewee to cut the crap and drop the platitudes. Instead he said, 'Well, sir, this must all be very sad for you. You have my sympathy. Did you keep in touch with Sir Conrad over all those years when he was away?'

'With Christmas cards, postcards, that sort of thing. We did eventually rather lose touch, though we'd sometimes meet in London when he was back. But then, of course, in the last year we've seen a great deal of each other. We've been colleagues, you might say.'

'A harmonious relationship?'

'Oh, yes. As I say, we were old friends.'

'I had the impression that you didn't see eye to eye on how the club should be run.'

'Can't think where you got that impression.' The Commander busied himself with his coffee cup: it clinked against his saucer as he picked it up. His hand was trembling slightly. Pooley wondered if it was an attack of nerves or the result of alcohol withdrawal symptoms.

'From Sir Conrad himself, actually.'

The Commander took a sip of coffee and replaced the cup on the saucer with both hands. 'I didn't know you'd seen him.'

'I saw him in pursuance of my investigation into the death of Mr Trueman.'

'I see.' The Commander rubbed his chin vigorously as an aid to thought. 'So you know all about it?'

'Let us say, sir, that the Admiral was frank.'

'Con was usually frank. And look where it got him.'

Milton said nothing. After about half a minute the Commander broke the silence. 'Very well then. I haven't much option really, have I? Here goes: the whole sad story.' He pushed his chair back slightly, leaned back and placed one cavalry-twilled leg over the other.

'If Con had a failing, it was that he could be bloody sanctimonious, even when he was a young man. Sometimes you'd be having a bit of a lark together and Con would draw himself up and say, "This has gone far enough", or, "Have you considered the implications of this course of action?" And he'd start talking about duty.' He saw Milton's enquiring eye. 'All right, all right. Maybe I was lackadaisical and a bit self-indulgent. Got drunk too much maybe, even by sailors' standards. But what could be really annoying about Con was that you'd start off together, a couple of sailors on shore-leave, and at the end of your binge, you'd be left feeling embarrassed at having gone too far. Con always knew where to stop, and he knew where you should stop as well, and if you didn't, he reminded you that you'd have been better following his example.'

'He was cautious?'

'Maybe the best way of putting it is that if you were abroad and on the town, Con would find a licensed brothel where the girls all had health checks, while the riff-raff might sometimes take the risk of picking up a likely-looking tart in a bar. He was a bit cold-blooded really.'

'It doesn't sound as if you liked him that much.'

'I liked a lot about him. I admired him, I respected him and I was flattered that I was his friend. And I think he was fond of me. We'd a lot of good times together. It was only when I did something particularly outrageous that the priggish side of him came out.' He sat up straight, swallowed the rest of his coffee and pushed the cup and saucer over to Pooley. 'I'd be grateful for some more of that, if you don't mind, Sergeant.

'We began to drift apart when we were posted to different ships. Then we got married. We met in the odd foursome and it didn't really work out. We thought his wife was stuck-up. A bit county – you know the sort. My wife wasn't like that. She was full of fun. I suppose the Meredith-Lees would have thought her common. She was only a typist in the navy. A great girl and we were very happy for the short time we had.'

'What happened?'

'She just dropped dead of a brain tumour at the age of thirty, leaving me with a ten-year-old girl. I did my best, but I suppose it was during that time that I began to drink too much and that finished off my promotion chances. By the time my daughter was eighteen and at university, I'd had enough of the navy and the navy had had enough of me. We parted happily when I got the job at ffeatherstonehaugh's.'

'When was that?'

'About fifteen years ago. Ask Chatterton. He'll tell you the time of day I first entered the building.'

'What was the club like when you came in as secretary?'

'Running down. I had a lot of plans. I knew it couldn't be restored to what it had been in the old days, but there was still room for a club where members had fun rather than did business. So I started in quite enthusiastically, but as you've probably gathered from Con, I didn't succeed.'

'What went wrong?'

'The committee.'

'Who were they at that stage?'

'Chatterton and Fagg and a few more like them who've since kicked the bucket. But it was those two who ruled the roost. Chatterton had the brains and Fagg the energy. And they were both agreed that the thing to do with the club was to use it for their private purposes. I knew what they were doing, but they had the authority. They weren't doing anything illegal and I wasn't much of a fighter any more by then: I suppose I just caved in. I had a conversation the other day with Con that reminded me of what I used to be, before I got corrupted by this place. I'm making no excuses. Just call it lack of moral fibre.'

'Is that what Sir Conrad said to you, sir?'

'No. In fairness to him, Con was kinder than that, even when he got me out of the secretaryship last year. Let's say he didn't use more force than was necessary. All I knew by then was that I just didn't want change.'

'You weren't concerned about the condition of the club any more?'

'Didn't give a tuppenny damn really. I was pretty permanently stewed, I suppose.'

'I appreciate your honesty, sir.'

'I haven't any choice really, have I? Anyway, I've been sober for a couple of days now and it changes your perspective a bit. What's encouraging is I haven't got the DT's. Not a pink elephant in sight. Mind you I haven't cut the stuff out completely, you understand. That'd be a bit too drastic, but I've cut the intake by about eighty per cent.'

'So who killed the Admiral?'

'Well, I won't insult your intelligence by suggesting a terrorist: that notion's been laid to rest. I simply don't know, Mr Milton. All the committee had motives. I think Con was strong enough and single-minded enough to do what I should have done years ago. He was threatening them with an extraordinary general meeting of the club. He'd assembled a lot of evidence about unethical behaviour. But I can't see how any of them was physically capable of setting a trap like that or even knowing how to do it.'

'Well, in view of their age, presumably all the members have some kind of military background?'

'Don't think so. Fagg and Fishbane, yes, but I think Chatterton was in intelligence, code-breaking, that sort of thing. And I'm pretty sure Glastonbury had a desk job. He certainly never talked about any time in the forces. But even with a military background, you don't know how to rig up bombs. Or if you ever have known you wouldn't remember. Maybe somebody employed a hit man. I don't know.'

'What of this evidence the Admiral had collected?'

'Well, as I told you yesterday, Chief Superintendent, there's nothing in the safe. So it's either at his flat or, more likely, he had it with him when he was blown to bits.'

'He had paper, certainly,' said Milton grimly. 'Or so our colleagues tell us. But where had he got the information from?'

'Account books seemingly, sketchy though they are. He had a taste for bookkeeping, had Con. Kept absolutely meticulous accounts, even in the old days when he was a kid. Even after a binge.'

'D'you mean wine, four and sixpence, women, one pound thirteen and fourpence and song, half a crown?' asked Milton.

The Commander laughed and looked at Milton gratefully. 'That sort of thing, yes. But the account books have gone too.'

'Well, leather-bound volumes were certainly involved in the explosion,' said Milton. 'So I expect that is that.'

'Nothing at his flat?'

'Nothing.'

'Any help you want I'll give you. But it won't be that much because I've been out of things for the last year and before that I had shut my eyes anyway. But I do know, in general terms, how Fagg manipulates the provender committee and Chatterton creams off the most expensive wines from the cellar to add to the committee's disposable income.'

'I should be most grateful, sir, if you could jot down any facts, figures or leads you think might be of assistance to us.'

'Certainly. Is that all?'

'Except for the matter of Mr Trueman.'

'But that was suicide, wasn't it?'

'The inquest said accidental death, since no motive for suicide could be found, as you know, sir. But we're still perplexed as to how the accident could have happened and we're still looking for any motive for murder or suicide.'

'You've plenty of motive for murder,' said the Commander. 'The state I was in at the time I'd have wanted to murder him myself. He kept talking about wanting to put things on to a sound financial footing, in which case none of us would have been able to afford to live in the club. At least, not live well in the club, if he'd had his way. He was trying to achieve too much, too soon, I think. More of a revolutionary than a reformer.'

'Was he murdered?'

'You're the police. You tell me how any of us could have chucked him over the balustrade even if the whole lot of us got together to do it. He'd have shouted. It has to be suicide. Something in his private life we know nothing about.'

'Very well, Commander. I'm grateful to you.' Milton consulted his list. 'D'you think you could ask Mr Chatterton to join us?'

'Certainly. And when I get a moment I'll get down to noting any facts I think could help you. I'm angry about Con. I'd like to help.'

'That's most kind of you, sir.'

'I won't get a chance to do anything till much later, you understand that, don't you? We're having a hell of a crisis with staff because of the media attention. Half of them didn't turn up this morning – the ones who're probably illegal immigrants and the ones who're afraid of being blown up. And the ones that did are completely bewildered at the siege of journalists outside and everything has to be explained to them in words of one syllable. I'm at my wits' end.'

'Good luck,' said Milton and smiled.

'Good day, Chief Superintendent. Good day, Sergeant.'

The Commander marched from the room with his shoulders back.

17

A few minutes later there was a tap on the door. In answer to Milton's shouted invitation, Amiss walked in. He bowed.

'Good morning, sir. Good morning, sir. The Commander has assigned me to you. If I can fulfil any of your needs just ring that bell behind you and I will be in attendance as quickly as possible.' He shut the door behind him. 'And if you laugh at me, you bastards, the coffee will be laced with arsenic.'

'You ask a lot of us, Robert,' said Milton, gazing fixedly at Amiss's uniform.

'Yes, well as you will appreciate, this is the spare uniform that fits me best, i.e., it was made for someone only three inches shorter than I am. No doubt you enjoy the effect of the exposed sock, the way the bum-freezer jacket now shows the waistband of the trousers – not to speak of the exciting way the buttons strain across my chest.'

'I'd never have noticed if you hadn't said,' said Milton, failing to keep the grin off his face.

'Lying sod. At least it's only till tomorrow. The tallest Turk has resigned and in a fit of unparalleled generosity the Commander has ruled that his uniform should be sent instantly to a fast dry cleaners. Apparently in the good old days the rule was that all the uniforms got cleaned every six months, whether they needed it or not. Now what d'you want?'

'More coffee, please,' said Milton. 'And perhaps when you see Chatterton leave us you might bring us the lunch menu.'

'How did it go with the Commander?'

'He sang like a little bird, once he knew the Admiral had already talked to us.'

'I wonder if the others will do likewise. Any revelations?'

'Nothing much we didn't know or hadn't guessed, apart from on the human side. What did you think, Ellis?'

'I thought he was pretty efficient at putting the blame on everyone else.'

'Yes, I know what you mean. He's offered to go away and come up with incriminating evidence, Robert. Facts and figures about unethical disbursement of club funds and that kind of thing.'

'Christ! You better make sure he doesn't get murdered as well. Although it would be a help in reducing the number of suspects by one, I suppose. Every cloud has a silver lining, what!'

'Oh, go away and get us the coffee,' said Milton. 'How are you feeling today anyway?'

'A lot better than the Admiral,' said Amiss.

Fresh coffee was provided and, at Milton's request, Amiss left the door open when he departed. A couple of minutes later Chatterton zimmered into the room.

'Good morning, gentlemen. I apologise for the delay in arriving. As you will see, I am somewhat encumbered, though not, I hope, for many days longer.' He levered himself into the seat nearest Milton and rested the frame nearby. Pooley got up and closed the door.

'Did you have an accident?'

'I had a hip replacement operation on my left side, after which I immediately broke my right leg. The combination was a bit devastating. I was stuck in hospital for three weeks and since then have been shuffling around behind that thing.' He jerked his head in the direction of the zimmer with an expression of deep distaste. 'Mind you, I try not to let it cramp my style unduly. Now how can I help you, gentlemen. I can't imagine that I know anything remotely useful, but fire away.'

'Why d'you think Sir Conrad Meredith-Lee was killed, sir?'

'Search me. I know you chaps keep denying it, but it seems to me it must be the IRA. They did the Carlton, didn't they? I remember that. Heard the bang. About six o'clock in the evening I think it was. I was having an aperitif. It would have been the twenty-seventh or twenty-eighth of June, nineteen-ninety. Stands to reason it was them. Security here's a bit lacking. Old Ramsbum's not up to keeping out gangs of terrorists.'

'I think, sir, there's little doubt that it was not the IRA or any other terrorist group. We are ruling out no possibilities of course, but the evidence suggests the crime was committed by a club resident.'

'One of those strange servants, no doubt.'

'Unlikely, sir. It seems much more likely that it was a member of ffeatherstonehaugh's general committee. I understand there were strong areas of disagreement between the Admiral and the rest of you.'

'There are always disagreements between committee members, Chief Superintendent, but I haven't heard of a club murder this century. It was only a little local wrangle. Different strategic visions of the club and that sort of thing. Meredith-Lee was a bit of a lefty – the sort of chap who would be all on for worker participation and that kind of rot. But we'd have brought him round when he got to know the club better.'

'I understand he believed the club to be badly run and the resources of the club to be used unethically, sir.'

'One man's ethics is another man's priggery,' said Chatterton carelessly. 'D'you think I might have a cup of coffee or is that reserved for the police force?'

'I beg your pardon, Mr Chatterton. How d'you like it?'

'Black, please. You see, the trouble with Admiral Meredith-Lee was that he was a newcomer. We shouldn't have let him become chairman. He didn't really understand the club. But there was a lot of boring administrative carry-on to be dealt with. Some nonsense or other to do with the nanny state. Not really the sort of thing that dear old Boy Glastonbury, who was then chairman, could have been expected to deal with. Especially not these days. But to appoint Con Meredith-Lee was a mistake. And it was a mistake to bring in that counter-jumper, Trueman. He didn't understand gentlemen. Wanted to run this place like a bloody accountant. That's not what Lord ffeatherstonehaugh would have wanted. Can't say I was sorry when that fellow topped himself.'

'The inquest verdict was accidental death, sir.'

'So what was he doing? Acrobatics on the balustrade or something? Anyway, that's your problem. As for Meredith-Lee's death, if you're asking me did I construct a bomb and blow him up, the answer is no. I think my doctors will confirm the unlikeliness of that. So you'll have to count me out of your calculations, I'm afraid. Sorry about that.' He sipped his coffee pleasurably. 'Anything else, Superintendent?'

'When did your association with the club begin, sir?'

'Eighteenth of July, nineteen thirty-eight. My godfather took me to dinner here and we played poker afterwards with a few of the members. I won fifteen pounds, fourteen and eightpence. That was a lot of money in those days and the others were so impressed, they took me into the sing-song and had me elected by acclamation.' The rather superior expression which Chatterton normally wore had softened. He resembled nothing so much as an old man reliving a glorious moment of his past. 'It was a great occasion for a shy young don.'

'Oh, I see. I hadn't realised that you were from an academic background.'

'I was a mathematics don at Cambridge living a rather sheltered life, but I was part of a group that enjoyed playing cards. I hadn't discovered roulette then. So ffeatherstonehaugh's was a great development for me. It took me out of myself. I used to come up quite often and stay for a couple of days and just revel in meeting high-spirited people who didn't care about university politics. There was a song they used to sing called "The Debauchee". Haven't heard it for years. Bit rude, but great fun.'

'Were any other committee members part of the club then, sir?'

'Blenkinsop, no. Fagg, no. Fishbane, yes. Glastonbury, yes. More coffee, please, young man.'

'And were you friends?'

'I fail to see the relevance of this, but yes, I should say that Glastonbury and I became friends. None of the others were ever more than friendly acquaintances and frankly, I've never taken to Fagg. He's a bit too vulgar for me.'

'But you and Mr Glastonbury were close friends?'

'Do I detect from your tone, Chief Superintendent, that you think us a couple of queers? What filthy minds the police have. We were and are friends. Before Glastonbury got past it, we used to play a lot of bridge and although he was never a real gambler, he used to enjoy going to casinos with me to play backgammon.'

'And during the war, sir?'

'During the war what?'

'Did you come to the club?'

'Occasionally. I was at Bletchley most of the time, code-breaking. Used to come up for the odd break. Saw Glastonbury and Fishbane once or twice.'

'And afterwards?'

Chatterton drained his coffee and shoved the cup and saucer several feet down the table with a practised twirl of the wrist.

'Went back to Cambridge. Had an undistinguished career as a university lecturer in mathematics. Was a fellow of a mediocre college. Got away from it all as often as possible. You think ffeatherstonehaugh politics are bad? Have you any idea what a Cambridge Senior Common Room is like? They'd murder each other over the choice of curtain fabric if they could get away with it. I was very happy to retire here. We don't meddle with each other. We run our own parts of the establishment without interference. We were a pretty united and single-minded committee until the Admiral fouled things up. I'm not going to pretend I'm sorry he's dead. I neither would nor could have murdered him, but I do not regard him as a loss.'

'So you've no light to cast on the murder?'

'None.'

'Did the Admiral talk to you at all about your conduct of the wine committee?'

'Ah! I wonder where you heard about that. From which of my colleagues? Yes, he had seemed to get the impression that something was awry. But that was because he had not attended sufficiently to the constitution of the club and its regulations as introduced by a legally elected committee. Our position was watertight. Not one that bleeding hearts would approve of, no doubt, but we, as the committee, were absolutely within our rights to sell off what we considered to be unnecessary stocks of wine in order to allocate the money to members' more urgent needs.'

'Like foreign travel, sir?'

'Certainly. For those who wanted it.'

'You weren't concerned about the conditions in which the servants lived? The kind of food they eat?'

'Wasn't my pigeon, old boy. I wouldn't have cared to live under the rule of Fagg myself, but I can't say it worried me that these people were getting short rations. There were plenty of other jobs for them to go to if they wanted to. Anyway, the point was that Fagg left me alone and I left him alone. That's been the rule about sub-committee chairmen for as long as I can remember.'

'Thank you, sir.' Milton was finding it difficult to conceal his distaste. 'I've nothing more to ask for the moment.'

'Very good. If you want me you'll find me close by. I'm not likely to be able to make a run for it. Good morning.'

Pooley got up and opened the door. Manipulating his zimmer with dexterity, Chatterton nodded at them both and left.

'Get on to his doctor, Ellis. I wouldn't trust that old wretch an inch. I'd like confirmation that he's as crippled as he appears to be, because, much as I'd like to, I can think of no way in which a man in his apparent condition could have pulled off this murder.'

'I'll see to it, sir. I was just wondering.'

'What?'

'The Cambridge connection and all that.'

'Oh, for Christ's sake, Ellis, that's a bit obvious, isn't it? I'm disappointed in you. You usually see more unexpected links. If he went to Cambridge, especially if he was homosexual, he has to be the Sixth Man or someone. Perhaps you're right. Perhaps we're in the middle of a nest of spies whom Meredith-Lee was about to unmask. But I wouldn't put any money on it, if I were you. I think we're in a nest of greedy, self-centred, corrupt old men, of whom at least one would stick at nothing to preserve his privileges. If you must exercise flights of fancy, I'd much rather you concentrated on working out how Chatterton could have committed murder. Now where's that damn waiter with the menu? I'm starving.'

18

'How do those old devils get through seven courses?' asked Milton of Pooley as they ate their grilled Dover sole.

'I don't know. I always thought I had a good appetite, but I remember being at a college feast once at Cambridge, where they had seven or eight courses and the elderly dons seemed to have less trouble than anyone else getting through it. I suppose it's what you're used to.'

'Well, the standard of the cooking is certainly impressive,' said Milton. 'I haven't had fish as good as this in months. How come you've got a decent chef?' he asked Amiss, who at that moment entered the room.

'Because of course the chef is well paid – as are his immediate underlings. The Colonel doesn't begrudge an artiste his due. At least not when his creations are going down the Colonel's own digestive tract.' Amiss flung himself into an armchair. 'God!' he said. 'It's absolute chaos out there. Twice as many members as usual have come in and poor old Gooseneck's trying to manage with half his usual staff. He's very decent though. Sunil offered to give up his lunch-time seminar and help out, but Gooseneck wouldn't hear of it. "My dear boy," he said, "the choice is between feeding *your* mind or *their* bodies: I give priority to the former." So I'd better not hang around here much longer. I should go and do my stuff. D'you want anything more? We've got roly-poly pudding today with jam and custard.'

'I'll pass, thanks,' said Milton. 'I'm not robust enough for that. Just coffee, please.'

Pooley's eyes glistened. 'Oh, I'll have the pudding, Robert. It's years since I've had roly-poly pudding. And coffee too, please.'

'I'll get you an especially big helping, Ellis. Incidentally, they're all still being careful about alcohol. I was trying to ply Fagg with extra claret and he almost bit my head off.'

'But he's always biting your head off, isn't he?' said Pooley.

'Not today, other than just now. In fact, he grunted something complimentary about it being dashed public-spirited of me to come back so soon. I nearly fainted. Glastonbury was nice of course. He always is. But Chatterton and Fishbane were pretty civil as well.'

'You should get blown up every day,' said Milton absently. 'Were any of them off their food?'

'What? You mean stricken with remorse or grief? Absolutely not. Guilt does not seem to be gnawing at the vitals of any of these old fuckers. However, self-preservation is definitely operating – hence the relative abstinence.'

'I suppose it does indicate that they've got something to hide.' Pooley sounded hopeful.

'Oh, for Christ's sake! We know that, Ellis. Even they know that the way they've been running the club is hardly likely to gain them a good press. Anyway, I can't stand around here chatting all day. I've got work to do.'

'On second thoughts, Robert,' said Milton, 'make it roly-poly pudding twice. I think I need to build up my strength for this afternoon.'

Colonel Fagg obviously believed that attack was the best form of defence. 'Disgraceful, disgraceful,' he said. 'You're wasting our time and yours when you should be hunting down those IRA swine.'

'There is absolutely no evidence, sir, to suggest IRA involvement.' Painstakingly, Milton once again explained the reasoning which had led the police conclusively to dismiss the likelihood that terrorists were responsible.

'That's all my eye and Betty Martin,' said the Colonel. 'It's a scandal, that's what it is, a scandal. You're letting these bombers out of jail every day of the week instead of locking them up. It's plain as a pikestaff. The bloody Hun-lovers were trying to blow this club up because it represents all that is best about England.'

Milton let pass that slur on his country. '"Hun-lovers"?' he said. 'I'm sorry, sir. I don't understand.'

'On the side of the bloody Germans during the war, weren't they? Treacherous beasts, all of them. We should have invaded. Then we wouldn't have all that trouble we have now. Shoot the ringleaders, that's what I say. That's the only way to deal with the enemy.'

'Ireland was neutral in the last war, sir.'

'Huh! Neutrality is as neutrality does.'

'Be that as it may, sir, I'm here to ask you some questions about Sir Conrad's death. I'm sure you will be as anxious as we are to have the matter cleared up quickly. After all, you don't want the good name of the club dragged through the tabloid press indefinitely, do you?'

The Colonel's wrath subsided slightly. He plopped himself down on the nearest chair. 'Muck-raking guttersnipes,' he said. 'Showing those disgraceful dirty pictures. Gives completely the wrong impression.'

'Well, the club does have a certain reputation for frankness in sexual matters, sir. Presumably that was why permission was given to the young lady to pose suggestively within the club's portals.'

As the Colonel began to swell up with rage, Pooley caught Milton's eye and shot him a warning glance. Milton reined himself in from giving any further vent to his attack of mischievousness. 'I can see you didn't approve, sir,' he said in a soothing voice.

'I should damn well think I didn't approve. Never could find out what was responsible for letting that trollop in. Of course I fired a couple of the likely suspects immediately, but I'm still not certain that we nailed the villain.'

'The likely suspects were, sir?'

'A couple of dago waiters. Those Mediterranean types, you know.'

It wasn't the occasion for a discussion of the English notion of innocence until proven guilty. Milton was developing a certain respect for the Colonel's ability to get him off the main point of the interview. There was a terrible temptation to follow the old buffoon down his byways of prejudice.

'To get back to Sir Conrad, sir, and taking as a working hypothesis that he was murdered by an insider, I would welcome your advice on what might have been the motive.'

'Motive, motive. There's no motive for this kind of random killing. Psychopaths, psychopaths. They're all around us these days. What are these chaps called who go around murdering lots of people they don't know?'

'Serial killers, sir.'

'Well, if it's not a terrorist, it's probably one of those chaps. We're all going to have to be very careful. Hope you're going to give the staff a good going-over. Especially the Indians. Very violent streak they've got, you know. Remember the carry-on after that communist fool gave them independence in nineteen forty-five?'

'Mr Attlee, sir?'

'No. The Hun . . . that fellow Mountbatten.'

Milton caught himself opening his mouth to defend Lord Mountbatten's right to be considered an Englishman, but he stopped in time. 'Rest assured, sir, that we shall be checking the movements and background of everyone in the club. However, at this moment I am addressing myself to the question of motive. Can you please tell us which members of the club might have had a specific motive for wishing to get rid of Sir Conrad?'

'How would I know? Hardly knew the chap. What're you suggesting? I don't go in for gossip. Tittle-tattle is for women and servants.'

Milton's temper was fraying. 'Since you had yourself a very good motive for murdering him, I should have thought that you would wish to help me identify anyone else who had.'

'How dare you, sir!'

Milton and Pooley noted with interest that anger was actually making a large blue vein throb on the left of the Colonel's forehead. 'I'll ring my lawyer and have you sued for libel.'

'I think you mean slander, sir: I haven't written it down yet. As you very well know, Sir Conrad was determined to reform the club in a lot of ways which you didn't like. You would not, for instance, had he had his way, have been able to go on running the provender committee in the disgraceful way you did.'

This sally produced a blustering but largely inarticulate monologue from which the words 'MP', 'head of Scotland Yard', 'no respect', 'outrageous', 'appalling', 'risked my life in the service of my king' and 'don't know what the world's coming to', cropped up from time to time. At the end of his tirade he seemed curiously tired, and emptied of invective. There was a long silence.

'Oh, very well then. Yes, of course I thought he was an interfering shit. Not enough to murder him, mind. I'm a good law-and-order man myself. All for hanging. You'll find people in favour of capital punishment don't go round murdering people.'

Milton chose to ignore this dubious proposition. 'Go on, sir.'

'Well, I wasn't the only one. Nobody on the committee liked what he wanted to do. But we'd have stopped him, the proper way. The members trust us. They don't want a club full of namby-pamby bleeding hearts.'

'Surely only Mr Chatterton had as much to lose as you, Colonel Fagg?'

'Oh, you know about the wine sales and all that do you? Perfectly legitimate of course. Like everything I did myself. But yes, I grant you that might have seemed a bid odd to the members if it hadn't been explained properly.'

'I should think the amount of money spent subsidising the residents would have seemed rather odd to members as well. It would be hard to justify living as well as you do while paying only a pittance for the privilege.'

'Lot of fuss about nothing. I suppose there might have been a bit of unpleasantness. Soon have won them over.' Fagg was shifting uneasily.

'But the other committee members were in the clear compared to you two really, weren't they sir?'

'Like hell they were. All decisions taken by one of us were ratified by all the others in committee. One for all and all for one, eh. The

Four Musketeers. Well, I suppose the five if you include Pinkie Blenkinsop.'

'What would you have done if the Admiral had won the day and put the club on a sound financial footing?'

'What d'you mean?'

'I mean that presumably you would have been required to pay for your bed and board in the normal way without subsidy. In other words, as happens in other clubs.'

'Oh, dare say we'd all have found the money somehow.'

'D'you have any income other than your pension?'

'Can't see what business that is of yours. I have enough, enough. I'd have a lot more if it wasn't for bloody death duties.' The remembrance of past wrongs seemed to strike him hard. He reached into his right-hand pocket and pulled out four snuffboxes. 'D'you mind?' he enquired, with unaccustomed civility.

'No, no, sir. Go ahead, please.'

Milton and Pooley had had this ritual described fully to them, graphically and with actions, but it still held great fascination. From the other pocket emerged no fewer than ten further receptacles. There were round ones, oval ones, rectangular and square ones, made of silver, gold and pewter. To Milton's relief, the Colonel did not investigate the contents of all of them: there was, apparently, a system. With considerable care he selected four, returned the others to his pockets, opened the chosen ones and sniffed in a discriminating fashion. Three more lids were shut and boxes returned home and finally a large pinch of the selected substance was taken to the right nostril, another to the left. Then after a hearty sneeze, Fagg appeared ready to resume his duties as interviewee. From the point of view of the audience, his appearance was not improved. He had managed to acquire a brown mark on his right cheek and in the centre of his chin, and a dark smear had appeared on the front of his shirt: this he had made worse by diligent rubbing. Another sneeze dawned and he reached yet again for his handkerchief, an object which Milton felt was about as disgusting as anything he had ever seen outside the occasional severed head in a motorway accident. When the sneezing fit was over, Milton resumed.

'Do you consider any of your colleagues on the committee to be capable of setting up a dynamite booby trap, sir?'

'No.'

'Would you have been capable of doing it yourself?'

'Dare say fifty years ago, when I was a second lieutenant. Though can't say I ever had call to.'

'Surely some of your colleagues, like you, have distinguished military records?'

'Stuff and nonsense. There's only Pinkie really. Oh, Fishbane did a bit. Others were all backroom boys. Nowhere to be seen when the shrapnel was flying. Suppose Meredith-Lee was the most active of all of them. Maybe he did it himself.' This appeared to tickle what Colonel Fagg would no doubt have described as his sense of humour. The laughter abruptly changed into sneezes and the handkerchief routine was gone through again. This time he had to wipe away tears and the handkerchief left an intriguing and almost symmetrical pattern below the deep, black bags under his eyes.

'You have no further information that might be of any assistance, sir?'

'No. Sorry, Superintendent, or whatever you are. Absolutely nothing. Have to count me out, I'm afraid. All very mysterious. Quite sure that you'll find in the end that I'm right and it was set up by murdering bog-trotters. Always keep them out of the club myself. Very strict recruitment policy here I can tell you. The thing about the Paddies is that some of them can pass as English if they've been brought up here. Bear that in mind when you're going over the staff with a fine-tooth comb.'

'Virtually all the staff appear to be foreign, sir, other than what one might call the old retainers.'

'Huh! Well, I don't know. There's that new chap, Robert. Check him out. You never know.'

'He was injured by the bomb, sir.'

'Exactly. My point, exactly. Chap might have just set the bomb and been taken unawares when it went off a bit early. Check it out, check it out.'

'Thank you, sir,' said Milton dispiritedly. 'I think we'll leave it at that for now.'

Amiss responded to the bell almost immediately. He looked at them and smirked. 'How did you get on?'

'I suppose you could say that we got a lot of interesting, philosophical reflections on national characteristics, the inadequacy of police methods, his own probity and old-fashioned virtues. Oh, yes. He did finger the most likely murderer.'

'Yes?'

'Robert O'Amiss. Piece of unimpeachable logic. He knows it's bound to be a Paddy: we say it must be an insider. Since he can point to no Irish employees, there must be somebody English who's second-generation Irish and passing for English. You follow me?'

'Just about.'

'So among what you might call the floating waiting population, there's really only you.'

'I knew that some day it would come out about my Irish grandmother,' said Amiss. 'Mind you, she was a Belfast Protestant, but I don't suppose that would cut much ice with Colonel Fagg. Well, before you clap the handcuffs on me, would you like me to procure you some tea?'

'What I could really do with,' said Milton, 'is a very stiff drink. But being a martyr to duty I'll settle for tea. We have got absolutely nowhere.'

'But it's a day of softening them up, sir, really, isn't it?' said Pooley.

'I know, I know, Ellis, but Christ, what a crew. What a bloody crew.'

'I think I'd better provide you with toasted teacakes as well,' said Amiss sympathetically. 'You don't sound to me to be in the right condition to spend time with Fishbane.' With a low snigger, he bowed and left.

19

'OK, Ellis, take out the tray and bring on the sex maniac.' Milton took a last bite of teacake and a last gulp of tea and lay back in his chair and closed his eyes. Pooley deposited the tray in the Coffee Room and went up to the gallery where Fishbane was awaiting a summons. From the bottom of the staircase he could hear Fagg's angry voice bellowing 'damn cheek'. By the time he reached the table where Fishbane was listening in silence to his enraged colleague, with splendid timing the Colonel had got on to 'bloody young whipper-snappers'.

Normally, Pooley was concerned to hide his upper-class origins from the general public as well as from his police confrères, but occasionally Eton came in useful when he wanted to discomfit a member of the public who was treating him like PC Plod. He summoned up from the past the accent he had spent years discarding and bowed to the two men.

'Colonel Fagg. Mr Fishbane. I beg your pardon, gentlemen. I am sorry to disturb you, but Detective Chief Superintendent Milton has asked me to tell you, Mr Fishbane, that he would be grateful if you would be so kind as to spare him a little of your time. Would you care to accompany me now or follow in a couple of minutes when you have finished your conversation?'

'I'll come now,' said Fishbane. Pooley thought he sounded rather relieved.

They walked down the first flight of stairs in silence. Then Fishbane asked, 'Have you been a policeman long . . . Detective Sergeant? Have I got that right?'

'Yes, that's right, sir. A few years.'

'And before that?'

'I was at university and then in the Home Office for a time.'

'What's your name?'

'Pooley, sir.'

'You're not by any chance related to the Worcestershire Pooleys, are you?'

Pooley cursed himself for letting his vanity give him away. 'Yes I am, sir,' he said, throwing open the door of the Rochester Room thankfully. 'Mr Fishbane, sir.' He scuttled round the table hoping there would be no further genealogical scrutiny.

'Good afternoon, Detective Chief Superintendent,' said Fishbane affably. 'I gather that your sergeant is related to my old friend Reggie Pooley. How close are you, Sergeant?'

Pooley gazed fixedly at the table. 'He's my father, sir.'

'Well, well. How extraordinary,' said Fishbane, somewhat tactlessly. 'But of course, now that I look at you, you have his colouring. How is he these days? I haven't seen him since school, I think.'

'He's fine, sir.'

Milton took pity on his embarrassed friend. 'Do sit down, Mr Fishbane,' he said. 'Can I order you some coffee or tea?'

'No thank you. I've just had tea, with Fagg actually. You seemed to have upset him rather. Gave him a frightful grilling, he said.'

'Well, I can assure you, sir, it is not my desire to upset anybody. But Colonel Fagg didn't appear to take kindly to the idea of helping us.'

'Poor old Fagg. I shouldn't pay too much attention to him, Mr Milton. Is it acceptable to call you that? Detective Chief Superintendent seems a terrible mouthful.'

'Yes of course, sir.'

'Good. Well Fagg is . . . I mean, perhaps I shouldn't say this about a chum, but he does lose his rag very easily. In fact, he's in a pretty permanent state of rage about everything. Indeed, come to think of it, about nothing. You are merely the latest grievance, especially since you, I understand, are insisting that the murder of Con Meredith-Lee was not the work of freedom fighters from the neighbouring island.'

'That is correct, sir.'

'Well, of course, dear old Fagg is a great man for believing whatever suits him and obviously the notion that this was an inside job is unlikely to appeal. How many suspects do you have, Mr Milton?'

'That's a somewhat leading question, Mr Fishbane. We don't have any suspects, but it has to be said that as far as I can see the people with the best motive were the five permanent residents of the club.'

'You are, of course, absolutely right. Had the victim been old Fagg himself, the suspect list would have been much longer and more colourful, in every sense of the word. But while I think it intrinsically unlikely that any of my co-habitees, if I may so describe them, should have committed murder, and I know that I didn't, I don't know that I can help you very much.'

'Perhaps you could tell us about your connection with the club and how you felt about the Admiral.'

'You mean my personal history? Hmmm! I joined some time in the late thirties when I was a young member of the Foreign Office.'

'Isn't this an unusual club for a diplomat?'

'For the usual kind of diplomat, yes. Let's say I was prone to a certain amount of raffishness which would have been frowned upon by my more sober colleagues. So though I was a member of the Travellers' and did my serious entertaining there, for socialising I infinitely preferred ffeatherstonehaugh's.'

'What aspects of the club most appealed to you, sir?'

'Oh, the lot. It was a bloody marvellous place. None of that wretched English puritanism about sex. No, ffeatherstonehaugh's understood the point of women all right. Knew they weren't for gracing suburban dinner-tables, but for having fun with.'

'When you say "fun", sir?'

'Oh, come on, Mr Milton. You've been round this club now for long enough to have learned something of my reputation. Perhaps you've even heard that my nickname among the older servants is "the satyr"?'

'No, sir.' Milton was taken aback as much by Fishbane's obvious pride in his priapic reputation as by the literacy of the nickname. It must, he concluded, have been a Gooseneck invention. 'I hadn't heard that. So did you remain an active member?'

'Oh, very witty, Mr Milton. Very witty indeed.'

'I'm sorry, sir. The pun was inadvertent.'

'You disappoint me. There was a period of about twenty years when I had little to do with the club. My lady wife would not have approved.'

'I didn't realise you were married, sir.'

'Was. Bachelors were rather frowned on in the FCO. It was felt that they might get into all sorts of trouble abroad, so we were, informally, encouraged to marry rather than burn, as it were. And of course, to marry somebody who would grace an ambassadorial drawing-room in due course. So foolishly I married someone from an impeccable diplomatic background who knew about servants, flower arranging and how to address the third wife of an African monarch.'

'Foolishly?'

'Foolishly. She was frigid and strait-laced and therefore somewhat ill-equipped to keep me on the straight and narrow. Oh, I was reasonably discreet and fortunately I was in a job where the hours were irregular – thus maximising the chance of getting away with dalliance.

'It was rather more difficult when I was based in London between foreign postings. Then Hilda could control the social life much more. Between keeping up with opera, theatre, art exhibitions and all the other things that the upper middle classes go in for, my playtime was severely limited. When I could, I frequented an excellent little establishment – now, alas, long gone – in Pimlico, where the ladies were both agreeable and comparatively inexpensive.' He smiled at the memory.

'Then we were sent to Moscow and the roof fell in. I speak metaphorically of course. Had a bit of difficulty in finding my feet, sexually, as it were, in that although prostitutes were twenty a penny, the kind of up-market lovelies that I favoured were harder to locate. So I suppose it was frustration that led me to break the cardinal rule of any diplomat behind the Iron Curtain in the good old days. I got involved with one of the filing clerks in the office. A local girl and very nice too.' He paused to remember. 'Perhaps she was a touch stocky, but she hadn't run to fat the way that most of them do. And there were definitely Slav genes, which gave her a rather exotic look. Yes, we had some good times together.'

Milton thought briefly about trying to speed up this self-indulgent narrative and decided to do nothing.

'That is, I had some good times. She, however, was on duty throughout, and she set us up for the KGB photographers. Next thing I knew there was old Boris sitting opposite me at my desk showing me a range of snaps that might, even now, command some good prices in the appropriate journals. Actually, I've kept a few: I enjoy nostalgia.

'The object, of course, was blackmail, but I wasn't prepared to play. I wouldn't say I'm a great patriot, but I wouldn't actually sell out my country. So I told Boris to forget it, broke the news to Hilda and to the ambassador and was transferred instantly back to London. I wasn't fired – nothing as ungentlemanly as that. Merely persuaded that resignation was in my best interests. All very civilised of course, and they were relatively generous with a pension, that sort of thing. But out I went and out of my life went my wife and children. Daddy having recently popped it, my wife was comfortably off in her own right, and she did a deal by which, in exchange for her making no financial demands on me, I would make no attempt to see my daughters ever again: the corrupting influence was to be kept away. I gave in because I had no cards to play. She was an implacable bitch and she would have poisoned their minds against me anyway. I got a job which just about produced enough money for me to live here.'

'What was the job, sir?'

'Secretary of a trade association – widgets and gaskets, that sort of thing. Absolutely ghastly. My members were the worst representatives of the then-prevailing largely rotten British management. They liked me because I told them dirty jokes, made good after-dinner speeches, did a reasonable job for them in terms of links with government and that kind of thing, and had a bit of class. Oh, God, it was frightful. They spent all the time just complaining about fair competition.

'So, since work yielded neither stimulation nor serious reward, I concentrated on my hobby. Never was much interested in anything except sex, despite my wife's efforts to civilise me. Essentially that's how I've spent the rest of my life, to date. Since I retired I've had more time on my hands and I pass it, you might say, in reading and reflection on my area of interest. The library here is particularly good for a man of my tastes.'

'So I've observed, sir.'

'Please don't become bourgeois about it and send the vice squad round: we've enough troubles. My predecessor as librarian did, I admit, go in for some rather unpleasant stuff towards which I have no inclination, but being a libertarian I'm certainly not going to act as censor. The perpetrator of the offence, as no doubt you would describe it, was called to account by his maker some time ago.'

'I'm grateful to you for being so frank, Mr Fishbane.'

'I'm not an idiot and clearly neither are you, so there isn't much to be gained by concealing from you that which you can easily find out, is there, Mr Milton?'

'Indeed not, sir. Perhaps we could now move on to the question of Sir Conrad's recent involvement in the club's affairs?'

'Well, I'm a bit torn on that. I'm not as much of a self-deluder as my fellow committee members. We have, of course, latterly been essentially running the club for our own benefit. In my own defence I can say only that I went along for the ride, as it were, if you'll forgive the expression, Mr Milton.' Milton managed a weak smile.

'Fagg and Chatterton were the leading lights and, of course, Blenkinsop was putty in their hands. I'm very happy to take whatever goodies are going. So, on the one hand I couldn't pretend to myself that Meredith-Lee wasn't justified in doing something to put things right, on the other hand I didn't want my comfortable life messed up. Hence the ambivalence. In some ways I remain permanently a diplomat, allegedly detached but with a tendency to go native, which, of course, is what I did here. However, I'm sure you'll agree that a bit of feathering one's nest is a long way away from murder. None of us is in that league of venality.'

'But didn't people feel very threatened?'

'Oh, I don't know about threatened. It's not as if they were going to be chucked out. Trueman might have done that if he'd had his way, but Meredith-Lee wasn't such an idiot.'

'But the quality of life would certainly have suffered,' said Milton. 'And surely to a serious degree?'

'Ah! The seven-course meals and the champagne and all that. I suppose people have murdered for less. I just can't see it. Chatterton's the only one I would have thought had the nerve, but then even if he hadn't been crippled, he wouldn't have the skill.'

'Easy enough to pick up I think, sir.'

'You'd have to have some experience with explosives – surely?'

'Did you acquire such skills during the war?'

'I was serving my country at my desk, Mr Milton.'

'Well, have you any theories, Mr Fishbane?'

'Just keep looking for a more credible suspect with a motive you haven't found yet, I suggest.'

'Do you believe there to have been illegality in the running of the club affairs?'

'I really don't think so. Chatterton's a very smart man and he understands small print. And one of the codgers on the committee when he and Fagg took over was a lawyer who was very thick with them. They pored over everything. Doubt that you'll find a loophole easily.'

'Didn't Mr Trueman?'

'Ah, now there was a man whom we all had a really good reason to murder. There was a rule no one had thought to have changed, to the effect that members might reside in the club indefinitely if the butler was agreeable. Well, of course, the secretary is technically the butler. There wasn't any problem with old Pinkie Blenkinsop, but when the matter came up Trueman refused to give a promise that we could all stay here until we were carried out feet first. "What happens if someone becomes incontinent or needs nursing?" he asked.

'Well, none of us has got enough money to go into a high-class nursing home – at least as far as I know – so of course the wind was up all of us. However, whether or not someone might have bumped him off is mercifully a hypothetical question, seeing that he had the decency to do the job himself. What a stroke of luck.' He stood up. 'I don't envy you your job, Mr Milton, but I hope you're having some fun out of ffeatherstonehaugh's. At least we're more interesting than the Athenaeum.'

'Thank you, Mr Fishbane. You've been most helpful.'

'Any time,' said Fishbane. 'Oh, by the way, Sergeant Pooley, give my regards to his lordship. Or rather, on second thoughts, perhaps you shouldn't. It might remind him of a few school episodes he will have made sure to forget.' With a charming smile Fishbane left them.

'What d'you think he might be talking about?' asked Milton innocently. 'Stealing sweets from the tuck-shop?'

Pooley had gone pink. 'You know bloody well what sort of thing he's likely to be referring to, Jim.'

'Ellis,' said Milton, 'I'm shocked. That is no way to address your superior officer. Now go and fetch Glastonbury and let's get these farcical interviews wrapped up for the afternoon.'

20

Pooley was expecting to find his quarry in deep slumber. In fact, he found him in a state of positive animation, in conversation with Chatterton about the dangers of travelling by public transport.

'No, no, my dear fellow. It's the germs, it's the germs. Those tube trains are full of them,' he was saying agitatedly as Pooley arrived at the table at which they were having tea.

'Excuse me, sir.' This time Pooley didn't resurrect his old accent. 'I'm sorry to disturb you, but could you perhaps spare a little time to come and talk to the Chief Superintendent?'

Glastonbury looked at him blankly. 'I'm sorry, young man. I'm sure I should know you. Have we been introduced?'

'We met briefly yesterday, sir. I'm Detective Sergeant Pooley.'

'Oh, I'm so sorry, my dear boy. Unforgivable of me. Hopeless memory for faces and names and everything else really these days. But you want to talk to me. Yes, yes, of course. Will you forgive me, my dear Cully. I don't want to keep this nice young man waiting.'

'Yes, of course, Boy. Off you go.'

'You might have an opinion on this, Mr . . . ' Glastonbury stopped and looked worriedly at Pooley. 'I'm sorry, what did you say your name was?'

'Pooley, Mr Glastonbury.' They set off again at a stately pace.

'I was just saying to my friend Chatterton that it's really very dangerous to travel on tubes these days. You see, all these foreigners come from abroad with germs we're not used to. It's not that I'm saying anything against them. It's not that they're not clean or anything. It's just that we haven't got any resistance to the kind of germs they're used to. Don't you remember Jules Verne's story about the professor who goes to the moon and accidentally kills off all its inhabitants because when he goes there he's got a cold and they're not used to it.'

'Yes, indeed, sir. A very memorable story.'

'So you see you can never be too careful. Now it's a long time since I went by tube, and there's not much you can do in the carriages except keep a handkerchief over your nose, but a useful tip is never to put your hand on the rail beside the moving staircase. That's one of the worst places for picking up germs, you know. All those hands.' He shook his head in agitation. 'I urge you, young man, to follow my example.'

Pooley's logical mind was baffled. 'But do you not fear being infected by one of the foreign staff here, sir?'

Glastonbury stopped in the middle of the second flight of stairs and gazed earnestly at him. 'No, no, my dear young man. You mustn't worry about that. Gooseneck absolutely assures me they always wash their hands before touching any food and anyway, I believe they are all selected extremely carefully. So I don't think it's anything we should worry about, do you?'

'Oh no, sir. Of course not. All the difference in the world between somewhere as spacious as this and a crowded tube carriage. I do understand that.'

Relief pushed Glastonbury back into motion. 'My friend Chatterton is a great daredevil you know. He thinks nothing of staying up till two or three o'clock in the morning in casinos, although I tell him it's very, very bad for one's constitution to have irregular hours. And I worry that the tension of gambling might be bad for the heart.'

'People vary,' said Pooley soothingly, 'and I have to say that Mr Chatterton does look extremely well.'

'Yes, he does look marvellous, doesn't he. And he says he's full of beans. I'm just afraid he might fall over again and hurt himself.'

'He seems to manoeuvre his frame very well. Now here we are, sir. Detective Chief Superintendent Milton is waiting for you.'

'Oh, thank you so much, my dear boy. You've been very, very kind and most reassuring. Good afternoon, young man,' he said to Milton.

Milton felt quite cheered at this form of address. 'Good afternoon, sir. Would you care to sit down?'

'Oh, thank you. Oh, yes. At the table. Very good, very good. It's easier to concentrate in a straight chair, I always find. I get a little sleepy in armchairs, I have to confess. Sometimes I wonder if I sleep too much, but my friend Cully Chatterton tells me that the need for sleep varies considerably from person to person and one must follow one's inclination.'

'I think he's right, sir,' said Milton.

'Now how can I help you, Mr . . . ?' He looked at Milton in distress. 'Oh dear. Oh dear. I don't know what's to be done about my memory.'

'Milton, sir. As you know, I'm investigating the murder of Sir Conrad Meredith-Lee and I wondered if you had any suggestions as to who might be responsible.'

'Are you sure it was murder?'

Milton stayed calm. 'Well sir, I think we can rule out natural causes and I can't see how dynamite could accidentally get under a table, so unless he committed suicide in a way that endangered the lives of other people, I think we must assume it was murder. Don't you agree?'

'Oh dear! I expect so, I expect so. It's just too sad. Such a nice man and awful to think of anyone being murdered, although it's a very violent world these days. People are always being blown up.'

Milton groaned inwardly at the thought of going through the terrorist loop again. He decided to cut corners. 'Mr Glastonbury, I'm afraid we are virtually certain that the Admiral was killed by a member of the committee.'

'But how could this be? You would be speaking of me or my friend Chatterton or one of the others.'

'Unlikely as it may appear, Mr Glastonbury,' said Milton firmly, 'I fear, almost certainly, one of you killed him.'

Glastonbury fell into babbling incoherence of a nature which Milton and Pooley found an interesting antithesis to the recent ravings of Colonel Fagg. The comprehensible phrases were 'oh dear's and 'oh no's and 'how terrible's and 'dear me's and 'surely not's.

Milton felt like a brute, but he pressed on. 'I'm sorry to distress you, sir, but your committee did not like what the Admiral was proposing to do.'

'I don't understand.'

'He was going to introduce changes to the club which would have made your lives much less comfortable.'

'Oh, I know he was suggesting ways of saving money, but I didn't really mind about that. I think eating too much is bad for us at our age. I often tell my friends that the especially important thing is to avoid cheese at night. It gives you terrible indigestion, you know. And you can have too much port. It often leads to gout. My old father used to suffer from it. I've warned Fagg about that. He suffers from gout, but he won't give up the port, you know. Won't give up the port.'

'So you were not personally alarmed by anything Sir Conrad suggested?'

'I can't remember very much, to tell you the truth. I expect I wasn't paying attention. I often don't, I'm afraid. It's a fault of mine. Tend to live a bit in the past, I'm afraid, at my age. I think a lot about the old days, when I was a boy and Father and Mother were alive.'

'But you sit on the committee, sir?'

'I have to. I believe we have to if we're residents. I'm sure that's what Fagg said to me.'

'But until a few years ago you were chairman, Mr Glastonbury.'

'Well, we took turns, you see. It doesn't matter who's chairman. I just did what I was told. I was never any good at committees. Not even when I was working. I did everything I could to avoid them. I don't like people arguing. It upsets me. So I don't listen.'

'What was your work, sir?'

'I was a librarian. I had a job in the British Museum, in the library there. I liked that. It was a very ordered life.'

'You're interested in books?' Milton was remembering what Amiss had said about the adventure books in Glastonbury's bedroom.

'I don't really read books, but I liked cataloguing them and arranging them and making sure they were well looked after and all that kind of thing.'

'Did you work as a librarian all your life?'

'Oh, yes, yes. I went into it straight from school. A friend of Father's helped me. I was a bit of a duffer. Couldn't get into university. Father was very disappointed.'

'And during the war?'

'Oh, they made me go into the army. I didn't want to. It's very dangerous. But I did my best. I don't think I was very good at it and I was invalided out very early. I caught something nasty in North Africa. So then I was able to go back to the library.'

'How did you come to be involved with ffeatherstonehaugh's, sir? If you'll forgive me saying so, it doesn't quite seem like your kind of club.'

'Well, I had a great friend at school who brought me here. He was killed in the war, but by then he had got me made a member. He said it would take me out of myself a bit. And we did have some jolly evenings. Then I met Cully Chatterton and he was very nice to me, so I felt at home here. I get into habits very easily, you see, so I soon got into the habit of coming here every night for dinner.'

'When did you move in?'

'When Mother died. You see, after Father went she sold the house in Derbyshire and moved down to London to be with me. It was very sad having the old home go, but it was very nice to be living with

131

Mother. We had a very nice flat in Bloomsbury, so I could walk to work. Of course, when Mother was living with me I didn't go to the club every night. Only on Fridays.'

'When did she die?'

'Fifteen years ago. Then Cully suggested I should come here.'

'Weren't you worried when Mr Trueman said that the residents would have to pay more and mightn't be able to stay if they became ill? Where would you have gone?'

'I wouldn't have minded about the money. I've got quite a lot of money, I think. But I don't like leaving places, so that would have made me sad.'

With little hope, Milton changed tack. 'But some of the members of the committee were upset, weren't they?'

'Fagg was upset, but he's always upset. I don't think he was any more upset, but I mightn't have been paying attention.'

'Mr Fishbane?'

'I don't know. I'm sorry. I don't remember him saying anything.'

'Commander Blenkinsop?'

'Oh, yes, I think Pinkie was upset when he stopped being secretary, but then anybody would, wouldn't they?'

'And Mr Chatterton?'

'My friend Cully is very philosophical, you know.'

'So you can't think of anybody who would have killed the Admiral or Mr Trueman?'

'Goodness no. I'm very sorry. I wish I could help you, but I'm sure you'll find it's all a misunderstanding.'

Milton sighed, stood up and held out his hand. 'Thank you, Mr Glastonbury,' he said. 'We'll be in touch. Goodbye.'

'Oh, thank you very much. And thank you, dear boy,' he said to Pooley. 'I hope you'll find whatever it is you're looking for. Goodbye.' And giving them a smile of absolute sweetness, he left.

Milton flung himself in his chair and buried his head in his hands.

'I think, sir,' said Pooley, 'that the term is "holy fool".'

'As opposed to Colonel Fagg, who is an unholy fool. Oh, God! I shall go mad. Go and find Robert, will you, and if he's free tonight, let's all meet. You two fix a location. Then collect me and we'll head off to the Yard to deal with the mess that's going on there.'

21

Amiss arrived at Pooley's flat at ten o'clock.

'You look knackered, Robert.' Pooley looked conerned.

'Knackered is right. I'm beginning to think Sister had a point. Maybe I should have hung on for a few days in there getting to grips with Alf Bundy's ailments. Might have been more restful than running round like a lunatic stuffing pâté de foie gras into the undeserving old ghouls who turned up in their dozens today.' He flung himself on the nearest sofa.

'Whisky?' asked Pooley.

'Please.'

'Half and half and no ice, isn't that right?'

'My dear Ellis, continue like this and I'll put a word in for you and get you a job.'

'You have eaten, Robert, haven't you?' asked Milton.

'Not only have I eaten, I have eaten adequately twice today. Commander Blenkinsop decreed that rations were to be supplemented by protein. We got chops for lunch and scrambled eggs for supper. Incidentally, has he come up with the goods yet?'

'I talked to him a couple of hours ago and he said that as soon as things quietened down he'd get as much down on paper as he could remember. He's a bit stymied without the account books, but he reckons he'll be able to pin-point roughly when some of the major wine sales occurred. That would help us track down details from the relevant auctioneers. He said he'd be able to help about subsidies and that kind of thing. Seems very keen to help.'

Pooley came in with the drinks.

'You're not looking too bright yourselves,' said Amiss. 'Surely the rest of the day was light relief after that collection of loonies?'

'It was saner,' said Milton, 'but less interesting. Mostly junk, in fact. Pep talk from my assistant commissioner, a pointless press conference, further inconclusive forensic reports, lots of people ringing up and calling in to tell me that they've got nowhere. Not to speak of trying to keep up with the other three murder investigations I'm in charge of. I had hoped that a further proper search of Meredith-Lee's rooms would have come up with something, but absolutely not. The lads I put on to it had to look behind every one of those bloody paintings for a wall safe. There wasn't one. Hunted through everything. Books, cabinets, drawers, anything relevant. Maddeningly, the poor wretch must have taken everything pertaining to ffeatherstonehaugh's with him to that committee meeting.'

'I can't imagine Blenkinsop's going to come up with anything to match what the Admiral had disinterred. After all, he'd been ferreting in the records for a good while.'

'Maybe not. But I'd be grateful for anything – even some idea of the scale of the funds they've been filching. I'm feeling very discouraged.'

'Oh, I don't know, Jim,' said Pooley. 'If Blenkinsop comes up with some facts, at least we'll have something to go back to them on. Put the pressure on.'

'How d'you put the pressure on Glastonbury, for God's sake? He wouldn't even notice.'

'What about the good old process of elimination?' asked Amiss. 'I mean, isn't it possible to say that Chatterton definitely couldn't have done it?'

'I wouldn't say that,' said Pooley. 'He's very agile considering the injury and he's also very smart.'

'Maybe he could have had Glastonbury holding the dynamite,' said Amiss. '"Oh dear, Cully, I've heard this substance is very, very dangerous. Aren't you afraid we might hurt someone with it?"'

Pooley sighed. 'I know,' he said, 'it's all very improbable. We'll get a medical report on him tomorrow anyway. Maybe there's a chance that he's better than he's pretending.'

'Well, what about Glastonbury himself?' asked Amiss. 'Surely he can't be a credible suspect?'

'He might be only pretending to be gaga,' said Pooley.

'Gooseneck says he was pretty dotty even fifteen years ago, when he became a resident, and that he's just got more so. You aren't seriously suggesting he might have spent fifteen years building up a simpleton's profile, in case it would come in handy if ever he wanted to commit a crime?'

'I have to agree with you,' said Milton. 'Ellis, don't let your fancy run away with you too much on this. The chap has a mental age of ten.'

'There have been murderers aged ten,' said Pooley.

'I don't have your imagination,' said Amiss. 'So for the purposes of this exercise I'm eliminating Chatterton and Glastonbury. Now, judging by what you told me earlier, Ellis, Fishbane sounds like the next candidate to go out.'

'I'd agree,' said Milton. 'He seems too sane really. It's a strange thing to say about a man whose libido is so out of control, but he seems psychologically very well balanced. At least that's how he came across. It's not as if murdering the Admiral was a sensible course of action. It was essentially an hysterical solution to a problem which could have been resolved in other ways. Ellis?'

Pooley nodded. 'So we're looking at Blenkinsop and Fagg.'

'That's difficult again,' said Milton. 'Blenkinsop is being extremely co-operative, and while I admit that his conversion into an upright citizen seems to have come with indecent haste, nevertheless, he was oddly compelling.'

'It will be enlightening to see if his new-found honesty runs to incriminating himself in any way,' observed Amiss. 'Hadn't Meredith-Lee found him with his hands in the till?'

'Indeed,' said Milton. 'I deliberately didn't bring that up yet. I'm giving him a chance to reveal his bona fides.'

'But essentially we're talking Fagg, aren't we?' said Amiss.

'The trouble with him,' said Pooley, 'is that he never seems to keep his mind on anything. Bit hard to imagine him seeing anything through.'

'Well, he saw the provender committee through pretty well.'

'Not the same thing,' said Milton. 'The murder needed a cool head – not the first quality I would attribute to the Colonel.'

'No chance that they'd have conspired to bribe Ramsbum or Gooseneck or someone to do it for them?'

'Out of the question,' said Pooley mournfully. 'Ramsbum was on duty that whole afternoon. There's no question about it. He just didn't have time. And Gooseneck has an alibi as well.'

'Which is?'

'He was with Sunil.'

'With Sunil?' Amiss was incredulous. 'What were they doing? Do I dare ask?'

'Well, they claim to have been in the Card Room all afternoon talking about the romantic poets.'

'Get me another whisky, for God's sake,' said Amiss. 'Everything just gets more ridiculous.'

'You're telling us,' said Milton. 'Absolutely everyone's been questioned now and we still have only five with a motive as well as an opportunity.'

'How many others had an opportunity?'

'The two Pakistani cleaning ladies,' said Milton. 'A Chinese waiter who's been with the club for a week. A Turk who's been there for ten days and the club handyman.'

'He's deaf and dumb,' said Amiss.

'Quite,' said Milton. 'Ellis will no doubt wish to offer this as a motive, but I can't see it myself. How, for instance, would he have gone about getting the dynamite?'

'Stop taking the piss,' said Pooley.

Milton blinked in mild surprise at this uncharacteristic leap into the demotic.

'Of course,' said Amiss helpfully, 'he could be pretending to be deaf and dumb. How long has he worked at ffeatherstonehaugh's, Ellis?'

'Thirty years,' said Pooley, grinning. 'I doubt if he could have kept up the masquerade for that long.'

'Therefore,' said Milton, 'since there appear to be only five possibles – all of whom we have decided are improbables – we're going to have to work quite hard. Quite apart from whatever Blenkinsop comes up with, I'm going to get my chaps tomorrow to get going on a major investigation into the backgrounds of all these people. Money, military records, careers, anything shady, usual sort of thing. And of course we'll have to go over all the old ground on timings and opportunities for both the Trueman and Meredith-Lee deaths.'

'I don't feel I'm being much use,' said Amiss. 'All I've given you so far is a little local colour.'

'You're looking for praise, aren't you Robert?' said Milton. 'You know it helps to know what to expect, and who's acting in character and who's acting out of character, and all that sort of thing. Anyway, it's early days. You may yet have the opportunity to find some incontrovertible evidence that will crack the case.'

'Mmmm,' said Amiss. He was relaxing over his whisky and enjoying himself. 'I see it all,' he said dreamily. 'I'll catch Chatterton red-handed tap-dancing on the gallery. Or will it be overhearing

Glastonbury delivering crisp instructions to Fagg about what to do with the detonators left over from their last operation? Fishbane, perhaps, will have been wildly in love with the Admiral's paramour, while Blenkinsop . . . What am I going to get on Blenkinsop?' He took another sip of whisky and gazed thoughtfully at the ceiling.

There was a ringing sound from Milton's suitcase. 'I wish these bloody mobile phones had never been invented,' he said as he fished it out. 'One never has an excuse to be free. Yes,' he said rather testily. His face changed as he listened. 'Right, Sammy,' he said, 'I'll be right there.' He slammed the phone down and said, 'Fuck.'

'Fuck what?' asked Amiss.

'My own stupidity mostly. I didn't think to put a guard on Blenkinsop.'

'You don't mean?'

'I do. Sunil found him ten minutes ago. Dead in the corner of the library.'

'How?'

'Apparently all he said was that he didn't know how he'd died, but it looked unpleasant. Come on, Ellis, we've got to get there. You'll have to go separately, Robert. What are you thinking? You've got a very faraway look in your eye.'

'I'm trying to decide if reducing it to four is a silver lining,' said Amiss.

'Only if he's been murdered,' said Milton. 'Come on. Let's go and find out.'

It was midnight before Amiss, back in uniform and trying to look official, was able to get any inside information. The police and their cohorts – photographers, finger-printers, pathologists and the rest – had drifted away; the corpse had been removed. Amiss had had his fill of the terrified squawking of foreign servants and the lamentations of old retainers.

'One of the old school,' Ramsbum kept intoning. 'God knows what'll happen to us now.'

If Ramsbum had been a human being Amiss might have suspected that he was seriously feeling grief. Blitherdick, usually a man of few words, had become lachrymose about Blenkinsop's enjoyment of a good wine. Amiss had to restrain his impatience, knowing as he did that a distinguishing feature of Blenkinsop was that he had enjoyed any wine, as long as there was enough of it. Gooseneck had been unsentimental, but a little sad.

'Every man's death diminishes us, Robert,' he observed, 'and I'm sorry that he should die now when he seemed at last to be recovering his dignity.'

Both he and Amiss had spent a considerable time comforting Sunil, who had been throwing up on and off for over an hour. There had been no opportunity to get from him an on-the-spot report of what had happened. Chatterton, Fagg, Fishbane and Glastonbury were huddled together in the Smoking Room, from which each of them had been extracted for a brief conversation with Milton. They kept ordering more brandy and all seemed genuinely upset. Blenkinsop had after all, as Fagg remarked, 'been one of us – not a damned outsider.'

A sense of mortality seemed to hang heavily on them. Their conversation was desultory. Amiss hovered in the gallery, hoping to waylay an informant. Eventually, he was rewarded by the sight of Inspector Sammy Pike heading out of the library and off towards the gentlemen's cloakroom. He shot after him at high speed.

'Psst . . . Sammy!'

Pike turned round and smiled warmly. He looked Amiss up and down appraisingly and said: 'Nice to see you again, Robert, but I'm glad the Super tipped me off you were here. I'd have got a nasty shock otherwise. By the way, I don't think much of your tailor.'

'Oh, shut up, Sammy. Beggars can't be choosers. Now come on, give.'

'Pathologist says it's murder, skilfully carried out, he thinks, with a sharp blow from a cylindrical object driven upwards from the base of the nose. Apparently that drives a couple of bones into the brain. It's a professional killer's trick, I gather. Haven't come across it myself before. Quick, but brutal.'

'So what instrument was used?'

'Dunno. It wasn't left there and I can't think what the chances are of finding it in a place this size. Still, we'll get dozens of men crawling all over this building again.'

Out of the corner of his eye Amiss saw the Smoking Room door open. 'Quick, Sammy, what about the information he was writing down for Jim?'

'There was nothing there, I'm afraid. Nor in his room, nor in his office. Either he hadn't started or whoever killed him took it away. That's the likeliest, isn't it?'

'Thanks, Sammy.'

Amiss hurried towards the Smoking Room, out of which was emerging a by now familiar though no less bizarre procession. The four old men were obviously on their way to bed. Fishbane and Fagg came first, Fishbane's six foot three inches of scrawny frame making an interesting counterpart to the roly-poly little Fagg, whose progress was retarded by his gouty limp. Amiss had a moment of sympathy for the old beast. It wouldn't do much for anyone's temper to suffer simultaneously from gout and piles, not to speak of bearing the life-long burden of being an unattractive midget. Fishbane nodded courteously, Fagg curtly. Amiss wished them goodnight and received civil responses. At least murder seemed to be a great improver of manners, he reflected. Behind came Glastonbury and Chatterton, but here there was a new development that Amiss found absorbing, for Chatterton had, that afternoon, been allowed to abandon his zimmer in favour of crutches and Glastonbury was therefore in a state of twittering panic.

'Oh, my dear Cully, pray take care, take care. Those things are treacherous, and you're not used to them. Please go more slowly. You mustn't be so reckless.'

'Boy, I've told you before, I'm used to crutches. Remember I had them twice before.' He stopped for a moment, deep in thought. 'Ah, yes. The first occasion was the fifth of September, it must have been. Certainly the first week in September, nineteen fifty. Don't you recall? It was when I had that skiing accident in Switzerland.'

The memory of that sent Glastonbury into deep distress. 'Oh, yes. I remember you telling me about that, Cully. That was dreadful, dreadful.'

Chatterton cut in. 'The second occasion, of course, was when I was hit by a car in Monte Carlo on my third visit there . . . let me see, yes, it would have been twenty-seven years ago, three days before Christmas. So I'm quite good with crutches. There is no need to worry. Goodnight, Robert.'

'Oh, yes, yes, yes. Goodnight, Robert,' said Glastonbury. 'Oh, dear. So disturbing. Everything so disturbing. Poor Pinkie. It's quite dreadful, terrible, terrible. Goodnight.'

'Goodnight, sir. Goodnight, sir.'

Amiss observed with interest but without surprise that Chatterton was as good as his word. He swung along on his crutches like a veteran, his dapper form complemented by the fleshy majesty of Glastonbury's. As they disappeared towards the lift a stampede of policemen emerged from the library and thundered towards the stairs. Milton and Pooley lagged behind. Sammy Pike reappeared and joined them and Amiss edged towards them, keeping an eye out for unwelcome observers.

'We're off, Robert,' said Milton. 'Nothing more to be done tonight. We'll have to wait before we can be absolutely certain of the time and manner of death, but from what we know already, it looks, yet again, as if any of those old buggers could have done it.'

'Nothing especially to look out for?'

'Incriminating documents in Blenkinsop's handwriting would be nice,' said Milton.

'And the murderer's cylindrical object,' said Pooley.

'A crutch?' suggested Amiss.

'I thought of that,' said Pooley. 'The circumference is about right, but apparently the object itself is too long. You don't get the thrust.'

'You'd be looking for something shaped like a truncheon or a torch,' said Pike.

'We'll have some better ideas when the preliminary pathology report comes in tomorrow,' said Milton.

'Will you be coming here?'

'I doubt if Ellis or I will be along tomorrow. Sammy will be running things. Give Ellis a ring before lunch-time and he'll bring you up to date. Goodnight, Robert. And please be careful.'

'I will.'

'I'll order some provisions for you tomorrow, Robert,' said Pooley.

'You mean in case Blenkinsop's successor puts us back on short rations? Well, that raises an interesting question. Who the hell is going to become the new secretary?'

'If the murder rate speeds up,' said Milton, 'perhaps you might put in for the job yourself.'

'I might be weary,' said Amiss, 'but I'm not suicidal.'

22

It was a dreadful night. Sunil snored loudly and Amiss didn't have the heart to wake him. It was bad enough, he felt, to be cast out by your family, be stuck working in ffeatherstonehaugh's, and be spending all your spare time working for a degree, without additionally having the stress of falling over dead bodies: the boy needed his sleep. In any case, Amiss's mind was racing, grappling with a situation devoid of any rational explanation. He desperately wanted to get up, make himself a cup of tea or get a drink and walk around and think; instead, he was trapped. Downstairs would be in darkness, so any light going on would attract the attention of the night porter. While the faded old creature who bore the main brunt of night duty would be too dozy to spot anything, Ramsbum was a different matter and Amiss was pretty sure that this was his night on duty. He could be absolutely guaranteed to report to Fagg in the morning that a servant had been out of bounds, and this was no time to get the sack.

The hours passed in fruitless speculation on one side of the room and loud snoring on the other. At around five, Amiss's need for sleep triumphed over his good nature and he hurled a paperback in Sunil's direction. Nothing happened. Four books later there was a grunt, a snort, a muttered 'Oh, sorry', and the noise stopped. Amiss cursed himself for a soft-hearted fool. Just because Sunil had had a nasty experience didn't mean that his sleeping pattern would have changed. After tossing and turning for another while, Amiss fell into a deep sleep from which he was woken less than an hour and a half later by his alarm clock. To his chagrin, Sunil had disappeared. He washed and dressed quickly and was downstairs ten minutes before breakfast began, hoping for a quiet word with Gooseneck about Sunil's condition.

He found them both sitting there. Sunil seemed a little febrile and was talking animatedly.

'Do join us, Robert,' said Gooseneck. 'We were just discussing attitudes towards death in our respective cultures.'

'Good morning, Robert,' said Sunil. 'I was just saying that it's easier for me than it would be for your average Englishman. I suppose you've never seen anyone dead, have you?'

Amiss decided not to mention the dead bodies he'd been coming across since he'd got chummy with Jim Milton. 'You're right. My family didn't go in for that sort of thing. Dead grandparents were whipped straight into coffins and the lids firmly closed.'

'Well, so far I have contemplated the dead bodies of one uncle, two great-aunts, a grandmother and a first cousin. As you'll know, had we been in India, we would have built a pyre and set fire to them. Here we're restricted to the crematorium. It's a good training for unpleasantnesses like last night and another area where I think Indian culture triumphs over English.'

'Don't judge us too much by contemporary mores, dear boy,' said Gooseneck.'You are an apprentice historian and therefore should know that it is only in this century that this attempt to sanitise death has stricken our race. It's not something on which one could fault the Victorians, for instance.'

Various depressed minions started to trickle in and just after seven-thirty, a man in a chef's hat arrived through the doors that led to the kitchens, carrying an enormous silver tray which he laid in the centre of the table. With a flourish he removed the cover and revealed to the incredulous eyes of the staff a feast of sausages and bacon. Most of the staff began to fall on this with cries of delight, but as he looked around, Amiss saw two sad brown faces at the other end of the table.

'Mr Gooseneck,' he whispered, 'what about the Muslims?'

'Your kind instincts do you credit, my dear Robert, but have no fear, I have no desire to torture our Islamic friends.' Through the swing doors came the same chef, this time carrying dishes of mushrooms, tomatoes and fried eggs. 'What's happened, Mr Gooseneck?' asked Amiss, when he had worked his way through the first stage of what was one of the best breakfasts he'd ever had in his life.

'I think you could call it the metaphorical baked meats for our secretary. Fagg has put me temporarily in charge and, limited though my power may be, I intend to ensure that those under my care are for once treated like human beings.' He smiled benignly around the table, a bit like Scrooge on Christmas Day, revelling in the joy of the Cratchits.

'What are you doing today, Sunil?' asked Amiss.

'College in the morning and then I'll be back to wait at lunch.'

'You don't have to, my boy.'

'No, no, please. I'm not going to leave you in the lurch. Maybe we could have a word in the afternoon, Robert. I've got a new toy I want to show you.' Gooseneck shot him a warning glance, but Sunil shook his head and said, 'No, don't worry. Robert's reliable. He won't split on us.'

'How's it going, Ellis?'

'May I ring you back?'

'If you do it quickly and say you're my doctor. Even Ramsbum can't object to that.'

'Sorry,' said Pooley when they connected a few minutes later. 'Had to find a quiet corner. Bloody awful in fact. None of those wretches were distinguished enough to get into *Who's Who* so one doesn't have anywhere to start from. And of course, because Jim was relying on Blenkinsop to know basic facts, he didn't grill any of them about their war records, their financial position, or career history. He wants us to try and get everything we can without their knowledge, in the hope that then we'll have some ammunition.'

'What have you got so far?'

'Well, it's a bit early, but I have dug up one piece of information that you'll enjoy. It's about Fagg's army record.'

'Oh good. I bet he turns out not to have been quite the hero he makes out.'

'Better than that. He never fought in his life. His entire career was spent in the catering corps. He was called up in nineteen thirty-nine, became an army cook and worked his way up. Not, I may add, to colonel. He only got to sergeant-major.'

'So he's a fake colonel.'

'So it would seem. The army are faxing me regimental lists, so we might be able to track down a contemporary or two.'

'Well, well, well. Well, well. How extremely pleasing. I shall beam on him as I serve him lunch and if the old bastard is particularly unpleasant I'll be able to reflect on how bad he'll feel when he's unmasked. I can't wait for the next revelations. Fishbane, perhaps, will turn out to have been an army chaplain and a founder of the League of Decency.'

'Shouldn't think so. He seems to have been corrupt from an early age. I rang up my old man this morning and asked if he remembered

Dickie Fishbane at school, and he exploded and started bellowing about degenerates and scoundrels. I tried to press him for some specifics, but he wasn't saying much. I did elicit the information that Fishbane was five years ahead of him and that briefly they were together in the school choir.'

'Nice-looking boy, your father?'

'You really have no respect for people's finer feelings. I don't want to know what Fishbane did to my unfortunate father all those years ago. Let's just say that my father talks a lot about queers and why they should be flung into prison and the key thrown away.'

'Well, you can't accuse Fishbane of being queer these days.'

'No, but he didn't have a lot of choice at Eton.'

'Thank God I was under-privileged and had to make do with girls. Anything else?'

'No. And on your side?'

'No, except that I'm engaging in prurient speculation about Gooseneck and Sunil and whether they're having an affair. Seems possible. Sunil went to public school and Gooseneck taught in a prep school. QED.'

Pooley clearly felt that this conversation was getting out of bounds. 'It would be more helpful, Robert, if you concentrated on something relevant.'

'You old prude, Ellis. I have to be allowed a bit of light relief. But yes, I'm off to serve lunch and find the blunt instrument and the missing notes. Oh, and you don't have to send me any more food. We're being fed even more royally than yesterday.'

'I'll just send you a little champagne to prove that though I may be a prude I'm not a puritan. Good day.'

'Good day, Ellis.'

'Are you free in half an hour?' Sunil sounded excited.

'Where will you be?'

'In Charles the Second. On the third floor.'

Amiss recalled a discreet chamber tucked away at the back of the building which appeared from its decor and its furniture to have been designed for the entertainment of a compliant lady.

'OK. See you.'

*

Sunil's toy turned out to be a lap-top computer. He showed it off shining-eyed. 'Isn't it marvellous, Robert. I've desperately wanted one of these, but of course, between the fees and books and everything else, I haven't been able to afford one.'

'Where did you get it?'

'Gooseneck gave it to me last night. Well, that is, he didn't give it to me, but he said I could use it until its rightful owner turned up.'

'Sorry, I don't follow.'

'Ah, right. The system is that Ramsbum and the upper servants divide lost property up among them.'

'What constitutes lost property?'

'Anything unclaimed left lying around the club or in the porters' cubbyhole. There's a lot of it, you know. All those absent-minded old people. So there's no end of umbrellas and coats and bags of goodies from Jermyn Street or Harrods. You wouldn't believe what they find. Gooseneck was telling me. They've had people leaving boxes of cigars and bottles of vintage port and silver-topped canes and even wigs and sets of false teeth, apart from all the other obvious things. But this is particularly marvellous. It was left behind a few days ago, Ramsbum doesn't know by whom, and no one's claimed it.'

'I find it almost impossible to imagine any frequenter of this club using a lap-top computer. It's also hard to believe that someone who would use a lap-top computer would forget where he left it.'

'I don't care.' Sunil was busily getting the machine to work. 'I'm just enjoying it. If it's snatched away from me, well and good, but if not, it'll be a great boon. I bought a spare disk for it this morning. I'll keep the one that was in it safe in case its owner turns up.'

'Shouldn't you look at the contents of the disk in case there's any clue to the ownership? Sorry if I'm sounding stuffy, Sunil.'

'Oh, I did look at that, Robert. First thing. But there's nothing. It's all incomprehensible. Looks like somebody's housekeeping accounts, with a lot of stuff about wine sales and trust funds.'

'Show me,' said Amiss. 'I have an idea.'

23

'You didn't blow your cover?'

'No. Sunil's a bright guy and he's sufficiently clued into club politics to have known about the question mark over Chatterton's conduct of the wine committee. It had come up vaguely in conversation between us. And of course he knew as well that the Admiral had been stirring it. So he just kicked himself for not having made the obvious connection.'

'So why didn't he ring us?'

'Because it was felt that I had got to know you two a bit yesterday. Anyway, I'm older and am seen as a man of the world.'

'OK. I'll send someone round for the lap-top now.'

'I suppose you can't let him have it back when the fingerprinting's been done?'

'You know I can't.'

'And I don't suppose you'd think of dipping into your patrimony to fund something similar for Sunil?'

'I don't mind subsidising you, Robert, but I'm not taking on your friends, however deserving they may seem.'

'Tight-wad.'

'That's how the Pooleys have held on to it down the generations. Now get off the phone, Robert, for Christ's sake.'

'When will we connect?'

'Are you on duty tonight?'

'Yep. We're still short-handed.'

'Well head for my place when you're finished. You've got the keys now. We'll all just turn up when we can.'

'See you.'

'See you. And, oh sorry, Robert. I should have said, "Very well done".'

'Oh gosh, thanks Guv. I'll try and keep up the good work.'

'Excuse me, Mr Gooseneck.'

'Yes, Robert.'

'Have you seen Sunil recently?'

'Not since lunch-time. He's due any moment, isn't he? It's almost seven-thirty.'

'I'm afraid he's had a disappointment.' Gooseneck raised an enquiring eyebrow. 'The lap-top turned out to belong to the Admiral, so it's been taken off to Scotland Yard for fingerprinting and all that while they analyse the contents of the disk. Then it'll presumably go to his heirs.'

'Damn! The boy was enjoying it so much.'

'I know he was.' Amiss looked as miserable as he felt. 'But unfortunately for him when he told me a bit about what was on the disk I had a blinding flash of inspiration.'

'I perceive that you're a public-spirited youth. It didn't occur to you to let sleeping dogs lie, if you'll forgive the cliché?'

'No, I'm afraid it didn't.'

'Oh, I expect you're right, my boy. My moral sense has been dulled by too many years here. I find it hard to raise more than a flicker of interest about who killed whom and why. I should, of course, in the event that they began disposing of those I like – you, Sunil, that rather delicious young Wu and that engaging Armenian. And me, of course.'

'But don't you think Sunil might have been in danger had it been realised that he had the run of the Admiral's computer?'

'Why?' Gooseneck sounded only very slightly interested. 'Was it full of incriminating material?'

'There certainly seemed to be a lot of stuff about club finances.'

'You are getting rather involved, are you not? Perhaps pulp fiction is your *métier* rather than poetry? Ah, here come the troops. I've ordered an extremely agreeable supper for us this evening – a fine steak and kidney pie.'

'What about the Hindus?'

'Sunil is a beef eater so there's only Sanjiv to cater for. He's happy with an omelette as are the two vegetarians. One has to be ever-vigilant in feeding what I believe are now referred to as "multi-cultural" gatherings.'

'No wonder Colonel Fagg kept it so simple,' said Amiss.

'Indeed.' Gooseneck looked thoughtful. 'If you do find the murderer, Robert, don't stop him in his tracks until he has seen off the Colonel.'

'But he may, of course, be the murderer.'

'That's an attractive thought and indeed he does have form.'

'How d'you mean?'

'I mean he has done time. Bird. Been inside. And what's more, for violence.'

'Really?'

'Well, I don't know what you're so surprised about, Robert. He's hardly the only one. The alumnae of Her Majesty's prisons now adorning ffeatherstonehaugh's include Mr Fishbane, Mr Mauleverer and, of course, myself.' He put his head to one side and regarded Amiss with interest. 'You appear surprised, my dear boy. Surely you realised I would hardly be here but for some catastrophe. Or perhaps I flatter myself.' He smiled genially. 'Here comes Sunil. Let us give him what solace we can. Should you seek further revelations, we can continue our conversation after supper.'

'Two years for buggery in nineteen sixty-three. Finished him as a teacher.'

'With adults or children?' asked Milton.

'Guardsmen, he said. He taught at a London prep-school and socialised enthusiastically in the area of Chelsea Barracks.'

'And Fagg?'

'Interesting. Grievous bodily harm, about twenty-five years ago. Nearly murdered his wife. Gooseneck couldn't remember what the marital row was about. He's a pretty detached sort of bloke. Doesn't take a lot of interest in other people anyway. Then there was Fishbane. Guess what he did time for?'

'Flashing?' asked Milton.

'Corruption of minors?' asked Pooley.

'No, but you're on the right lines. Living off immoral earnings, no less. Apparently, he ran a small but superior bordello in Pimlico until the vice squad descended.'

'He talked about visiting such an establishment,' said Milton.

'Well, there you are. He presumably bought into it with his Foreign Office gratuity. Marvellous. Oh, yes. We mustn't forget Mauleverer, the one who's always demanding to know if the haddock is finnan, the salmon wild and the beef Aberdeen Angus. He was done for four years for fraud. Pity he's not a suspect.'

'He wasn't even in the club on the days of the murders,' said Pooley morosely.

Milton was already on the phone to the Yard issuing instructions. 'Thanks, Robert,' he said when he returned. 'A very useful day you've had. You'd have earned your money if you were paid any.'

'Well, come on, come on. What did the Admiral's disk yield?'

'Lists of auction houses with dates and receipts. We'll have to check them out of course, but it looks as if Comrade Chatterton has sold over a hundred thousand pounds' worth of wine in the last ten years.'

'Wow!'

'He seems also to have been given sixty thousand in travel grants. Fishbane appears to have had an entertainment allowance of around twenty thousand. Then there are notes and figures relating to the library with a lot of question marks. Meredith-Lee appears to have seen a discrepancy of twenty to forty thousand pounds. Look, here's the print-out. Look at the list headed "Missing. First editions, question mark. Best drawings, question mark. Rochester manuscript, question mark. Toulouse-Lautrec". And then it just says on the next page, "Fagg angle".'

'Anything else important? It looks pretty incomprehensible.'

'There's quite a lot. Summaries of the kitchen accounts for the last ten years, for instance.'

'Grotesquely extravagant, presumably.'

'Looks like it. Then there are summaries of income and expenditure in all departments. The subscription income is interesting. Look how it's gone down spectacularly over twenty years.'

'Where do you go from here?'

'Tomorrow we'll be putting on the pressure to gain access to bank records – club and personal. Then of course there'll be a team checking with the auction rooms. And there'll also be at the club tomorrow morning an antiquarian bookseller, a dealer in manuscripts, and an expert in drawings, to see if there's been the hanky-panky suggested by those few notes about Fishbane.'

Milton returned the typescript to his briefcase. 'I have to admit to being rather staggered by the number of jail-birds the club accommodates. Presumably most clubs frown on chaps with records, Ellis?'

'Good Lord, yes. You normally get drummed out if you disgrace yourself. Or you resign first.'

'Not so in ffeatherstonehaugh's,' said Amiss. 'Our great founder laid down a rule in his will that anyone who went to prison would not have to pay his subscription during the time that he was unable to use the club premises, and that any unused portion of his subscription should be held over until his release.'

'How d'you get thrown out of ffeatherstonehaugh's anyway?' asked Pooley.

'Ah! He thought of that too. Ten members may present a petition claiming another to be either, (a), a bore, (b), a Roundhead, that's with a capital 'R' you understand, or (c), an admirer of Mr Gladstone. A vote is then held on the last Friday of the following month and members drop white balls or black balls in a box bearing the member's name. The decision is made on the basis of a simple majority.'

'Well I don't know about (b) and (c)' said Milton. 'But they appear to have got a bit lax on (a).'

'Funnily enough, Gooseneck says that the only votes in his time were attempts to oust Fagg, but the majority of white balls was so immense that the opposition seems to have got discouraged and given up.'

'Who counts the balls?' asked Pooley.

'The secretary,' said Amiss. 'And the late Pinkie Blenkinsop's loyalty was, of course, to the purveyor of the flesh-pots.'

'He didn't seem too bad a man all the same,' said Pooley. 'I rather liked him in spite of myself.'

Amiss sat up angrily. 'I'm supposed to be the one that makes excuses for people, Ellis. You're the absolutist. Well, let me tell you that on this occasion I would welcome a little more intolerance from you. He might have put up a good show the other day, but that was because he was frightened. If you actually had to live belowstairs and see the obscene way people were treated, you might be a little less sympathetic towards a man who claimed just to be following orders because he was weak. Some things are inexcusable.'

Milton looked at them both. 'Give him another drink, Ellis,' he said, 'and then let's vote him out of our club for being sanctimonious.'

24

Breakfast was particularly tiresome that morning. The strain seemed to have got to the aged suspects. Amiss suspected they had been hammering the port harder than ever the previous night. Waking Glastonbury had on this occasion required him to bellow his nanny impersonation four times, causing old Mauleverer to come staggering out of his nearby bedroom asking if the club was on fire. Mauleverer had then proceeded to snatch the cover off the dish on Amiss's tray, sniff disparagingly and explain to him that the ham was underdone and the eggs too hard. By the time Amiss had sorted Glastonbury out and returned to the dining-room Mauleverer was well into his 'Is-the-haddock-finnan' routine with a bewildered Vietnamese whom Gooseneck had omitted to brief. Not to be outdone, Fagg had then plunged into his 'What's-your-name-then-and-where-do-you-come-from-you-bloody-foreigner?' performance. On being told that the name was Ng and its owner Viet-namese, Fagg had started bellowing, 'North or South? North or South? Are you a bloody red? And why is your hair so long? Are you queer as well?' As the frightened boy bolted to Gooseneck's side, there was a scream from Fishbane's corner where an unwary Pole had reaped the consequences of turning her back to view the drama. In turn she fled to Gooseneck, who after uttering a few more words of comfort, strode over to Fagg's table and said, 'Shut up.'

'How dare you shout at me! Don't you know who I am?'

'Of course I know who you are, you appalling oaf. You've been plaguing the life out of me and everybody else for as long as I've worked here. You have had your day. Now shut up and stop insulting my staff.'

Fagg emitted an interesting glugging sound, rather as if he were repeating the name of the insulted Vietnamese over and over again. Amiss wondered if apoplexy would ensue, but all that followed was silence. Fagg began to pretend to read his newspaper with great attention. The rest of the breakfasters, who had been gazing on with fascination, returned also to their newspapers, with the exception of Fishbane, on whom Gooseneck now turned.

'If you ever again touch one of my staff,' he said clearly and loudly, 'I will instruct the largest and toughest of her colleagues to knock you down. Is that understood?'

'Perfectly, my dear man.' Fishbane spoke with commendable urbanity. 'You've made yourself absolutely clear.' He returned to his newspaper.

As Gooseneck strode masterfully back to his accustomed position, Amiss heard Mauleverer muttering mutinously: 'That's all very well, that's all very well, but nobody's told me if the haddock's finnan.'

Gooseneck turned on his heel and stood over him. 'Of course the haddock's finnan, you old idiot. Has been probably since the foundation of the club. The kidneys are lambs', and yes – they have been grilled with the fat still on them – the marmalade is thick-cut, the food is superb and the waiters are underpaid. Is there anything else you wish to know?'

Mauleverer avoided Gooseneck's eyes. He looked covertly at the members to his left and right: they gave not a flicker of recognition. 'That's fine,' he said. 'Thank you very much. I'd be grateful if you could tell the waiter that I would like the haddock.'

Petrified, all the old men gazed at their food or their newspapers: the silence was palpable. After relaying the message to Ng, Gooseneck looked over at Amiss and gave him a long, slow wink. Amiss made him a deep bow followed by a noiseless, but enthusiastic clapping of hands.

'It's Robert. Have you a moment?'

'Yes.'

'Any news?'

'Some. We've got Fagg's career well and truly sorted out.'

'Go on.'

'Hang on a minute. I'm just looking for the biographical summary Ellis has given me. Albert Anthony Fagg, born nineteen fourteen, Sevenoaks, Kent. Father ran a butcher's shop in which Fagg also worked until called up in nineteen thirty-nine. By then he was married to Ethel Midgley, whose father was a cobbler. She went off with a GI during the war and he divorced her in nineteen forty-six.'

'Well, poor old sod. Maybe he was quite nice till then.'

'Posted to the Army Catering Corps serving the Pioneer Corps.

152

They weren't glamorous enough for you to have known about them: they consisted of the people who weren't medically A1. Fagg fitted in: his eyesight was very poor and he had flat feet. So his whole war was spent with them in England, or, much later on, in Italy. He emerged as sergeant-major. There's a reprimand on his record for improper treatment of a prisoner of war.'

'Any details?'

'No. Can't have been too serious. Probably just abuse. And one court martial on a charge of pilfering rations. The case was dismissed. No other details. Ellis managed to track down one contemporary who described him as, quote, a horrible little shit who thought he was Napoleon, unquote. The same chap also revealed that he was given the nickname Colonel because he was so self-important.'

Amiss exploded with laughter. 'I feel a grudging respect for his brass neck,' he said. 'It takes real guts to carry off such a successful fraud. Go on. Go on.'

'Back to father's shop. Married Julia Short, the daughter of the fishmonger.'

'He certainly had a clear view of his place,' said Amiss. 'But how the hell did he come to join ffeatherstonehaugh's?'

'It's a long story, which Ellis extracted from Gooseneck this morning. Apparently, Fagg turned up as the protégé of one Captain Fanning of the Pioneer Corps, an Irish member of ffeatherstonehaugh's whom Gooseneck remembers as an occasional visitor and noted practical joker. He apparently introduced Fagg as his colonel.'

'And the wife?'

'Had a bust-up in the late fifties when he beat her up so badly he was sent to jail.'

'Well, wasn't he unmasked?'

'No, it doesn't seem to have been reported in the national papers, just the local Kent newspaper. Gooseneck found out about it through a retired old retainer who lived in the area. After that Fagg was divorced. He sold the shop, of which he was the owner by then, and moved into ffeatherstonehaugh's as a resident. The rest we know.'

'So his private means?'

'Can't be much. Old-age pension and whatever remains of his modest capital.'

'Unless he's played the stock market with great brilliance.'

'Unlikely, since . . . Come in. Yes. I'll be up at once. Got to go, Robert. Bye.'

Amiss wandered disconsolately out of the phone-booth, full of unanswered questions and a desire to be part of the action. The blunt instrument obstinately refused to reveal itself and he doubted if there were any more revelations to be got out of anybody. He was aching to tell his friends about the Gooseneck episode, but since it was of human rather than police significance he didn't feel entitled to waste their time during a busy day. He had enjoyed being able to tell Sunil all about it at lunch, though he had been a little worried by the way Sunil had then gazed at Gooseneck throughout the meal with evident hero-worship. They couldn't really be, could they?

He walked slowly back to his gallery-duties, by this time in the afternoon virtually non-existent – and had just got to the top of the stairs when he saw Gooseneck advancing towards him carrying a large package.

'I was looking for you, Robert. Come into the library for a minute. There's something I want to show you.' They retired behind the erotic-drawings cabinet and Gooseneck tore open the cardboard to reveal a lap-top computer. 'Look, I couldn't resist getting this for Sunil. Won't he be thrilled?'

'Of course he will.' Amiss's unease persisted. He couldn't warm to the notion of a Gooseneck–Sunil love affair: the potential for pain seemed too great.

Gooseneck had put the machine back in its box. He leaned against the wall and surveyed Amiss appraisingly. 'You don't seem very enthusiastic, Robert.'

'Oh, I am. I am. It'll be marvellous for Sunil. It's terrifically generous of you.'

'I know what's wrong with you. You think I'm screwing him, don't you?'

Amiss realised he respected Gooseneck too much to lie. He looked at him squarely and said, 'Yes.'

'I thought you did. Of course, you're quite right. But as I think people always say at such a time as this, it isn't the way you think it is.'

'And how do I think it is?'

'I suspect you believe me to be a corruptor of minors. And in that, of course, you are technically right, as the age of consent is twenty-one.' He took out a packet of cigarettes and offered one to Amiss, who took it, accepted a light, drew deeply and then said, 'Oh Christ, I'd forgotten. I've stopped.' He stubbed it out and threw it in the fire.

'Goodness! I must have unnerved you, dear boy. Well, in sum, I do not lay hands on my staff, however much they attract me. Much of my paltry income goes on rent boys – one of my few weekend leisure activities. They're already corrupted. Sunil, however, fell in love with me and I with him through our discovery of a common taste in literature and a strong need for affection. Sunil is an unregenerate homosexual – you note I do not say "gay", a word which has been infamously ghettoised – and he appears to find me, at this stage of his life, to his taste.' He inhaled deeply, expelled the smoke and threw the cigarette in the fire. 'Might I draw your attention to a poem by Rochester? Perhaps you know it? "A song of a young lady to her ancient lover".'

'I've read it.'

> 'Ancient person,' [*began Gooseneck*], 'for whom I
> All the flattering youth defy,
> Long be it ere thou grow old,
> Aching, shaking, crazy, cold;
> But still continue as thou art,
> Ancient person of my heart.

And so on: the sentiments, if not the sex, of young Sunil.'

'I'm sorry, Mr . . . Damn! What the hell am I supposed to call you now?'

'A fair question, Robert. With my new-found self-respect I may decide to refuse any longer to be called by that ridiculous name. Although I really don't notice it any more. My real name is Harry Cameron. Sounds a bit like the hero of a boys' school story, doesn't it? Please call me Harry, except when on duty. It might confuse the natives.'

'Very well. I was about to say, Harry, that I was accused by some friends last night of being sanctimonious. It seems to be the effect this place has had on me. Sunil is lonely and I'm sure you're good for each other.'

'A pretty and affecting speech. I shall see you at supper, shall I? Simple but excellent sausages and mash for the pork eaters.'

'Have you had any reactions to this morning's turn of events?'

'You will have observed that at lunch they were all well behaved. I haven't heard a peep.'

'I thought they were having a council of war this afternoon,' said Amiss. 'Four of them got together over a couple of decanters of port and I listened to what I could. Fishbane and Fagg seemed simply embarrassed. Chatterton pulled their legs slightly and said they had better be careful not to get on the wrong side of you again and Glastonbury didn't know what the hell anyone was talking about. I think they're cowed.'

At that moment Mauleverer tottered in and made for the armchair beside the fire. 'Ah! Gooseneck,' he said, showing no surprise at seeing the head waiter standing in the library wearing a slightly battered but decent sports jacket and corduroy trousers and lighting a cigarette. He sat down and addressed Amiss. 'Can you get me some tea, young man? And a slice of fruit cake, please. Make sure it's Dundee, and moist.'

'Certainly, sir,' said Amiss.

'Oh yes, and would you be so kind as to fetch me *The Economist* from the table over there?'

'Certainly.'

There was no *Economist* on the table. All the other serious journals to which the club subscribed but which no one read lay there, virgin. Amiss looked around the rest of the room and returned to Mauleverer.

'I'm sorry, sir,' he said. 'It's not here. Somebody must have taken it.'

'Taken it? *The Economist*? There isn't anyone left in this club who reads anything more demanding than the *Racing Times* or tits and bums magazines. Are you sure?'

'I'm sure, sir. But I'll look in the Smoking Room. Perhaps somebody took it in there.'

'Oh, it may be. It may be,' said Mauleverer. 'Perhaps our friend Fagg is looking for enlightenment about the role of the Vietnamese in the Second World War, or by chance Glastonbury is investigating recent discoveries of esoteric viruses.'

'I'll check it out, sir.' Amiss and Gooseneck withdrew.

'Mauleverer's all right,' said Gooseneck. 'He was only ever annoying – not actually bad.'

'What about his fraudulent activities?'

'He ripped off a firm of disreputable City stockbrokers to the tune of about a million pounds and spent it on high living – yachts, mistresses, that sort of thing. I think actually he's in the true spirit of the old ffeatherstonehaugh's. Perhaps if he'd been around more, he might have held the club together. I shall see you shortly.' He moved towards the lift and then turned back and said, 'Oh, by the way. From now on, you use the lift whenever you like. If anyone protests, refer them to me.'

'My hero,' said Amiss.

'I have a hypothetical blunt instrument for you, Ellis.'

'Yes?'

'This week's *Economist*. It's gone missing from the library.'

'That's it,' said Pooley. 'The forensic people told us that they had found a trace of paper in his nostrils. I'll find out whether *The Economist* is the right size and weight. Keep looking for it.'

'Presumably it was thrown out by the murderer,' said Amiss. 'Anyway, you're the scavengers.'

'I'll have to get the facts first,' said Pooley. 'If they think you're right I suppose we'll have to send in another team to scour through the garbage again. Goodbye.'

'Ellis!' shouted Amiss. 'Stop!'

'What, what? I can't stop and talk, Robert. I'm in a hurry.'

'Will I be seeing you tonight? I'm going mad here. I have to know what's going on.'

'Oh, yes, yes. The usual, I suppose. Turn up when you can and we will when we can. Bye.'

Amiss returned to the gallery and gave Mauleverer his tea and cake along with apologies for the delay.

'No, no, don't apologise,' said Mauleverer. 'It's quite all right. Just one thing. Tell me, is the tea Sri Lankan? And strong?'

'Of course, sir. That's what you always have in the afternoon.'

Mauleverer smiled affably. 'Don't be too hard on me,' he said. 'You and Gooseneck must allow us our little eccentricities and then we will allow you yours. Perhaps you would now be so kind

157

as to fetch me a copy of the *Financial Times*? I trust Cully Chatterton has not appropriated it in order to check out casino share prices.'

25

Amiss was fretful and impatient as the evening wore on. Supper was spent in silence, for Sunil was absent and Gooseneck was at the far end of the table doing his managerial duties by a couple of nervous new waiters. Caught between Ng and Wu, who together had about seventeen words of English, all to do with food, Amiss retired into feverish speculation and self-questioning, oblivious to the excellent meal and the multilingual cries of appreciation around him.

'I don't need you tonight, Robert,' said Gooseneck at the end of supper. 'We've only got a handful of customers. I think Blenkinsop's death has scared off most of the outsiders.'

'Oh, but I don't mind staying on none the less.'

'I don't need you,' said Gooseneck firmly. 'You've been working ridiculously long hours and you should take time off when it's available. Go and read a book or go to the motion pictures or do whatever it is you like to do in your spare time, preferably outside this benighted building. You're in the place far too much.'

Amiss trailed off miserably, wondering how to fill in the hours until meeting Milton and Pooley. He went upstairs to look for Sammy Pike, who'd been directing operations in the club all day, but he and his men had left. He was unable to resist ringing the Yard for an update of news. Milton's direct line didn't answer: Pooley's did.

'Oh, I'm so glad you rang, Robert. I tried to leave a message for you, but that old cretin wouldn't take it.'

'Ramsbum?'

'Yes. My fault. I forgot the rules and said I was a friend and he said he didn't hold with servants having friends.'

Amiss was too inured to Ramsbum's awfulness even to get cross. 'Well, what was the message? What gives?'

'I'm sorry. You're not going to like this, but we can't make tonight.'

'Oh shit!'

'We've got endless meetings and there's an absolute mass of material coming through that's got to be sifted and sorted and we're not going to get out of here before midnight. Due back eight hours later. We just won't be fit to talk, Robert. I'm sorry.'

'Any news so far?'

'Yes. Looks like you're right on *The Economist* – right size, shape and paper. But Sammy holds out no hope of finding it. They've had an absolutely fruitless day at the club. Look, I've got to go. We'll be along tomorrow. Probably mid-morning. Try to be on duty.'

As Amiss emerged from the phone booth, Ramsbum was standing with his hands on his hips, looking wicked. 'Look here, young Robert, this isn't good enough. Someone tried to leave a message for you earlier. I 'ad to tell him that servants have no right to have messages left for them unless they've got a dead granny. You know that perfectly well. If I were to do my job properly I'd report this to the Colonel.'

'Oh, piss off, you old fart,' said Amiss. He stomped up the stairs into the Great Saloon. He felt utterly bleak. The cavorting nymphs and shepherds, the Regency bucks, the courtesans, even Rochester, struck a sordid note in a vast building out of which life had long gone. He trudged up the stairs to the deserted gallery and thence into the empty library where Blenkinsop had died. He wandered around looking for distraction or solace, but he was too restless for the serious journals and too sated with the literature of sex. If I really were a poet, he thought, this would be the time to write my elegy. To depress himself further he took out Johnson's *Lives of the English Poets* and re-read his denunciation of Rochester:

> Thus in a course of drunken gaiety, and gross sensuality, with intervals of study perhaps yet more criminal, with an avowed contempt of all decency and order, a total disregard to every moral and a resolute denial of every religious obligation, he lived worthless and useless, and blazed out his youth and his health in lavish voluptuousness; till, at the age of one and thirty, he had exhausted the fund of life, and reduced himself to a state of weakness and decay.

'Oh, fuck,' said Amiss. 'I need a drink.'

*

Twenty minutes later, out of uniform, Amiss walked past Ramsbum in silence and headed for the bright lights of Piccadilly. He was in a state of complete indecisiveness, seeking distraction but with no inclination for it. He wandered aimlessly until he reached a cinema offering three films, two about sex and one about death. He found the themes too reminiscent of ffeatherstonehaugh's to be bearable. He drifted on to Piccadilly Circus. Eros, recently refurbished, perched brightly in the centre, surrounded by hordes of the kind of people who got youth a bad name. He went into Regent Street to get away from them and on an impulse decided to have a cocktail at the Café Royal. He leaned on the bar and ordered their 'Original Champagne Cocktail', a concoction of brandy, Grand Marnier, angostura bitters, champagne and other odds and ends, and appraised his surroundings.

The place was essentially rococo, full of half-naked plaster ladies decorated in blue paint and gilt, while the furniture was red plush and cane. Very Fishbane, thought Amiss. The walls were festooned mainly with photographs of the famous dead who in their heyday had frequented that bar: Noel Coward and Fred Astaire and minor royals and bright young things. They gazed out at their audience toothily or greeted each other frothily and insincerely. Wandering around, Amiss chose as his favourite record of bygone days the affectionate picture of Lady Throckmorton and the Maharajah of Jaipur.

He looked around for a comfortable seat and chose one beside two extremely attractive young women. It might have been an association of ideas that led him this time to order 'Between the Sheets', whose mixture of brandy, white rum, cointreau and lemon juice gave him little pleasure. The two girls, however, were great compensation. He became riveted by their lively dissection of an acquaintance. In Charles's favour was his family (loaded), his family dogs ('utterly divine beagles'), his sister Sarah ('an absolute sweetie'), his horsemanship ('won the point-to-point last Saturday'), his job (wine shipper – took him away to 'heavenly places'), and his car ('absolutely fabulous little MGB'). Against him were his looks (poor old Charles inherited Granny St John's nose), his stupidity ('honestly, Peter said he was always the dimmest boy in the class') and his passion for practical jokes ('I mean, darling – apple-pie beds at our age!').

Amiss was meditating ordering a third drink and trying to muscle in on them, when they both jumped to their feet crying, 'Charles, you absolute poppet. How wonderful to see you,' and flung themselves upon a tall, braying person with an absolutely hideous nose.

Plunged back into gloom by this new evidence of the innate hypocrisy of the upper classes, he marched over to the bar, demanded and paid his large bill and walked out. He stood irresolute on the pavement, half tempted to get the tube to his friend O'Hara's pub, where distraction was absolutely guaranteed and the carousing would go on till 4 a.m. However, he was reluctant to render himself completely useless the following day. He idled back to Piccadilly Circus and strolled up Shaftesbury Avenue, reading the notices of plays he would never get round to seeing and looking at pictures of actors whom he didn't recognise. He strayed into Soho. After long exposure to the ffeatherstone-haugh library he was unmoved by even the most comely of the hookers. After five attempts, he found a pub without deafening music or fruit machines, but its peace was soon shattered by the arrival of the drunken dregs of somebody's leaving party. Screams of laughter about what Sharon had said to Mr Boyd and what he had said to Sharon seemed promising, but despite assiduous eavesdropping, Amiss could make no further sense of their conversation. In the end he was driven out by their noisy incomprehensibility.

By the time he reached Piccadilly Circus again it was ten-thirty. The young – both foreign and domestic – were sitting in their dozens around Eros, gaping – most of them in silence – at each other. As he passed into Lower Regent Street, Amiss wondered if any age group was exempt from the misanthropy which appeared to have over-whelmed him. He recognised that he was suffering from a surfeit of institutional living, sexual frustration and a severe lack of the company of those he loved, but this awareness brought little comfort.

He turned into Pall Mall and looked appraisingly at the clubs as he passed them: it seemed months since he had first ventured into clubland with Pooley. He looked at the stately Athenaeum, from which seemed to emanate the certainty that God was in his heaven and all was right with the world, and he tried to imagine how its members had coped with ffeatherstonehaugh's wicked travesty of their noble building. He ambled past the Travellers' and the Repeal, and saw a cheerful group descending the stairs of the Reform. Presumably a go-ahead club like that, the only gentlemen's club in London to have admitted women as equal members – and that after only a hundred and forty years – would have coped better than most with the ridicule that ffeatherstonehaugh's architectural pastiche must have brought. He began to smile as he contemplated the outrage that must have prevailed when the joke was first made public and so reminded himself what a very good joke it had been. As he sauntered into his dwelling, he even favoured Ramsbum with a smile: he received in exchange a glower which combined venom with wariness.

He was in bed reading when Sunil arrived.

'Evening, Robert.'

'Evening, Sunil. How are you?'

'Fine, honestly. Nothing to worry about. I think I exorcised poor old Blenkinsop's corpse tonight, working on an essay on nineteenth-century protectionism. It was really interesting.' He sat at the end of Amiss's bed, put his briefcase on his knees and opened it. He took out a pile of papers, dumped them on the bed and pulled out his computer. 'It's an absolute dream working with this, Robert. I could play with it all night. I'll be able to do my essays on it now Harry's going to get me a printer.' He stood up and carried the machine over to the chair by his bed and came back and picked up his papers. He removed several photocopies and put them by his bed. He began to put the rest of the pile back in his briefcase.

'What's that magazine, Sunil?' asked Amiss suddenly.

'Magazine? Oh, that's *The Economist*. D'you want to borrow it? I'm nearly finished.'

'Where did you get it?'

'In the waste-paper basket in the library. Why?'

'I'll tell you in a minute. When?'

'The other night.'

'You mean the night you found Blenkinsop?'

'Just before. I went in to borrow a book from those shelves down

162

the end on the right where they've actually got some serious Victorian novels and poetry.'

'Yep.'

'I had assumed the place was empty, as usual. I got what I wanted, turned round, saw *The Economist* sticking out of the waste-paper basket and put in in my case along with the book. And then I was just going when I saw Blenkinsop.'

'Well, well,' said Amiss. 'D'you know something, Sunil. As a scavenger you're having a really bad week.'

26

'No fingerprints, except Sunil Gupta's.'

'Shit!' Milton banged his fists together in frustration. Then he shrugged. 'It was too much to hope for. No one would have been crazy enough to discard a murder weapon so openly if it was going to incriminate him.'

'Damn it. We should have thought of checking them for gloves that night.'

'The murderer wasn't necessarily wearing gloves,' said WDC Hutton. 'There are quite a lot of fudged prints on the cover. Someone could have just wiped the magazine vigorously after use. Sorry we couldn't help.'

'Thank you anyway, Melinda. You can go now.'

'Goodbye, sir. Goodbye, Ellis.' Pooley was too preoccupied even to notice her departure. He began to stride up and down. 'It wasn't really much of a risk, if you think about it, sir. For a start, we wouldn't have been likely to look twice at a magazine in a waste-paper basket. It wasn't as if it was rolled up or anything. Sunil said it was quite flat. And look at it. There's only that one line near the binding that shows it's been rolled up and that slight squashing at the top.'

'I think you're being over-influenced by Edgar Allan Poe, Ellis. I'll bet you're thinking of the envelope that was hidden from the police by being displayed openly on the mantelpiece.'

'"The Case of the Purloined Letter", sir? Well, yes. I was thinking of that.'

'I always thought that was nonsensical. It entirely relies on the assumption that people don't look for evidence in the obvious places, whereas I'm sure that's only true of imaginative folk like yourself. Now with due deference to our colleagues, many of them are extremely thick and can be utterly relied upon to go for the blindingly obvious.'

He rang the bell. Amiss was with them within half a minute. 'Christ!' he said, 'I thought you'd never call me.'

'How about some coffee, Robert?'

'In a minute, in a minute. What's the score?'

'Still three-love,' said Milton gloomily. 'No useful fingerprints on the *The Economist*.'

'Shit!'

'That's what I said. Ellis, you must have covered about half a mile by now. Slow up. You're making me feel tired.'

'Robert,' said Pooley, 'would you think the odds were good that Blenkinsop wouldn't be found until the morning?'

'Excellent, I'd have said. None of the members was likely to use the place. They'd all have tootled off to bed and it would have been Ramsbum's job to switch off the lights, not to look around. He could easily have missed him.'

'And by that time someone could have rescued the magazine, couldn't he?'

'Sure, even if they went up to bed at the same time. They'd only have to pop down in the lift, collect the offending item and destroy it. Come to think of it, they'd only have to burn it in the Smoking Room. There was a fire there that night.'

'That's probably what was intended.'

'So the murderer was taking a calculated risk,' said Milton, 'not an outrageous one.'

'The sort of risk Cully Chatterton would take,' said Amiss.

'Yes. And he was physically capable of doing the job. However, after exhaustive conversations with his doctor it still seems definite that he couldn't have done Meredith-Lee, let alone Trueman.'

'Two different murderers?' suggested Amiss. 'Or a conspiracy? Or back to Glastonbury holding the dynamite?'

'Just because Chatterton and Glastonbury are friends doesn't mean they have to be partners in murder,' said Milton. 'Fagg and Chatterton seem much more likely – Chatterton providing the brains and Fagg the brawn. And they certainly seem to be the ones with the most to lose, judging by what we dug up yesterday. Robert, will you for Christ's sake get the fucking coffee.'

'Oh, all right. I'll get the fucking coffee.' Amiss left reluctantly. He was back in five minutes. 'Here,' he said, 'I've even got you biscuits. How's that for coals of fire?' He poured out three cups of coffee, sat down in an armchair and sipped his.

'What d'you think you're doing?' asked Milton.

'Being interviewed. That's what I just told Gooseneck. Now come on. Just give me the headlines. What did you find out yesterday? And if you don't come across I won't find you any more clues, so there.'

'You're a great man for your pound of flesh,' said Pooley.

'Pound of flesh, pound of flesh. You deposit me in this stinking mausoleum and leave me to rot from boredom and frustration while you're whooping it up with your mates at the Yard.'

'Now chaps, now chaps,' said Milton. 'Stop squabbling. You're like a pair of kids.'

'Sorry, Vicar.' Amiss got up and refilled his coffee cup.

'You won't be surprised to hear,' said Pooley, 'that they're all in a pretty parlous financial state. Except Glastonbury, that is. He's comfortable.'

'What's comfortable these days?'

'Quarter of a million pounds of capital which keeps increasing because he rarely spends anything. It's all in a building society. He showed us his savings book.'

'Yes,' said Milton wearily, 'and explained at enormous length that he did enjoy going to the building society and they were all so nice there and it was a little treat for him, quite a little outing. Really, the only thing that he did do outside ffeatherstonehaugh's, except his little bit of gardening.'

'Gardening? What gardening?'

'He looks after his mother's grave in Highgate Cemetery. He explained at equally great length that Mother had decided that she wanted to be buried in London so that he could look after her, but that arrangements had been made at her request that on his death both she and he would go back to Derbyshire to be buried with Father.'

'And Nanny,' said Pooley.

'Quite right, Ellis, How could I have forgotten? Apparently, the grave's looking very nice at the moment. Pansies.'

'Seems appropriate,' said Amiss.

'So he could afford to live in a relatively luxurious old people's home,' said Pooley. 'His motive is therefore rather slim.'

'Except that he'd have to leave here and Cully.'

'With that amount of money he'd probably have enough to keep Cully in an old people's home as well.'

'What's interesting,' said Milton, 'is that Glastonbury was apparently the only honest one of them, but he's also the only one that's reasonably well off.'

'Unless they've been salting it away in Swiss bank accounts,' said Amiss.

'No,' said Milton. 'They were too careful for that. You see, they weren't actually stealing. What we inferred from the Admiral's notes was correct. Chatterton's had about fifteen to twenty thousand a year for travelling and accommodation, Fishbane somewhere about five to ten thousand for hospitality.'

'Christ! That's a lot of whores,' said Amiss.

'Perhaps just a few expensive ones. Sammy was too delicate to ask.'

'Sammy?'

'Yes. Sammy did the interviews yesterday. Except for Glastonbury. We kept him till this morning because we didn't want him upset by a stranger.'

'How can so soft-hearted a policeman get to be a chief superintendent?'

'Because I pretend to be a brute.'

Pooley looked impatient. 'They were all reasonably open with Sammy about money, except Fagg, but he apparently gave in when Sammy threatened to arrest him. All he claims to have is his old-age pension and the interest on about twenty thousand quid. Fishbane has no capital at all and a pension of about ten thousand a year. Chatterton's got about the same. Outlook grim outside ffeatherstonehaugh's, eh?'

'Very. Why isn't Fagg claiming anything?'

'He has no outside interests. But he is ripping the club off more than the others in the sense that he is the driving force behind the sheer gluttony of the place. The others humour him and there isn't anything else he wants. But, in so far as we can understand the Admiral's notes, the club is running at a loss of over a hundred thousand a year, despite the very generous ffeatherstonehaugh endowment, and losses are rising steadily because of the lack of new members and the wholesale subsidising of the old. Hence the wine sales and what turned out to be substantial library sales as well. Fishbane admitted quite cheerfully that in his official capacity he's been selling off some of the club's greatest treasures – including the Rochester manuscript.'

'Which one? I didn't know we'd had one.'

'It's allegedly his farewell. Written in his own hand, it is claimed.'

'My God! How suitable,' said Amiss. 'How marvellously suitable. I've learnt quite a bit of it off by heart. I was thinking it should be carved on the Admiral's grave.'

'Well, go on. Recite it,' said Milton.

Amiss jumped up and struck an attitude.

> 'Tired with the noisome follies of the age
> And weary of my part, I quit the stage:
> For who in life's dull farce a part would bear,
> Where rogues, whores, bawds, all the head actors are?
> Long I with charitable malice strove,
> Lashing the court, those vermin to remove,
> But thriving vice under the rod still grew,
> As aged leachers whipped, their lust renew;
> Yet though my life hath unsuccessful been,
> (For who can this Augaean stable clean),
> My generous end I will pursue in death,
> And at mankind rail with my parting breath.'

Both members of his audience clapped. 'Excellent, Robert,' said Milton. 'Delivered *con brio*. And in the Rochester Room too.'

'Mind you, it's a bit general. A pedant would want to change it from "mankind" to the "members of the general committee" and "parting breath" to lap-top computer. But that would lack a certain *je ne sais quoi*, I feel.'

Pooley was tapping his foot. 'Anyway, that manuscript went, along with quite a lot of first editions, drawings and even a Toulouse-Lautrec.'

'What about the stuff in Fishbane's bedroom?' asked Amiss.

'Some is apparently his own, but he quite cheerfully admits that quite a lot of it belongs to the club. Said he just borrowed it.'

'Anything more on backgrounds?'

Milton sighed. 'Nothing significant. We're still digging. In fact, now that we've seen Glastonbury and you, we're going to bugger back to the Yard and continue.'

'D'you know what I'd like to do, Jim?' said Pooley.

'No.'

'Just read through everything all over again, starting with Trueman. Just to see if I can take a fresh view.'

'If you can find the time, Ellis. Come on. Bye, Robert.'

'When will I see you?' wailed Amiss.

'Oh, Christ! Don't panic. Ring one of us this afternoon. We'll make a date. And keep yourself busy. Pick some brains.'

'If I can find any to pick in this dump,' said Amiss. 'Another few days of this and I might be prepared to go back to the Civil Service.'

'I don't know if that would be wise,' said Milton. 'The food isn't as good.'

'And you don't get living accommodation,' said Pooley.

'Oh, push off,' said Amiss. 'And leave me alone in Château Despair.'

27

During the next few hours evidence began to pile up against Chatterton. First, there was the telephone call from Paris from Milton's friend in the Sûreté, Philippe Daguerre.

One of Milton's strengths was his ability to circumvent the bureaucratic process: his loathing of the byzantine procedures of Interpol had caused him to develop his own relationships with like-minded individuals in the major European police forces. Daguerre owed him a considerable favour for the work Milton had done in nailing a French killer who had been pleading a London alibi: he delivered.

'Your friend Chatterton has problems, it seems.'

'What sort of problems?'

'He has no money. In fact, he has a debt of more than a million francs to someone very unpleasant.'

Milton was quivering with eagerness, but he knew better than to cramp Daguerre's style, which included a liking for teasing introductions and dramatic pauses. 'How interesting, Philippe. Congratulations. Tell me more.'

'I have a very good friend in Monte Carlo. It wasn't a problem to find out about Chatterton. It is unusual in a casino to see an old man with a metal support at four o'clock in the morning. And the risks he was taking! There was much comment.'

'I'm not surprised.'

'Also, this was not typical.'

'Sorry, Philippe. You've lost me.'

'My friend found a croupier who remembered Chatterton from a preceding visit. He remarked how his style was changed. He had been a courageous but safe gambler. This last time he is not prudent. In all, my friend thinks, he probably won six million francs and lost seven.'

'Good grief! And he owes the missing million to whom? The casino?'

'No, no. You do not have the bills with a casino. It is not a restaurant. I am told the debt was paid by an *habitué* who is not a nice person. Very strange company for an English gentleman – and, I believe, well-educated.'

'You intrigue me greatly, Philippe.'

'I am pleased, Jim. Now this unpleasant person is well known to us. He is a gambler whose activities are financed by drugs.'

'As you say, very strange company for Mr Chatterton. Does your undesirable gambler want his money back?'

'Always he will want his money or services furnished in exchange. I think that your Mr Chatterton was of some service.'

'Jesus!' said Milton. 'Drugs in his zimmer!'

'I beg your pardon?'

'You have given me an idea, Philippe, which I must now pursue. I'm extremely grateful.'

'It is nothing, Jim.'

'Ellis, just a quick word.'

'Yes, Robert.'

'Chatterton was in the library in the middle of the night that Blenkinsop died. Could have been trying to retrieve the magazine.'

'How d'you know?'

'Gooseneck saw him. He'd stayed up late. After he'd put Sunil to bed, he went off to the kitchen, where he sat reading and sipping port. He was feeling a bit unsettled so he didn't go to bed until one o'clock and on his way he stopped by the Smoking Room to pick up a newspaper to read in bed. He was in there when he heard the lift. He didn't want any confrontation, so he stayed in the background and saw Chatterton swinging down the gallery to the library. Apparently, he was in there only for a half a minute and then straight back into the lift and upstairs – not carrying a book. That's what Gooseneck found a bit odd.'

'Mmmm. Thank you, Robert. Food for thought.'

'See yer.'

'See you.'

'I've tracked down the zimmer, sir. I've sent McGuire around to pick it up from the hospital. They're certain it's the same one.'

'It's going to be a waste of time, Ellis. Chatterton's not a fool.'

'People do slip up, sir.'

'What a fatuous remark. Oh, for God's sake, Ellis, stop looking like a wounded puppy. You're so fucking thin-skinned. Go ahead, of course, but ten to one you'll find a perfectly ordinary frame with no special compartments. He'll have done a swap.'

'I'm more of an optimist than you are, sir.'

'I know that, Ellis. That's why it's nice to have you around.'

'Really, Mr Milton, you're putting pressure on me to agree that a man of seventy-six, while three-quarters crippled with two serious fractures and unable to walk except with the support of a zimmer, could construct a bomb and strap it to the underside of a table.'

'No, I am not, Mr Selwood. I'm asking you to come to the scene of the crime and watch somebody going through the motions of planting the device – with an open mind.'

'I'm a very busy man.' Milton said nothing. 'Oh, very well. When d'you want me?'

'As soon as you can manage it, sir.'

'Six o'clock then. Do you want me to bring an aged cripple to practise with? Or can you provide your own?'

'If any aged cripples are necessary, sir, you can rely on us to provide them.'

Their goodbyes were positively friendly. One thing that doctors and coppers had in common, reflected Milton: gallows humour.

'Come in.'

Pooley walked over to Milton's desk and put a pound coin in front of him.

'What's this for?'

'You bet the zimmer would be clean, sir.'

'Oh, dear. Cheer up, Ellis, You're the optimist. Anything new from your reading?'

'No.'

'Any thoughts?'

'I don't think we're leaning hard enough on Fagg, sir. We shouldn't be losing sight of the fact that he's got the biggest motive of all for keeping ffeatherstonehaugh's going in the old way.'

'Fair enough. We'll go and bully Fagg this afternoon. It'll get us out of the office. Chatterton we can leave until Mr Selwood has done his stuff. Ring up and make an appointment.'

All the fight had gone out of Fagg. He sat with his head in his hands, pathetic and close to tears, unable any longer to lie about his past. The repulsive brown stains bespattering his garish club tie accentuated his forlorn appearance.

'I liked living like a gentleman,' he said. 'So I had to pretend to be one.' Pooley trembled visibly, and Milton, seeing him desperate to get a word in, nodded.

Pooley glared at Fagg and in a clipped tone, said, 'May I remind you, sir, of a quotation from Cardinal Newman. "It is almost a definition of a gentleman to say he is one who never inflicts pain." If I may say so, you did little else.'

Milton scowled at Pooley. This was no time for him to be springing to the defence of his own class. Pooley saw his face and subsided in embarrassment. He had however stirred Fagg up again into action.

'Don't you start lecturing me, young fellow, about what a gentleman is or isn't – like all your bloody stuck-up kind. I was patronised for seven years in the army because of being lower-middle-class. Oh, yes. They're all fine and romantic about the working class, but there's something very funny about a butcher from Sevenoaks, especially a small, fat butcher with bad eyesight. And don't think I didn't know why they called me the Colonel. They thought it was a great joke. And when Captain Fanning brought me in here and passed me off as his colonel, he was making fun of me more than he was making fun of them and I thought it was bloody clever of me to turn it to my own advantage. I wonder how he'd feel if he knew that I had taken over his club.'

'Did you start out with that intention?' asked Milton.

'No. I just liked coming here sometimes and pretending to be one of them. It was when I was in prison that I decided on a plan. Do you remember Scarlett O'Hara in *Gone With The Wind*?' Milton and Pooley gazed at Fagg in total astonishment.

'Er, yes,' said Milton.

'There's a scene when she says, "I'll never be hungry again". I always remember that. I might have been common, but I knew about food and drink and every day in jail was a misery to me, more than to most. Best part of two years being locked up for losing my temper with a trollop I never should have married, who only married me for my shop.'

'So what did you set out to do?'

'What I did. To turn it into the sort of place that suited me. It was a matter of finding another few people to be partners. It wasn't that difficult. I was a businessman remember. You could say I was the entrepreneur and people like Chatterton were the expert advisers.'

'You do realise, don't you,' said Milton, 'that you stand out as having more to lose than any of the other residents of this club?'

'How d'you mean?'

'You care about it most and you're the least well off.'

'So?'

'Listen, Mr Fagg.' Milton's dropping of his erstwhile title was not lost on the old man. 'Mr Chatterton was physically incapable of committing these murders; Mr Glastonbury has plenty of money; Mr Fishbane will have sufficient to live in reasonable comfort. You're the obvious suspect.'

'I didn't have the expertise.'

'Prove it. You could easily have picked up those tricks. You were in the army long enough and you've got a record of violence. Give me a good reason why I shouldn't arrest you, because I can't think of one.'

Fagg's eyes bulged. For a moment Milton thought he was going to go into one of his rages, but then he appeared to be thinking. 'You're only saying that because you think I've no money.'

'It's a strong reason.'

'Well, you're wrong. I wouldn't be in penury. I've stashed some away.'

'How much?'

'Maybe half a million.'

'Where did you get that?'

'I told you. I'm a businessman. It was all legitimate. I just didn't tell anyone. I got commission from our suppliers.'

'Half a million pounds' worth?'

'I've been chairman of the provender committee for more than twenty years. We get a lot of expensive food. I don't spend any money. It's all in a high-yield account. Now are you going to arrest me?'

'Not today,' said Milton.

28

'No, no, no, no, no, no, no,' said Selwood. 'A thousand times no. You have just confirmed that it would be completely impossible to do this job without getting on one's knees, crawling under the table and then lying on one's back. Chatterton couldn't have done that without someone to help him down, push him under the table and get him up again.'

'No matter how agile he was, sir?' asked Pooley.

'No matter if he was a bloody acrobat.'

'Thank you, Mr Selwood,' said Milton, 'We were just checking.' He nodded to the DC who had laid on the demonstration and, with Pooley and Selwood, walked out of the committee room.

'Extraordinary place this,' observed Selwood, as they climbed the stairs to the ground floor. 'Oddly enough, my father was a member. Can't say it was ever to my taste: I'm inclined to respectability. But he loved it. In fact, he sent me Chatterton—years ago, when he broke his leg somewhere abroad.'

'Friends, were they?'

'Friendly. There was a little group of them who used to jaw on about the war and all that. When they weren't gambling.' He shook his head. 'That was my old man's downfall. I wish he'd stuck to wine, women and song.'

Milton was enjoying this unexpected candour. 'Had your father been in code-breaking too?'

'Good Lord, no. Man of action. Out in North Africa with David Stirling and all those lunatics.'

'You mean the SAS?'

'That's right. And you know what that crowd were like. A hundred and one ways a boy can kill.' Selwood laughed merrily. 'Not surprising that I rebelled by trying to put people back together.'

'Did he have any other old colleagues in the club?'

'One or two, I think. Can't remember any names. But most of his cronies were just chaps who enjoyed listening to that sort of thing—like Chatterton. It's quite interesting if you've got a taste for adventure yarns and all that crap, which, let's face it, lots of chaps do. Look at all these rubbishy books you get at airports these days. Full of boring stuff about electronic devices and Semtex and computer hardware and software and state-of-the-art military aircraft. Boring as hell if you ask me. Rather read Graham Greene any day—wounded minds rather than bodies, you know. Makes a change. My pater thought me a right wimp.'

They reached the far end of the Saloon and Selwood held out his hand. 'Right. I'll be off now, Mr Milton. Sorry to have dashed your hopes.'

'It was a very long shot. Thank you again and goodbye, Mr Selwood.'

'Goodbye, Sergeant.'

'Goodbye, sir.'

'Goodnight, Master Selwood,' came Ramsbum's voice from half-way down the stairs.

'What d'you mean, "Master Selwood", Ramsbum? You silly old bugger,' Selwood said genially. 'I'm fifty-eight.'

'You'll always be Master Selwood to me, sir.'

'Just as Lieutenant-Colonel Selwood will always be Lieutenant-Colonel Selwood, I expect. Ramsbum, I think you should be pickled, bottled and sold to Americans, but it's nice to see you all the same. Goodnight.' He disappeared swiftly into the street.

'Good man, Mr Selwood's father, was he?' asked Milton.

'Oh, yes.' Ramsbum's eyes went moist. His on-duty accent began to slip. 'Knew 'ow to enjoy 'imself, did the Lieutenant-Colonel. Many's the night 'e'd lose 'undreds of pounds to Mr Chatterton at poker and all 'e'd say was, "Bugger me, I've lost again."'

'Did he do anything except gamble, Mr Ramsbum?' asked Pooley.

'Well, 'e wasn't a one for the ladies, if that's what you mean. Quite right too. They're a waste of bloody money. Not that Mr Fishbane would agree with me.' He chuckled like the father of a much-loved delinquent son. 'But 'e liked a good chat in the afternoon over the port, reminiscing about old times. ''E was a war 'ero you know. Military Cross.'

'Very impressive,' said Milton. 'Where did he win it?'

'North Africa. He was with them SAS. Ooh! Must of killed dozens in unarmed combat.' He stopped and considered that statement. 'And dozens more in armed combat. And that's what he talked about. Ooh, yes! Sometimes he'd show 'ow it was done. Call up a servant to practise on. Did it to me a few times. It was a privilege.'

'What exactly did he do?'

'Well, 'e'd show 'ow he could break your neck in four different ways with the side of his 'and. Kill you with one blow of the fist to your chest. You know. The usual.'

'Oh, I know the sort of thing, Mr Ramsbum,' said Pooley. 'My dad used to go on about it,' he added mendaciously. 'How to get a sentry from behind and chuck him over the edge of a roof, a sea wall, that kind of thing.'

'Yes. Yes, 'e was good on that. I remember . . . ' Ramsbum

stopped suddenly and gazed in deep suspicion at Pooley. 'What are you on about?'

Pooley tried to look innocent. 'Just comparing notes, Mr Ramsbum.'

'You gettin' at something? I know what you're thinking. True-man. That's what you're thinking. Well, you listen to me, you young smartypants. I said I saw him jump and I'm sticking to that.' He turned his back on them and stalked downstairs. 'Hell!' said Pooley. 'I'm sorry, sir. I blew that.'

'Too fucking right you blew that. The old bastard won't say another word now about who was in the admiring group. You've got to learn to control your impulsiveness.' Milton sighed with exasperation. 'Oh, stop looking suicidal, for God's sake, Ellis. It's all right. We've got a lot to chew on. Now we should really talk to Chatterton, but I can't do it. The Commissioner's called an emergency meeting for seven o'clock to review progress. Apparently there's been some bitching from the Ministry of Defence. They're taking it personally that the Admiral's murderer hasn't been found yet. Come on. We'll have to go.'

'I've got a couple of ideas, sir.'

'A commodity you're never short of, Ellis.' Milton sounded slightly acid. 'But run with them by all means.'

'Easiest thing in the world, old man,' said Pooley's old school friend.

'For a geriatric?'

'Certainly for a geriatric. You have to get them to lean over, then you grab them by the heel, flick of the wrist, Bob's your late uncle.'

'Would you be able to do this if you were dependent on a zimmer?'

'Now that you mention it, Ellis, it's not a matter I've given any thought to. The SAS don't usually put people into action when they're crippled, though perhaps with all the defence cuts, that may become necessary. But since you ask me, no. I think the minimum requirements are to be able to stand up steadily on your own two legs and have the use of your arms. If you can manage both those things and you've got the know-how, you could prob-ably do it when you're a hundred.'

'And the other trick? The one with the magazine?'

'A doddle, if you know how. Even your zimmered friend might be able to manage that, if he were sitting down at the right angle to his prey.'

He chortled. 'I must say I'm looking forward to hearing which of our old boys can still do his stuff so efficiently in his twilight years.'

'Well, it's not necessarily one of your old boys, Dominic. It looks as if someone might have picked up some tricks from one of them in sessions at the club.'

'Forget it, Ellis, You don't pick this sort of thing up. You've got to have been trained, and trained, and trained, and done it, been there. Learning it is hard. After that, it's like riding a bicycle. You don't forget. If you're not looking for one of ours and it sounds as if you are, then you're looking for some other kind of trained killer. Take your choice.'

'Thanks. You've been a big help.'

'Think nothing of it. I always feel the only justification for sending people to Eton is that they will never have to pay for advice. Good luck.'

'Cheers.' Pooley put down the phone, jumped up and began to walk round and round and round the office, oblivious to the sneers and sniggers of his colleagues. Half-way through his sixth tour of the perimeter, eyes focused on the floor, hands in fists, he straightened himself and rushed back to his desk. It took him a couple of minutes to find the file he needed and three more to race through the forensic details. He dropped the papers and made a short and unsatisfactory phone-call. Slamming down the receiver with a curse, he banged his fists together with frustration. Then he thought for a moment, crossed over to Sammy Pike's desk and began to plead.

'Dominic. It's me again, I'm afraid.'

'Not at all. Delighted to hear from you. Any progress?'

'I won't know for another half-hour or so, but I've had another thought. You know the bomb I told you about? The straight-forward one?'

'Yes.'

'Would one of your old boys have easy access to dynamite?'

'Depends when he left us. You see, lots of them make off with supplies.'

'What sort of supplies?'

'Ammunition, detonators, dynamite, firearms. Whatever they can get away with.'

'What for?'

'A rainy day. Our chaps tend to be pretty far along the right wing of the political spectrum. Even, dare I say it, paranoid. Bit like your chaps I suppose.'

'You can say that again.'

'With ours it takes the form of expecting the IRA to invade the mainland or the proles to riot at any moment. They like to be prepared and they feel a lot more secure if they've got a few weapons to hand in their bottom drawer.'

'Well, you wouldn't keep dynamite in your bottom drawer, would you?'

'I think I'd prefer to keep it in my potting shed. But if it's wrapped up properly, say in tarred oilskin, that kind of thing, you could keep it for a very long time.'

'How long is very long?'

'Maybe ten years.'

'What about topping up supplies?'

'One ex-SAS man can always get help from another.'

'Bit like Old Etonians.'

'Exactly.'

'Thanks again.'

'Don't mention it.'

Milton had just flung himself into his chair and yawned heavily when there was a knock and Pike and Pooley came in. Wearily he noted that Pooley was in eager mode.

'I think I've got it, sir. I mean, got him. Well, nearly.'

'Sit down. Both of you. Now go gently with me, Ellis. I've just had a very, very hard meeting and I don't want my hopes raised and dashed. Be circumspect and begin at the beginning.'

Pooley took a deep breath and explained about Dominic. Milton listened, first with amusement and then with growing interest.

'And then?'

'I saw nobody seemed to have fingerprinted the shoes.'

'I'm getting a bit dizzy, Ellis. Which shoes?'

'Trueman's shoes, sir.'

'Oh, sorry. Of course.'

'So I asked Sammy to make them do it immediately. They wouldn't do it for me.'

Pike smiled that slow, solid smile that always made Milton feel secure. 'I'm afraid they kicked up a bit of a fuss, sir. Got a lot on. But I thought young Ellis was on to something, so I took your name in vain.'

'Well, don't keep me in suspense.'

'Lovely set of prints around the heel of his right shoe. Glastonbury's.'

'Glastonbury's!' Milton shook his head. 'Gimme a break, Ellis. Surely they could have got there innocently, perhaps when he was kneeling by the corpse.'

'But he didn't. It was Fagg and Blenkinsop who knelt by the corpse. By the time Glastonbury got downstairs Trueman had been declared dead. Blenkinsop ushered Glastonbury back upstairs to spare him the horrid sight. That's in Blenkinsop's and Fagg's evidence.'

'This is too much for me. Ellis, are you now going to tell me Glastonbury was a devil of a chap in the SAS?'

'I don't know if he was a devil of a chap, sir. But he was in the SAS.'

'How come we've only just found that out?'

Pooley looked at the floor. 'Er, it was an oversight, sir. It's entirely my fault.'

'Oh, come on, Ellis,' said Pike. 'It wasn't your fault at all. I'm afraid DC Pierce mucked it up, sir. He was the one doing the donkey work on Glastonbury. And when he found a B. Glastonbury in the Scots Guards invalided out of North Africa in early forty-one, he thought that was that.'

'But he's not B. Glastonbury, is he? Surely Boy has to be a nickname?'

'That's right, sir. He's "C" for Cyril.' Pooley was at ease now that somebody else had done the sneaking. 'So when I re-checked this evening, there he was. Transferred to Eleventh Commandos and in there at the formation of the SAS. He was invalided out in December nineteen forty-two.

'With what?'

'Seems to have been a nervous breakdown.'

'Got any details on him yet?'

'No. We're hunting down contemporaries.'

'But I still don't get it. Surely . . . ' He looked at his watch. 'My God!' he said. 'It's half-past nine already. Didn't we promise to see Robert?'

'Yes. He'll be waiting for us.'

'D'you want to come along, Sammy? We'll thrash this out.'

'Only if you need me, sir. Don't really think it's my sort of thing. I wouldn't have anything to contribute. If you don't mind, I'd rather go home to my wife.'

'Don't say such things, Sammy,' said Milton. 'Makes me feel nostalgic. I haven't seen Ann for six weeks. All right, see you tomorrow. Come on, Ellis. Let's go.'

29

'Just a sliver, thank you. I don't need feeding up any more.' Amiss accepted the slice of pizza and nibbled on it delicately.

Milton and Pooley, ravenous, got through several mouthfuls before resuming the story. By the time they'd finished their meal, Amiss had been brought up to date.

'But I cannot seriously begin to regard that gentle old blockhead as a killer.'

'Like riding a bicycle, remember?'

'And you don't know what he was like before the breakdown?'

'Should know very shortly,' said Milton, looking at his watch. His telephone rang seconds later. 'Yes, right. What's his number?' He put the receiver down. 'They've found someone who served with him. I'll go next door and ring him from your phone, Ellis. I hate these bloody gimcrack things.'

He shut the door behind him, leaving Pooley and Amiss in a fever of speculation. Within five minutes he was back.

'Interesting,' he said. 'Who would have guessed?' He sat down and poured himself another glass of wine. 'This fellow I've just been talking to, Wilson, was an NCO in training with Glastonbury, first in the Commandos and then in the SAS. Remembers him well because, he said, he was so gentle and yet so lethal. He was a brilliant technician, very attentive, never questioned anything, anxious to please, always did what was required of him.'

'Just followed orders,' said Amiss.

'Exactly.'

'Did he actually kill people?' asked Pooley.

'Yes. He was involved in a number of desert raids. Wilson says he did his job like the rest of them. But he said one thing he did remember clearly about Glastonbury was that one always had the feeling he didn't quite know what he was doing. He was just doing it.'

'Sounds a bit like a psychopath,' said Amiss.

'No. I asked that. A psychopath wants to kill. Glastonbury didn't enjoy it. He just did it to oblige his superiors.'

'And the breakdown?'

'Back to farce,' said Milton. 'Wilson said he recollected it vividly because of its sheer incongruity. Apparently Glastonbury went to pieces after a letter from home telling him his nanny was dead.'

Amiss reached for the bottle. 'Invalided out owing to death of nanny? Well, it must have made a first for the SAS. Even a last.'

'This ties in with what I'd got from his librarian colleague,' said Pooley.

'You didn't tell me about that,' said Amiss.

'Well, it wasn't terribly significant, or didn't seem so then. He was meticulous, obliging, obedient, pleasant, did any job that was within his capabilities scrupulously and efficiently.'

'But wasn't all there,' offered Milton.

'What his colleague said,' said Pooley, 'was that although he wasn't in, he was much more useful than most of the people who were, as long as you never expected him to stray beyond his areas of technical expertise. Incapable of thinking for himself.'

'And if he trusted you?'

'He would do anything you asked. That's what his fellow librarian said. That he was so obedient to his superior as to seem like someone who had been brainwashed.'

'Christ!' said Amiss. 'Nanny has a lot to answer for.'

'So, I expect, has Chatterton,' said Milton.

*

Amiss awoke at four in the morning with an idea about which he could do nothing for another three hours. He tossed and turned until after five o'clock when he began to slide into sleep. At that moment Sunil turned on to his back and burst into loud snores. With uncharacteristic venom, Amiss picked up three paperbacks and hurled them hard across the room. Sunil emitted a yelp and turned over, then stayed silent. Amiss fell fast asleep. When his alarm woke him at seven, he greeted Sunil monosyllabically and, pausing only to brush his teeth, leaped into his uniform and ran downstairs to a telephone. It took Pooley a couple of minutes to answer.

'His mother's grave,' said Amiss.

'His what?'

'You heard. At Highgate. We couldn't fathom where the stuff was kept. Must have been befuddled by wine. Don't you remember Glastonbury's gardening?'

'Good Lord, how could we have forgotten? This answers lots of problems.'

'Storage space.'

'Privacy.'

'Probably protective clothing. Since he doesn't keep any gardening tools at the club, he must keep them at the graveyard.'

'Thanks, Robert. I expect we'll see you this morning.'

'You'd bloody well better. My nerves are in shreds.'

The sun came in through the windows of the Rochester Room, its brightness at odds with the mood of the three men inside.

'I wish one could get desensitising injections,' said Milton.

'Me too,' said Pooley.

'At least nobody will hang him,' said Amiss.

'No. But he'll have to end up in Broadmoor or somewhere and he'll be separated from Chatterton, who is not mad, just wicked.'

'Well, be that as it may,' said Milton, 'we have to get started. Robert, you must leave. Ellis, get Chatterton. He should have reached the saloon by now.'

Chatterton looked perfectly cheerful when Pooley ushered him in. 'Hello again,' he said. 'What a lot we seem to be seeing of each other.'

'Please sit down, sir. Would you care for some coffee?'

'No, thank you. I've just had some. How may I be of assistance?'

'You're a man of considerable intelligence,' said Milton, 'so I don't propose to drag this out or even lead you into it gently. We know that you have run up an enormous debt in Monte Carlo, that you're smuggling drugs in order to work it off, and that Glastonbury killed Trueman, Meredith-Lee and Blenkinsop at your instigation and using the techniques he learned in the SAS.'

Chatterton placed the tips of his fingers together and rested his chin on them. He looked squarely at Milton. 'Would you care to produce some evidence for these interesting allegations?'

'Certainly. Here is a sample. Glastonbury's fingerprints were around the heel of Trueman's shoe, something we didn't know until yesterday, yet he had not been near the corpse. His mother's grave contains a great deal of weaponry, including dynamite. For your part, we know about your Monte Carlo activities in detail, and on the home front, we have, for instance, a witness who saw you at one o'clock in the morning after Blenkinsop's death in the library in search of the murder weapon.'

'QED,' said Chatterton.

'QED.'

Chatterton threw his head back and gazed at the ceiling for a couple of moments. 'It certainly sounds as if you've done for poor old Boy. The grave's a real clincher. You've obviously got a lot less on me. However, I was never one of those stolid, dogged mathematicians who was prepared to spend half his life working out proofs. Trouble was, I wasn't gifted enough to be the other – the intuitive – kind with much success. So I'll spare all of us the long-drawn-out arguments over evidence. I could deny all knowledge and leave you to interrogate Glastonbury, but well though he's done so far, he wouldn't last long in the face of the kind of pressure you're likely to bring to bear. Therefore I'm prepared to say, "It's a fair cop, Guv'nor" and fill in the details, if you'll do me one favour.'

'Which is?'

'Let me break it to Boy.'

'Very well. I agree. Now I fear I must deliver a formal caution before you begin.'

'About my words being taken down and used in evidence against me?'

'Yes.'

'Please let's take it as read, Chief Superintendent. I abhor meaningless ritual. You can probably trace that back to those thousands of meals at High Table which were preceded by the mumbling of grace by our atheist Master. I have my failings, but I'm not a hypocrite.'

'Please note that the caution has been given, Sergeant.'

'Yessir.'

'You're very smart for a policeman, aren't you? My bad luck – or judgement. One tends to assume all you chaps are seriously thick.'

Milton kept his expression solemn.

'Now you've already got the gist and you won't be needing much detail. Boy and I will plead guilty. In his case it should be possible to argue diminished responsibility.

'I suppose he and I seem an unlikely pair, but in fact we suit each other very well. At Cambridge I lived in a world of aridity and intellectual combat: it was nice to meet somebody who hero-worshipped me. Besides, we were sexually terribly compatible. I should think it will be a little hard for you, Chief Superintendent, let alone your young companion here, to imagine that almost fifty years ago Boy and I had a passionate sexual relationship. I can see you're doing sums, Mr Milton. It was not when we met first before the war, it was after he came back from North Africa, broken up by the death of his nanny. Risible, isn't it? But not to him. He was a man who could form only intense, loyal, self-abnegatory rela-tionships – his nanny, his parents, his sergeant-major and me. He always did what he was told.'

'How did he get into the Commandos?'

'Good with his hands and obedient. A definition of a good lover, as far as I'm concerned, although for the last couple of decades we've mostly just been friends. He's not intellectually stimulating, dear old Boy, but one way or another, he's the emotional centre of my life and his wittering hardly even gets on my nerves.'

'Why did you do what you did, sir?'

'Suggest that he kill Trueman? Gambling instinct, I fear. I was leaving for Monte Carlo, quite perturbed about what this new idiot secretary was proposing and convinced that the even tenor of our lives was going to be fatally disrupted. Boy could have financed us in a decent old people's home, but that was not for me. Besides, I've never wanted to take his money. Sentimental old devil, am I not? So

I had some coffee and a drink with him after lunch that day and gave him a little of what we used to call white snuff.'

'That was?'

'Cocaine. I've taken to that a bit over recent years. It's an awfully good pick-me-up I find, especially at my age. It beats vitamin supplements, I can tell you. It certainly does wonders for Boy – livens him up no end. He knew not to talk about it. He understood about our secrets. It was a secret that we went to bed together and it was a secret that we took white snuff. I went up in the lift to my bedroom to pick up my passport and money and stopped by on the way down just to say goodbye again. He was sitting just by the lift. Then there was an altercation at the other end of the gallery and Trueman came in our direction looking cross. He stopped in front of us and said, "One can't close one's eyes to reality". Almost his last words. Quite funny really. And I said, "Indeed not, Ken. And speaking of reality, there's a very nasty crack in the plaster work in this pillar." Trueman, eternally conscientious, switched his attention to the damaged fabric. I shuffled over, pointed out the worrying cracks – you could always rely on there being lots of these anywhere in the building – and summoned up Boy. All I had to do was gesture and whisper, "Get him, Boy". That was what his sergeant-major used to say. He did very well. It was a lovely clean operation.'

'Even fifty years on?' asked Milton.

'He had in a sense had frequent refresher courses. We used to have lots of Auld Lang Syne with an old SAS man called Selwood, a pal of his drops in from time to time, and anyway Boy's always gone on rehearsing his skills. It's a bit of a joke with us. You see, Boy wasn't afraid of physical challenge himself. He worried about me, but where he was concerned, it was germs that made him anxious. Anyway, Trueman had gone, the others were responding to his scream from the other side of the gallery, and I was able to fade into the lift without being seen, merely taking the precaution of saying, "It's a secret, Boy. Now, pretend to be asleep."'

'The debts in Monte Carlo, sir?'

'Nerves and cocaine, I fear. I had taken a large risk, most impulsively and with absolutely no guarantee that the fingerprints wouldn't be found or that Boy wouldn't forget it was a secret and admit everything disarmingly. He had it in his sweet and simple mind that Trueman was dangerous, like the germs, so I hoped that would keep him guilt-free. But I took more cocaine than usual and, therefore, far more risks. Hence being down a million francs, hence smuggling heroin in a zimmer. Very good way of doing it, I may say. Quick swap in the gentlemen's lavatory at Heathrow and I was clean as a whistle.'

'The Admiral?'

'Oh, Boy had his little stash of this and that in his mother's grave. It made him feel secure. I used to arrange for it periodically to get topped up, or updated, as they say. It took very little to make him happy. He just wanted to know we would be all right if the revolution came. So we had the dynamite, the detonators, the protective gloves and the rest to deal with boring old Con Meredith-Lee. Boy does this sort of thing terribly well when he's high. Ditto of course the job he did on Pinkie Blenkinsop. Although that confused him a bit at first because he thought Pinkie was his friend. However, once I explained that Pinkie was my enemy, there was no more problem. The trouble was that he was discovered too early – before I could burn the magazine. I've been worried about fingerprints, even though I rubbed the cover of the magazine thoroughly before discarding it. Any other questions?'

'How long do you need, sir?'

'Fifteen minutes, if you'd be so kind. I need five minutes to get to him and wake him up and ten minutes to explain.' He retrieved his crutches and swung himself to his feet. 'Thank you for being so civilised,' he said. 'I never expected that of the police.'

'Aren't you afraid they'll make a run for it, sir?' asked Pooley, as soon as Chatterton had left.

'Sammy's got people on duty front and back and I just haven't got the bottle to face Glastonbury before Chatterton's done his stuff. Tell me when it's time.' Milton lay back and shut his eyes and said, 'Why the hell couldn't it have been Fagg?' Pooley began to pace as quietly as possible, round and round the Rochester Room.

Lurking in the corner of the Coffee Room, Amiss observed Chatterton walking through without police escort. He was about to seek an explanation when Gooseneck emerged from the kitchen, hailed him warmly and engaged him in conversation about what measures should be taken to render life at ffeatherstonehaugh's more attractive to the staff. Amiss had no option but to be helpful.

'Very useful, my dear fellow,' said Gooseneck. 'You're quite right about tackling the accommodation immediately. Let's go upstairs and take a look. This place is in such disarray that I should be able to get a troop of carpenters and painters in without our dear Colonel even raising an eyebrow.' Unhappily, Amiss trailed with Gooseneck out of the Coffee Room and into the Saloon.

'My God! What's going on?' said Gooseneck, for standing round the Saloon in positions of frozen horror were Ramsbum, Blitherdick, Sunil and Ng, all of them staring up at the gallery, on the balustrade of which teetered the great form of Glastonbury, pulling at an invisible object.

'Now, Boy, now,' called Chatterton's voice, and with a huge heave Glastonbury summoned up all his strength to haul his friend alongside him. Chatterton's remaining crutch clattered all the way down to the Saloon floor and Glastonbury supported his weight.

'Jump, Boy. Now.' And with his arms tightly enclosing Chatterton, Glastonbury jumped. Amiss turned his head away just too late.

Epilogue

'Holmes and Moriarty at the Reichenbach Falls?' asked Pooley.

'A colourful analogy, if not very apposite,' said Amiss. 'This wasn't a struggle, and Chatterton and Glastonbury were friends, not enemies. And anyway this time neither of them's going to return. Oh, Christ! I really wish I hadn't seen it.'

The three of them sat in Pooley's flat, exhausted after a day of emotional turmoil.

'Jim, why did you let Chatterton go?' asked Pooley suddenly. 'You were taking a frightful risk.'

'I was giving him time to do what he did.'

'You knew?'

'Doesn't that happen with your humane detectives in crime fiction, Ellis? I simply didn't feel I could put Glastonbury through the process of the law if there was an alternative. That may be criminal: I think it's humane.'

'But it's got you in trouble.'

'Not big trouble. Easily smoothed out. Very minor reprimand. Anyway, I don't care. I'm more at peace doing it this way and somehow I can live with never becoming an assistant commissioner.'

'I wish we could be celebrating,' said Amiss. 'Damn it. We got there, between us, and here we are, plunged in gloom.'

'So cheer us up,' said Milton.

'I thought that was Ellis's job. I can't be very jolly, I'm afraid. It was all a very sad scene. I was even sorry for Fagg and Fishbane. They're completely dazed.' There was a depressed silence. Amiss jumped up, took the bottle, poured lavish amounts of whisky into their glasses and said, 'Sod this. Time to look on the bright side.'

'We've cracked the case,' said Pooley.

'Glastonbury doesn't have to go to Broadmoor,' said Milton.

'And I can stop being a waiter,' said Amiss. There was another silence.

'Mauleverer and Gooseneck are going to take charge of the club,' said Amiss.

'Two jailbirds?' said Pooley.

'Reformed. They might turn it into a good club again.'

'It's not going to happen,' said Milton, 'Its ethos is not going to fit the 1990s, I fear.'

'You're probably right. But they're game to try, and they're both extremely bright.'

'What are you going to do now, Robert?'

'Serve out my week's notice. Gooseneck is distraught that I'm leaving, but he'll have Sunil to console him. Then, poverty notwithstanding, I'm going to visit Rachel: I'm tired of loneliness and celibacy. Additionally, she pointed out cheerfully that in Delhi I'll probably see enough violence and death to put ffeatherstonehaugh's in perspective.'

'Haven't you got something rude from Lord Rochester to do that for us now?' asked Milton.

Amiss beamed. 'I thought you'd never ask. I've nothing relevant, but I do have a verse I learned the other day that I found diverting. The trouble is that Ellis probably won't like it. It's a bit close to home.'

'I'm not a fan of Rochester,' said Pooley. 'You two will say it's because I'm a prude. But don't let me stop you.'

'This is perfectly clean. But you still won't like it.

> 'How wise is nature, when she does dispense
> A large estate to cover want of sense.
> The Man's a fool, 'tis true, but that's no matter,
> For He's a mighty wit with those that flatter.'

'If it was flattery I was after,' said Pooley stiffly, 'I'd hardly associate with you. I think that's really rather cheap.'

'Aha! He's got the answer to that as well. "Fools censure wit, as old men rail at sin".'

'They'd have been a lot better off in ffeatherstonehaugh's had they been railing at sin rather than committing it.'

'Ellis, why don't you become a fucking lay preacher?'

'Like your hero, Inspector Romford,' added Milton.

Pooley looked at him in horror. 'You don't mean I sound like him, do you? But he's . . . '

'A self-righteous wanker,' said Milton.

Pooley looked at Amiss in supplication.

'Sorry, Ellis. He's right. You need to watch it.'

'Oh, very well.' Pooley rose, took the whisky bottle, refilled all three glasses and sat down again. 'I can take a hint. Bring on the dancing girls.'

They clinked their glasses.